O BEAUTIFUL

BÉCHAMEL

A perfect combination of raised blue veins on Martin's right foot spelled *M*. His mother traced it out for him before he could read. She sang "Mary Had a Little Lamb" and other songs that featured the letter. Her normal voice was light and distracted, but when she got to an *M*, she'd lean down into his face, close her lips, and sing louder, buzzing almost. She'd squeeze his foot, holding the note, until her breath gave out. Then she'd lose interest. She'd race through the rest of the song, barely audible, and rock Martin quickly in the hard, white rocker.

The *M* grew larger as Martin did. Now, at the end of a long day of walking, he'd find it pulsing beneath his socks, huge and livid. It was certainly a sign, but of what? His mother had said it was there to remind him who he was, should he ever forget. She herself had a mole on her wrist that helped her tell left from right, or used to. But surely these engravings of the body have more to say than that, thought Martin. Surely one must attempt to obey them.

The building he lived in now had thirty identical floors, each with apartments designated A through P. At first he had hoped for an M apartment, even though M's were far too expensive. "What on earth will you do with three bedrooms?" his mother had asked. "Are you out of your mind?" In the end, he had settled for a one-bedroom J, but it made him uneasy. It was like ignoring horoscopes, even if you didn't quite believe in them.

Over the years he had looked upon people whose names began with *M* as possessing some special potential affinity. He had slept with a man named Max on no other evidence than his promising initial. After thrashing around in the sheets for an hour, he'd suddenly forced Max to look at his foot.

"What?" said Max, panting and droopy-eyed.

"On my foot, look, an *M*."

Perhaps that's what scared Max off.

■ ■ ■

SO Stella's announcement was a little unnerving. "Don't be a baby about this," she said, surprising Martin at the theater on the day his new show moved into New York. "Just hear me out." She kissed him hello, on the top of his head, causing him to smile and then to shiver. Martin, who had been scratching methodically at a set of blueprints, put down his mechanical pencil.

"Don't be a baby about what?"

"There's a guy named Matt I want you to meet." She handed Martin a Styrofoam box.

"In here?" he said, tapping the lid.

"No, my dear, in there is lunch. Japanese. It's like a briefcase—you should like that."

Inside, there was a piece of raw fish, a tiny fried object, a mound of rice spiked with red and green.

"Oh my Lord."

"I thought you liked Japanese. I thought you'd like the presentation at least." She took off her coat, facing away. "No matter. I guess I can eat it."

"I guess you can," said Martin. He studied her tense, liquescent body. "That's a nice dress."

Stella picked at the collar. "Perry Ellis sale," she said. "Ninety-eight dollars. There's a pull in it somewhere." She sat down and looked at the bright, empty stage. "What's going on? Where is the set?"

Martin made a beagle face. "One of the trucks got in an accident on the way from Philadelphia. The side sheared off, stuff flew out. Apparently there were looters. People stopped their cars and took what they saw on the road. The driver said he saw a woman running off with a ficus before he blacked out. Who knows what else? They hired a new truck, but it hasn't come in yet, and we're falling behind."

"Falling behind," Stella repeated. She cracked apart the fused chopsticks and started to eat.

They were sitting in the balcony of the Mark Hellinger Theater. Onstage, electricians were installing what lights they could. Standing on top of ladders and scaffolds, they reached high above their heads into the darkness with their tools, as if to clean the underside of an enormous animal.

"Are you pretending you didn't hear what I said?"

Martin shrugged.

"It's not a death sentence, Martin. You said you wanted to meet people is all. I'm complying. I'm *trying* complying."

"I didn't say people."

"Well, what then?"

"I mean not plural. Not *people*. Not random people. Not humanity at large." He frowned. "What *is* that, zucchini?"

One bite more and whatever it was was gone. "I'm not discussing humanity at large," said Stella. "I'm discussing one particular *piece* of humanity. One particular nice, *good-looking* piece, if you really must know." She flipped a vegetable over and back between her chopsticks until it was completely denuded of its dressing. "Someone I myself might like. A nice *person*, if you get my drift. A nice *person*. A very nice *person*."

There was entirely too much emphasis in her voice, and Martin picked up his pencil. "Why should he like me?"

Stella sighed. "Oh, Martin. With an attitude like that, I really couldn't say." She closed the empty Styrofoam box. "I love this stuff, this Japanese *stuff*. It's not like eating. Or rather, it *is* like eating, but not like eating food. It's like eating an idea. You know, Martin—" She pointed to the stage. "*That* would make a wonderful something."

One of the electricians had dropped a sheaf of gels from the top of his ladder. Amber, blue, green, and pink squares were swooping through the air, hesitating then sinking. Stagehands leaned in from the wings to watch. "Beautiful," said Stella. "If you like that sort of thing."

The gels all landed. The hammering and the chirping of wrenches resumed.

"Well, I should be going," said Stella, rising. "But why don't you come with me tonight? There's an open studio. It might even be good."

Martin made a doubtful face then shook his head no. "Artists," he said. "You can have 'em."

"Oh, but I do," said Stella.

STELLA used to be fat. When Martin first met her, she wore bright floral outfits with wings and dropped waistlines. *Slimming* was the word she employed to describe them; she said it sadly but hopefully, knowing it was at best only marginally true. In a store, she'd hold a dress to the mirror and demand an opinion. "Slimming?" she'd ask.

Martin could not bear to tell her that the dress would heighten, not disguise, her problem. All the colors, all the shapes and panels and pleats: they drew the eye unfailingly to the place it least was welcome. Even when the outfit was less commandeering, Stella made up for it, fussing and arranging. Just to sit down she had to wrap herself up like a restaurant napkin, fold all the pieces over and over according to some intricate plot in her head. Then she felt compelled to talk about it. The tag itched. The wide, stiff belt pinched at her side. Couldn't she leave well enough alone?

No, she couldn't leave well enough alone—because she wasn't. *Well enough alone.* Lacking companionship, she made lovers of her clothes, which mistreated her, as men did, but never ran away. She could count on them to touch her, to come alive upon her flesh.

Once, just as a concert was about to begin, she leaned toward Martin and said she was feeling a draft.

"Where?"

"My dress," she hissed.

Martin had to laugh. It seemed entirely plausible to him that the dress might contain its own private weather: tropical depressions, a simoom blowing up from the south.

"What's so funny?"

He wanted to say, "Your dress doesn't fit, it doesn't suit you in the least, and that's why you feel so uncomfortable in it." That was the truth. But she took criticism so poorly, he didn't dare risk it. Instead he took her hand and whispered, "You know I think you're beautiful, Stella."

"Don't patronize me. I'm not a child."

Stella could not take a compliment. When people told her, as they inevitably did, what a fine-featured, lovely face she had, she wrinkled it up in a horrible mask to prove how wrong they were. "Right," she'd say. "And what about my hair?"

In fact the hair was beautiful, too, shiny and black like licorice; but she cut it herself without a mirror and stuffed it up in a purple beret. She set about almost scientifically to disguise her most attractive features. Martin had once seen her from across Broadway, elbowing her way through traffic with a sour look on her face. She was wearing medals and false epaulets on a belted pea-green blazer, and she looked like a compressed Latin American dictator.

He had been shocked to glimpse her like this, so cruelly revealed in the light of day. Usually he got to see her in circumstances she controlled: alone, in an apartment, in the dark corner of a neighborhood restaurant, or at dusk at Lincoln Center by the fountain. She always arrived early and discovered Martin before he discovered her. "Martin," she would announce, "Martin. Here." And there she would be, waiting, in a shadow.

But across Broadway he had seen her without her approval, like the awful time he had glimpsed his mother through the frosted shower door. He held his hand to his mouth. "Oh my Lord," he muttered, the breath of it warming his palm. He had not before realized how ungracefully she walked, how fierce, how heedless. Poor Stella, he thought, and then, ashamed, ducked beneath the bright umbrella of a pretzel vendor's cart.

It was a betrayal to notice any of this, and more a betrayal, noticing, to hide. She wasn't an object to be studied, and pitied, at a distance. Martin knew how much she suffered with her weight. Had she been less willful, less defended, she might have blown apart from the humiliation of it. Instead she managed to stay together—wrapped up, it was true, cinched in by her clothing. But no matter how she achieved her cohesion, at whatever cost, she deserved respect for succeeding. Martin, who stood alarmingly tall at six-foot-five and weighed alarmingly little at one hundred and eighty pounds—who had nothing tangible to make complaint of—had half her humor, half her drive.

He blamed it on growing up rich. All things came easy, even heartbreak, and money poulticed every wound. Were he to lose a job, he would not go hungry—he would not, in fact, eat any differently from the way he ate before. Were he to lose what little remained of his family, he would only be richer, he sometimes thought. There were truths but no consequences: consequences were what poor people suffered. Rich people never touched ground long enough to stir them up.

As a teenager he had thought he would someday grow out of the feeling, but now, at twenty-seven, he knew he would always regard his life as a fiction. Stella was one of the few things in it that uncontestably passed as real. Before he met her, nothing around him was constant enough and near enough, both at once, to keep him in place. Among his family, he felt like a comet in irregular orbit. Among his college friends, he felt merely insufficient. They were lofty, or unreliable—by which he meant they dared to change. They moved constantly closer to achievements Martin could barely credit, let alone attain. Their horizons were so wide. The life they hoped for was like some magnificently squalid village in India Martin had no desire to visit. Mystics or no. But he could not argue the merits of his narrowness. Even if he could, his friends were not the types to join him in it.

But Stella was. She didn't waver from her established role. From the time he had met her, three years before, at the midtown gallery where she sold him a chair, she had kept to her script. "If I sit on this," she had said of the graceful Sheraton, "I'll have to sell it as a collage. But you go ahead. You've got the right lines."

Martin had laughed without thinking. Her joke deflected consideration of the pain involved in its construction. He merely sat on the chair as invited and admired the satinwood marquetry. "It's beautiful," he said.

"If you like that kind of thing," said Stella.

They met a few times more while dickering a price. If the gallery wasn't busy, they'd sit—on modern, purple swivel chairs. She'd gone to Yale, majored in art history, written her thesis "on Rubens, of course." In their third conversation, when the name of a common acquaintance came up—as if this alone afforded permission—they finally decided to meet for dinner.

At the time, Martin was still suffering under the delusion— or perhaps by then it was only a hope—that he might yet find some way to be straight. Stella, it turned out, had no such ideas about him. She had made the correct assumptions from the start. "Really, Martin," she would tell him later, "who else is coming into galleries just because he likes the art?" As a result of her certainty she was completely exuberant that first night at dinner, while Martin sat listening, stiff as an umbrella. "Heh-heh," he would laugh, sharply, at right angles.

It was a tiny nouvelle French restaurant—this was 1981. Everything in the room save Stella was excruciatingly dainty. The breadsticks were almost two feet tall, delivered to the table in a cerulean vase. Martin noted these details for possible use in a show someday, a contemporary comedy, Neil Simon perhaps. Then, over an appetizer so self-conscious it seemed to be spelling its own name on the plate, Stella mentioned to Martin the name of their mutual acquaintance.

"Miriam Sutter," she said. "She's pregnant, you know. She's keeping it, too. Though I couldn't say why. Something about *human life*, I suppose. Whatever that means."

Martin looked amazed. "But how did it happen? I mean, Miriam Sutter?"

"If you prick us, do we not breed?" asked Stella. "I don't mean *you*, of course."

Martin liked that. He was known, it seemed, without having had to make the effort. All that painful wrangling with pronouns, all that agony over colors and signs—obviated. There was no need. There was no use, and there was no need. The umbrella of his spine opened up a bit and rendered him buoyant, for a time, at least, with Stella in restaurants.

BUT after he saw her across Broadway that day, Martin noticed a change in Stella's behavior. She spoke less when they met, and drew him out instead. Not quite imperceptibly, the frequency of their meetings diminished. Had she seen him hide? Sometimes he thought she must have. For now she called only at times she knew he was out and left messages on his machine that said, "Nothing important, no need to call back." And often he didn't. He wasn't one to insist. Only when time seemed to be swelling up dangerously between them did he drop in at the gallery, leave a note at the desk. Even so, he got no response. Weeks went by—it might have been months. At Christmas, he mailed her a homemade card with heartfelt wishes, awkwardly worded.

The card, or perhaps the new year, did the trick. The fifth of January, 1983, she showed up at his apartment unannounced. "That doorman of yours," she said as she entered. "He'd let in the Mansons."

"He remembers you."

"And you, Martin? Can you forgive me? I've been an alarming jerk." She lay down on the sofa and put her feet up on its arm.

"Of course I forgive you."

"Then that's done," she said. "I'm mending fences right and left. Well, only left, really. I'm giving up on the right. I'm mending fences on the left and building *trenches* on the right. Wait, what does that mean? Is mending fences patching up friendships? Or patching up what divides them?"

"Good fences make good neighbors."

"Do they? Do they, Martin?" She scanned the apartment briefly to see what might be new. "Pretty flowers," she said.

"I was a little worried when I went to the gallery and the woman didn't seem to know you. Did you get my message?"

"Not exactly."

"Not exactly?"

Stella took a deep breath and exhaled ostentatiously. "Martin, I quit three months ago. I started my own place with Patrice and Ellen. In the East Village. It's all contemporary—trash, probably. Constructions, you know. Abstract. You'd hate it. My grandmother died in September and left me some money—that's when this all started. I got back from the funeral and turned off my phone and sat around and just thought. Oh, Martin, I'm such a louse not to have told you. And I could have used your help, too. The place was a mess when we signed the lease. Dropped ceilings and all. There was tin underneath, but we didn't know how to strip it. Patrice did something that turned it brown."

Martin stared. "Patrice?" he said.

"This French guy I met. We had an affair, I'm sure I don't know why. Green eyes, I suppose—well, you know. Oh, Martin." She pursed her lips before resuming. "I got pregnant, of course, the one time I didn't have my diaphragm with me. What a joke that I should prove so fertile."

Martin stared at her, attempting to determine how far along she might be or if, God forbid, she had given birth and was even now secreting on her person a hitherto undetected infant. The way Stella dressed, it was difficult to tell. "And what—well, when—I mean," he stuttered.

"Don't look so scared, it was only a few weeks."

Martin said, "Oh." He looked at the floor.

"And don't be disapproving, baby," Stella said with surprising conviction. "Please, I couldn't stand it now. And anyway, we Jews are allowed. Encouraged, even, I would almost say." But now her voice guttered. "There was a stainless steel bowl."

Martin opened his mouth to speak, but nothing intelligible

came out. He was thinking: How could so much happen so quickly? How could so much happen at all? And then his breathing became irregular; the sound of wind picked up in his inner ear. He feared he might faint—something he did occasionally, and had done since childhood, for no known reason. He closed his eyes, as his mother had once suggested might help. He imagined a Brandenburg Concerto playing, but slow as a dirge. He exhaled on the downbeats and soon enough the wind subsided.

"Are you all right?" Stella asked. "It's not that fainting thing again, is it?" She didn't quite believe in the fainting.

"Just a little startled. Can I get you something?"

"Do you have bottled water? I'd love bottled water."

Bottled water must have been Patrice's innovation. Each new lover brought a new drink with him; once it had been Frangelico. Martin stocked them all, but this new request he was not yet prepared for. Iced tea, he decided, would have to do.

Though Stella had disappeared before, she had never disappeared for so long. What was the purpose of these vanishing acts? Was she incapable of changing—as Martin was—except in the dark? Was life something she feared would embarrass and dismay him, as he had once feared his wealth would discomfit her? For Stella was wealthy, if mere movement, if turmoil, was tender. And in these terms Martin was poor, but happy. Nothing speakable happened to him. During the time Stella had been out of touch, yes, he had fallen in love four times, but he'd never mentioned it to anyone—not even to those he had fallen in love with. And so here he was, just as he had been, Frangelico, vermouth, Midori in the cabinet, while Stella was trailing an entirely new cast of characters on the couch.

"Was it awful?" he ventured.

"Ask me no questions," Stella replied, "and I'll tell you no truths." She bit her lip. "Doll," she added.

From the kitchen pass-through, slicing a lemon, Martin peered at her between the hanging copper pots. Something else had changed besides the names in her stories. He noticed ankles where her legs had formerly run directly into her shoes. "You've lost weight," he said carefully.

"The abortion," she replied. "I don't recommend it." She idly opened a magazine.

But as the weeks passed, a waist began to appear in the midst of her dresses when she turned within their massive volumes. Her chin started poking from its collar of fat until the fat disappeared and only the chin, hard and square, remained. Her features emerged like new terrain from an ice age receding. There was a bigger, dramatic nose, and larger, apparently greener eyes. Specific breasts took form where a vague sloping plane of chest had been. And muscles moved slightly but unmistakably beneath the fabric of her sleeves.

Stella was thin. She had gone into hiding and altered herself completely. The tent dresses and muu-muus were replaced with clothes so simple as to almost not be there. A sheath of black was all you would notice, a few pieces of jewelry as punctuation. No bright sashes, no berets. The hair was cut in an expensive salon whose name she perversely refused to divulge. She ran three times around the reservoir each morning, whatever the weather, allowing no exceptions. And Patrice had apparently been shed with the weight.

When complimented on the transformation, she changed the subject. When complimented on her clothes, she told Martin where she had bought them, what percent off, how long the sale was likely to last. She trained him to avoid making comments at all, but he still shook his head a little when he saw her. How could people change so quickly? How could people change at all?

Stella ignored his wondering looks. She dropped an opinion or a random piece of gossip, like food into a fishbowl. "If I have to go to another lunch with Caryl Crower, I'm giving up the business," she'd say. And then they'd talk about that.

A S if it were the natural consequence of her physical transformation, Stella quickly became successful in business. In April she sold an entire roomful of oils to a movie star who was seeking investments. The commission was enormous. Talk got around, articles appeared, and within a few months she was a *figure in the art world*. The movie star, reconfirmed in his doubtful taste, returned for more. He bought out a show of vorticist drawings, had them delivered to a bank for safekeeping.

Stella was pleased—Martin could tell because she affected ennui. Oh, she didn't care so much about celebrities; celebrities were erratic, she said. But they brought in the others, the society wives with their decorators, the lone-wolf professionals on their way up. These were the people who followed trends, who redid their homes every five years.

Soon limos lined Sixth Street from noon to four, absurdly sleek amidst the crumbling tenements. But the incongruity was part of the draw. People started saying to her, "You just can't find things this *vital* on Madison Avenue." And Stella would nod. It was true, you couldn't. What she sold was nothing if not vital, even if the quality varied tremendously. But the quality was irrelevant, she found. Anything she pointed to became desirable to her clients: broken plates, graffiti on glass, mutilated books. Occasionally it was even unnecessary to point. A stockbroker visiting the gallery between installations asked to purchase whatever might be coming in soon that was large enough to put above his sofa.

From the way Stella told these stories, from the tone she employed in describing the transactions, a stranger would have assumed she had a low opinion of art in general, and nothing but a mercenary interest in the whole dirty business. Martin knew better. It was all a smoke screen. The comments she made were meant to obscure her almost embarrassing reverence for beauty, a reverence constantly threatened by the very means of promoting it. But the means were fascinating, too. The game turned her on—prices and reputations, rumors and feints— though it was a game in which it was better that people not know how deeply she actually felt. Passion caused discomfort, Stella had learned. Better they should think the fire was long extinguished in her, lest they try to douse it themselves.

So Stella proceeded with baronial sangfroid. She got Ellen married and shipped Patrice back to France, then bought them both out at a fair but low price. If she was a figure in the art world before the change, she was now a remarked-upon, recognizable figure. When Martin escorted her to one of her obligatory openings or parties, he was surprised to find that everyone knew exactly who she was. They kept tabs on her from the moment she entered the room. Hoping she would speak to them, they prepared their introductions; you could see their lips moving over the syllables of her name.

This all happened as usual the night after Stella's Japanese lunch at the theater. Martin accompanied her to a loft in SoHo to see bleak, red paintings by members of a collective. A statement of purpose taped to the wall suggested war in Central America as the exposition's theme, but Martin suspected an overstock sale on bala red was the real motivation. In any case, the paint-streaked artists turned as one when Stella appeared like Venus in their midst; the host tried to introduce her around, but could never get further than *I'd like you to meet.*

"Well, of course," said a man with bright yellow hair. "Stella Klein. Imago Gallery. I loved your neo-expressionist show." He smiled, but suddenly seemed unable to continue.

"Did you really?" said Stella.

"Well, I mean, it was uneven, of course, in some respects, but that's to be expected, new artists and all." He looked as if he might spill his drink. Then he lurched ahead. "How about this stuff? Do you like this stuff here? I'm not in the show," he hastened to add.

"I haven't yet looked," Stella lied.

It used to be she had an opinion on everything. She'd walk into a room and, as if the decor were about to attack her, fend it off with criticism. Now she mostly let others do the talking. Martin could see in her face that she still passed judgment, but she was content, or determined, to keep it to herself.

"Tell me what *you* do," she said to the man. "I think your name's familiar. Is it?"

As the evening ground on, artist after artist, each of them male, would shake Stella's hand, announce himself in a manner affected or sullen, then halt. That's as far as his social skills would take him. If he didn't head off for the bar at once, he'd just end up staring.

Stella would bail him out. She'd say, "What kind of work are you doing right now?" She'd suggest he drop by with portfolio or slides. Then she'd turn to Martin and say, "Excuse me, the phone, did you see where it went?"

And she'd call her machine for the tenth, twelfth time.

As soon as Stella left the main room, Martin would begin to sip again from his empty glass of soda. He slunk around guiltily as if he had forged a ticket to get in. He looked for a wall to lean against, but all the walls were taken up with art or with artists. There was nowhere to go except the bathroom, and that was impossible. He'd been to the bathrooms at openings like this; there were never any working locks, and he always walked in on some black-haired painter staring at himself while he urinated.

So he toured the show once again instead, looking mostly at the way the artists signed their names, and wondered why none of these good-looking men ever said a word to him. As a matter of statistics, if for no other reason, you would think someone would have something to say. Mere entropy should ensure a random collision. You would think at least one. *One out of ten*. But no. Not one.

Martin got up his nerve to approach two men who had earlier managed a halfway pleasant conversation with Stella. But as he neared them he heard one saying, "That Klein woman—what's her story?"

"Fag hag," said the other, chuckling.

Martin slapped him in the face and stood there staring, his chin all atremble, until the man started to laugh. Stella returned from the phone in time to see Martin turning away in disgust. "Mixing as usual," she said, and grabbed his arm.

As the victim of many related phrases, Martin could not tolerate affronts to others. Even the casual racist comments let drop by cabbies aggrieved him. But this was nothing compared with his rage when his feeling for Stella, and hers for him, was so maligned. It was no one's place to judge the value, the competence of their affection. To dismiss it as worthless; to dismiss Stella, even worse, as perverted.

Still, the ferocity of his response was surprising. He was not her lover and not her protector. He did not idolize her, as so many now did. He knew her too well not to find fault. She was headstrong and overdramatic. She moved from one tragicomic encounter to another in a way Martin could only describe as happy-go-crisis. She had no cake, and she ate it, too.

But after many years he had been permitted glimpses of the tiny, heroic things she did without crowing. He had followed her through streets at midnight, after a party, in search of the dog who depended on her for a meal once a week. When found, the mutt had leaped toward her knapsack, anticipating the lamb chop she'd wrapped for him in foil. She took him home to bathe him, too; how often this happened Martin could not determine.

Shelters and soup kitchens were part of Stella's shadow world, and kindness to the homeless on East Sixth Street. There were fewer of them begging near her West Side apartment, but the boy who slept outside the shoe store got fed.

Even now she was leading Martin from the scene of his crime to the refreshment table. "My hero," she said, dropping pigs-in-blankets into her knapsack.

By ten o'clock, Martin had seen more unbelievable need shining from pale faces than he'd ever seen anywhere except in his mirror. Stella was feared, pursued, courted. She was the key to these artists' dreams for themselves. This woman, whom Martin could probably lift on his outstretched forearm—so light she was, so ready to disperse—had them all in her thrall. She might have scorned them and still been admired, but she took her power as a grave responsibility. She slighted no one, and would not duck out, no matter how much she, or Martin, wished to.

Her sense of responsibility extended beyond the artists to the art. She visited each piece in the show at least once, and returned to those that piqued her interest. She affected the casual air of a shopper. If she found herself making a third appraisal, she scribbled the artist's name in her datebook, there to share a crowded page with grocery lists, appointments, and fantastic doodles of men and women kissing. When she did this, people in the vicinity buzzed with excitement, and looked jealously or appreciatively at the painting she had honored.

"Now?" Martin asked.

"No. Not quite yet."

When finally she determined it was permissible to leave, half the party followed her out. They called cheery farewells into the shutting freight elevator, or accompanied her down to the dark, industrial lobby. There they shook her hand weakly but repeatedly.

The man with yellow hair tagged along as far as the cab. It was cold, he was shaking, he'd left his coat inside, but he stood there smiling more than was natural. "I'll bring those slides then. Is Thursday all right?"

"Morning, please, if you're alive in the morning."

He leaned against the cab as if to keep it from leaving.

"Well, nice to have met you," said Stella.

"Nice to have met *you*. And you, too, Marvin."

Martin saluted from deep inside the cab. "You too."

The artist hesitated. "Are you going uptown by any chance? Uptown? West? We could—"

"No. New Jersey," Stella lied.

"Well then, nice to have met you."

"Thursday," she said.

"Yes, you too."

"You too."

"You too."

Stella smiled until the driver took off. Then, at once, she shut her eyes.

"You too," said Martin.

Her hair was up and her dress was plain and black, as usual. She unclipped her earrings, then folded her hand so a silver bracelet could be slid off her wrist. Not opening her eyes, she took off her ring. "Martin, my pearls, could you get them, please?" They were her grandmother's pearls: a willful anachronism, considering her crowd. She dropped her head forward.

Martin undid the clasp and let the pearls drip into her palm. "Here, Mommy."

She threw all the jewelry into the shapeless green knapsack she carried everywhere, even to parties. She slipped off her shoes. The meter clicked, and she eyed it suspiciously.

"It's a bomb," Martin said.

"Ach."

She swiveled around and lay her head in Martin's lap. She put her black stockinged feet up to the window. For minutes, they didn't speak. Martin twirled a plait of her fallen hair around his finger, and by the time they reached the Pan Am Building it was holding a curl.

"Why do all these men approach you, and never the women?" he asked at a light.

Half asleep on his lap, she sighed. "I imagine they must want to hurt me, baby."

Though she was attractive and powerful now, she still had a terrible time with men. They abandoned her, they evaded her, they were simply, incontestably absent. For this Stella took some of the blame. "I can only sleep with men I don't like. I can't help it," she'd say. "I'm drawn to them like a fly to a flyswatter. Or are they drawn to me like a flyswatter to a fly? It's an interesting question. When one is not a fly."

This was Stella at her most philosophical. But in the midst of some man's unparalleled treachery, her sense of mistreatment had the proportions and mythological tendency of a classical painting. Martin imagined it in its terrible gilt frame: *The Rejection of Stella*. In the lower left corner she lay naked, twisted in grief, while a horde of ocher-muscled men dashed off into the upper right.

She whimpered fitfully into his lap, for alone with Martin, Stella could still be Stella. She could rant and cry. She believed she had to steal things because no one would give them to her, and even her thinness could be taken away. She was still fat, fat as ever, beneath the black sheath of fabric, the hard, white pearls, the expensive, mysterious, luminous haircut.

MARTIN said hello to the night doorman, a handsome fellow, short, Hispanic, with a neat angular mustache. Though he wasn't much older than Martin himself, he had three young children; every evening at ten o'clock, when his shift began, he removed a photograph of them from his wallet and placed it neatly in view, by the intercom. He and Martin had never spoken until the afternoon a little girl in Martin's show came to visit; Delia introduced herself and then introduced Martin. From then on, the two men always said hello when they met; and once, on a Sunday, when Martin saw him walking up Madison Avenue with his family, they even managed to talk for several minutes. The man proudly introduced his wife and his children, whom Martin recognized from their picture, and said to his taciturn six-year-old daughter, "Mr. Gardner has a pretty little six-year-old, too."

It took weeks for Martin to figure out and correct the mistaken impression Delia had quite purposely given: that she was his daughter by a marriage now ended. And though the fiction that falsely connected Martin to his doorman had been revealed, they continued to behave exactly as if it hadn't, and Martin found himself with a friendly acquaintance at the door of his own building, where previously there had been polite anonymity only. Delia had done this; perhaps any child could.

It certainly made Martin think, as he rode up in the elevator, how much easier it would be to meet nice men if only he had a child. But there was a flaw in this logic, and by the time the elevator reached the fourteenth floor, he had resigned himself to more traditional methods of torture. He decided to consider the blind date Stella had suggested at lunch.

There was this to be said for the so-called Matt: his name began with an *M*. But Martin had largely outgrown the compelling voodoo of that letter. On the other hand, he had not yet found some other voodoo to replace it. Nothing dragged him into disastrous affairs—or any affairs; he had become inadvertently but contentedly celibate. It was three years now, he calculated. And this was fine. It was true he was lonely and, much to his surprise, aroused almost constantly by sexual thoughts. But he felt he had handled these burdens with grace. He did not actively pine for anything different. If he was aroused, he had the privacy and the God-given means to do something about it. I take matters into my own hands, he liked to think; it was a formulation somewhat defiantly vulgar, for though he did not seriously concern himself with the morals of masturbation, it did seem a breach of taste to formulate a defense of the necessary act in words.

Still it was true: he was in this as in everything else self-sufficient. His coworkers relied on him without hesitation; any man whose shoes were so clean need not be hounded to get something done. He worked in a timely, efficient manner— that's what a seventh-grade teacher had written. He did not talk back, or much at all, really; he brooked criticism well. In fact, he lacked none of the adolescent virtues. Well, almost none.

But it was in the domestic sphere that Martin truly took pride.

He was an excellent, entirely self-taught cook. He could sew a button, or a hem, if need be. He had decorated his apartment, elaborately, on his own: the Sheraton chair Stella had sold him held court in a room filled with other antiques, damask curtains, a prop chandelier. No one who visited failed to comment on how much "realer" it seemed than their own apartments— though it was not entirely clear that "real" was a compliment. Strangely, it seemed to mean its opposite, *unreal*: an apartment inappropriately decorous, stately. Something some adult would live in—but beautiful, yes, certainly that.

Despite its willful beauty, Martin had come to wonder whether it could ever satisfactorily house any human life other than his own. Such a human would have to be small and infinitely neat, entirely at ease with a long-outmoded taste, silent, incorporeal: exactly opposite in all important traits to the kind of person Martin could imagine loving. And so, Martin realized, he had boxed himself in. No one could pass his mutually exclusive tests; he must not want them to. And this, too, was fine. He liked the queen-size bed to himself; he was tall after all, and slept at a diagonal.

Still, when he took off his socks that night, there was the venous *M*, pulsing and livid. He turned off the light and tried to clear his mind. Across the street, in the fourteenth-floor apartment opposite, a man sat writing in the glow of a yellow lampshade. Love letters, Martin imagined, that's what he's writing. And the phrase brought him back to the *M* on his foot.

He could not sleep, or refused to. He lay in bed trying to manufacture an image of this Matt that combined all the uncombinable traits he required: an image of a man by whom he might find himself, both at once, moved and undisturbed.

D E L I A was uncharacteristically late getting ready the next day— she was unable to choose an outfit sufficiently novel. Her father, David, had let Martin into the apartment before leaving hastily, his raincoat flying. Maria, her mother, could be heard in Delia's bedroom, attempting to hurry the girl along.

Martin looked at his fancy watch, which told him, among other things, the time in Ghana. "We should get going!" he called, putting on a cheery voice.

"Come in here!" Delia shouted peremptorily. "There's plenty of time."

This was true. Martin had been escorting Delia to rehearsals lately, when their schedules matched; she had seen for herself that lateness was something he defined abstractly. No one was clocking him, and even when he left ten minutes past schedule, he was one of the first to show up at the theater.

"Help pick my sneakers!" Delia commanded.

Though he was scrubbed and well combed, Martin was not yet awake enough to relish participating in Delia's sideshow. "White is never a mistake," he answered lazily, entering the bedroom; from that moment on, Delia ignored him.

"You look strange," said Maria, who was sitting on a corner of Delia's unmade bed.

"I do? Really?" He peered into the mirror.

"Not mirror strange," Maria said.

They had known each other for six years now—the newborn Delia had been cast in a soap commercial when Martin was just a set decorator—but sometimes Martin wasn't sure they knew each other at all. Maria made baffling, laconic pronouncements: slightly menacing self-improvement koans. She had moral certitude derived from who knew what, and most surprising as far as Martin was concerned, she seemed to think he would understand what she said. Sometimes he had the feeling she was talking to someone standing directly behind him: someone older, someone with an Asian outlook on the world.

"Well, I guess I *feel* strange," he said. "I didn't think it showed."

Maria snorted minimally, as if to say that everything showed.

"I'm wearing these," Delia announced, holding up sneakers of a floral design.

"Excellent choice," said Martin, though in fact he worried they would conflict with the mad assemblage of floral patterns she had already chosen for the rest of her outfit.

"Even if Martin doesn't mind," said Maria, "Mommy has to get herself off to work."

"Then go then," said Delia quite practically. "Who's stopping you?"

Maria sighed, but her face barely altered. She did not move. Her long brown hair did not swing forward: it was parted in the middle, pulled up loosely, and cinched in the back by a brown leather buckle. She turned to Martin. "So?" she said. "What are you troubling yourself about?"

Martin saw he would have to say quickly and directly what he had hoped to say at leisure later. "Do you think I ought to go on a blind date?" he asked.

Delia looked up from tying her sneakers.

"See, Stella is trying to set me up with this guy, his name is Matt, but I'm not sure—"

"Yes!" said Maria, interrupting. "By all means. By *every* means." Then she left the room to put on her coat.

A NEW TRUCK arrived from Philadelphia overnight, but much was damaged and much was missing. No one could find the second-scene drop. "Where's the Manhattan skyline?" Martin kept asking. The stage manager distinctly remembered seeing it lowered from the flies at the Forrest, remembered seeing it rolled and tied, but after that she'd lost track. It must have gone into the ill-starred truck and, unlikely as it seemed, been pilfered with the ficus.

The drop had been Martin's creation, one of his most visible contributions to *Jet Set*. The designer, an elderly Russian gentleman whom Martin was assisting, had blanched at the idea of doing it himself. "I can't face all those lines," he said. What the show required was so detailed and tedious and relentlessly complicated, he just turned a vague sketch over to Martin and sighed. "Take my backdrop. Please," he said. He preferred to spend his energy on a blurry romantic scene of the Alps, on a Beaux Arts ballroom. Anyone would have—anyone but Martin.

Martin had jumped at the opportunity. He'd work through the night without moving from his drafting table. He'd fall asleep amid pencils and rulers, electric eraser, and onionskin. His paraphernalia slept alongside him, except for the glass of seltzer, ever so slowly giving up the ghost, and his patient calculator, remembering its answer. After an hour, he'd wake up, resume; he'd look outside at the actual skyline, reject it, make it more rigid for his drawings. When the room turned light, he'd slink to bed and dream of cornices, courses of brick, reticulated skies.

It was everything Martin most enjoyed, and nothing he feared. Straight edges, complex perspectives, flat surfaces: his métier. A teacher had told him long ago that the soul of art was in the curve, but he couldn't draw one properly until the day he sat down with tape and a compass and trained his hand by mechanical repetition. Years later curves still came grudgingly; in this backdrop he had an excuse to banish them altogether. "Not a curve in sight," the painters who realized his design had said, looking at the blueprint admiringly.

Now it needed repainting. With previews beginning on the first of March—three days away—Martin found himself working all hours at the scenery studio in the bombed-out South Bronx. The same four painters had been assigned to the task; with two thousand individual windows to copy, three hundred buildings, millions of pinpoint stars and bulbs, the three days left would be just long enough.

And so, for the second time, Martin was helping to lay out a twelve-inch grid on a piece of canvas the size of a house. Each square of the grid was labeled in pencil to correspond with identical squares on the original blueprint: A-1 through Z-67. One square at a time, working radially out from various centers, the painters would enlarge and transfer the image. Manhattan would develop upon the canvas, a colony of rectilinear amoebas.

Over Martin's protests, Stella came to the studio for a look— she had to look at everything, it seemed. She watched the men and women creep around with their brushes. "This is right up your alley," she said to Martin, walking along the beige periphery. She pointed toward a tall building in progress. "What is that one going to be?"

"Citicorp."

Stella stood above one of the workers, a well-built man with an olive complexion and little round glasses. As it was hot in the studio, his shirt was off; the hair on his chest, Martin had noted, grew in the shape of a perfect martini.

The man's name, astonishingly, was Cy, for this is what everyone did in his presence. He looked up from the tiny window he was painting. "See the triangular roofline?" he said. "I'll get to it in about an hour. Then you'll really be able to tell."

"L-26," Martin said.

Stella knelt down in a dry patch of canvas to examine Cy's technique at close range. She addressed him intimately. "Where I grew up, that's how the town was divided up. My father worked at X-10. My mother worked at Y-12."

"Where was this, Mars?"

"No, but close. Oak Ridge, Tennessee. X-10 was the nuclear pile. Y-12 was biomedical research. You know, the Manhattan Project. Like your Manhattan Project here, except with a bomb."

"A bomb could be arranged," Cy said, apparently referring to *Jet Set* itself. Indeed the show was a bit ludicrous, but nice to look at, and fairly tuneful.

Stella smiled. Martin, warily, made introductions.

"So how is Martin as a boss?" she asked.

"A stern taskmaster."

Stella laughed.

"No, he's all right."

Martin mimed cracking a whip. "Tote that barge," he said, and then dragged Stella into another room.

Cy was one of Martin's secret loves. Their intimacy had proceeded rather slowly, however: they had shaken hands once, and Martin had paid him a compliment on his work. Stella, in one minute, had gotten miles further. She had deliberately leaned on his shoulder to get up, had touched the beautiful skin without hesitation. She was so direct in her indirection—and yet this was nothing more than Martin would have done if he could. Indeed, since he was forbidden to touch, he found himself compensating, it embarrassed him to realize, by breathing in deeply when this fellow passed by. What was he doing? Hoping to catch a scent of—well—he didn't know what.

"Would you like me to set you up on a date?" Martin asked.

Stella hummed a little and seemed to consider.

In the inner office, Martin's plans were rolled up in scrolls. He spun one out for Stella to examine, but her attention had turned to a wall of windows. Through its motley panes, the Bronx was alternately revealed and obscured. A crumbling tree, a closed bodega, then a milky pink warp of glass. A game of jump rope. Frosted vagueness. Another tree, limp. The Bronx was coming back, people said, but Martin always wondered, as what?

Stella was appraising the view as if it were art. "This would make a wonderful something. Photo at least. Well, maybe not. Anyway, Martin, what about Thursday?"

"Thursday."

"Next Thursday. You know what I mean. What about dinner? Dinner seems a good way to do it, don't you think? You'll have all these little tasks so you won't go crazy, and he'll of course be impressed with the food. I'll keep the conversation moving. So are we settled?"

Martin was silent.

"Good."

"But why? Why am I doing this? I'm content, Stella. I'm quite content."

"You are not content. Will you please accept that you have these feelings, you're allowed to have them, they aren't shameful or bad?"

"I've come to terms with all that."

"You think you've come to terms because you've withdrawn from temptation. But in your own heart you still believe your desires are unnatural. I'll tell you what, Martin: *All* desires are unnatural. What's natural is just to lie there and molder. So please get off your chicken divan and start thinking up a menu. We'll be at your door at seven-thirty."

Martin shook his head. "The show will just be starting previews. And what would I make? Lamb chops? Veal? Is he vegetarian? Who *is* he anyway?"

"He's a guy who comes into the gallery a lot, just to look, because he likes the art." She raised her eyebrows pointedly. "I don't know, it worked for me before."

"Dumb? Smart? Callous? Caring? Any distinguishing features of any sort? I mean, gay people don't match just because they're gay. It's not like matching shades of black. What if he doesn't know music, or poetry? What about then?"

"Martin. All I can say is, he says smart things and he looks like a model. If you want a guaranteed Robert Browning, go to Westminster and kiss the marble. This is what I've got that's alive. And look, Martin, *don't* overdo it. Just think calm thoughts, don't try to resist. That's the key. Let it happen, whatever it is. Imagine you're someone else completely."

"Any suggestions?"

She thought a moment. "Gandhi," she said.

MARTIN studied his *Joy of Cooking* and Julia Child. Every menu he attempted to devise seemed a wild overstatement of intentions he did not have. Starch or spice, cream or chocolate—

all of it seemed so lush and pretentious. Oysters too obvious, curry too aggressive. Chicken divan kept coming to mind, but only because of Stella's joke. There was nothing he could make. They'd have to go to Papaya King and guzzle fetid hot dogs.

"Gandhi, Gandhi, Gandhi," said Stella on the phone. .

Eventually he cobbled a menu together. He read it over and over, aloud. Vichyssoise, salad, Pommery chicken, carrots bécha-mel, chocolate mousse in chocolate cups—it made him sick merely to imagine.

But he was resolved to go ahead with the terrible plan, if only to avoid disappointing Stella. And Maria, too, had seemed so certain. *By every means*, she had said, and looking at his elabo-rate menu—it was designed more like a trap than a dinner—he knew he was complying.

He called the elderly Russian designer on Thursday morning to beg off work. "I have the flu," he said. "I'm sorry." He covered the mouthpiece of the phone and coughed lamely. He called Maria and said she'd better plan to take Delia to rehearsal herself the next morning—just in case he got delayed.

"I'd be only too happy," Maria said, with something that passed for a leer in her voice.

Martin sat at his drafting table and prepared a master plan. He laid out on graph paper the various tasks he would need to accomplish in order to have everything ready by seven-thirty. There would be shopping first, then dessert to assemble. Once the mousse was in the freezer, and the chocolate cups safely drying, he'd peel the potatoes and start the soup. Next would come the salad—or no; save the salad for late in the day. He put a question mark next to this notation.

Now there was a decision to be made about the chicken. He could buy the breasts already cleaned, but they cost more that way and the butcher never did an adequate job. Even if Martin asked him to, he would not remove the stringy white tendon on the underside of the fillet. When cooked, it turned rubbery and made Martin sick. Therefore, despite the time it took, he would do it himself. *Clean chicken*, he neatly wrote, then added a prim exclamation point.

Initial food preparation would go on until midafternoon. When everything that could be done was done, he would vacuum and straighten the apartment. If things moved quickly, he'd sneak a nap before his shower, and still have plenty of time to dress. According to his chart, he'd be finishing the béchamel at exactly the moment the doorbell would ring. It was like a moon shot.

At quarter past seven, right on schedule, Martin whisked the béchamel until it thickened and turned perfectly smooth. Reading the recipe carefully from the book, although he already knew it by heart, he then put it into the oven to finish. Twenty minutes, it supposedly took. Everything else was already done. He walked around the apartment checking, adjusting the angles of prints and furniture. He dried the inside of the sink with a towel. Was there anything else? His shirt smelled funny, that dry-cleaning smell. He put on cologne. He tried to wash it off.

If the name Matt entered his mind, he banished it. He did not imagine what might happen between them. He did not let himself think what he wanted. He thought only about the food and its schedule, which was embarrassing enough. He felt unbearably homosexual. There was nothing that wasn't unpleasant to consider. His appearance: too tall, too neatly dressed. His smell: a mixture of naphtha and musk. He perched on a chair and then jumped away because he'd been perching just as his mother would. Is there no one I'm allowed to be? he thought.

Out the window, across the street, the man on the fourteenth floor turned on his yellow light. He set to work calmly, as he did every evening. He seemed to be typing another letter. Then he stopped. He got up from his desk and turned off the light. Martin went to another window for another view, as if changing a channel, but nothing of interest was playing there either.

At seven-thirty the sauce was done, but Stella and Matt had not yet arrived. Martin opened the oven door and studied the little blue pot inside. Should I take it out? he wondered. What if it cools too much, will it curdle or something? He started to reach for a cooking mitt, then changed his mind. Maybe they'd show up soon, he thought. He stared at the pot again. It burped. Well? he wondered. What do I do? Maybe I ought—

The doorbell rang and Martin grabbed the pot. He tried not to scream as he spilled its contents all over the floor. His hand turned red immediately. From outside the door he heard Stella saying, "Martin? Martin?"

He bit the thumb of his unburnt hand. He had used a pound of butter for cooking; there was none left now to conscript as a salve.

"Martin? Martin?" Stella called. "Are you all right? I'm letting us in."

Martin heard the dead bolt shift; he ran to the bathroom. An impression of the pot's knobby handle was now developing on his palm. He washed it under cold water.

"Martin? Martin?"

"What a great place!" a man's voice exclaimed: a sweet, reedy, high-pitched voice.

"Martin?"

He answered heartily, falsely calm. "I'm back here, Stella, show Matt around. I burnt myself a little is all. I'll be there in a minute."

"Oh, Martin, you didn't." She stalked into the bathroom.

"Go back, go back!"

"Do you have first-aid cream? Here, let me get it." She took a tube from the medicine cabinet and applied the stuff gently to Martin's right hand. "Quiet," she warned, and gestured with her head toward the living room. "Be a man, Martin. Stop moving around." He clamped his lips shut, and his eyes, and his legs.

Several minutes later, the two of them emerged from the

bathroom. Stella said, "There, all fixed, all better," and made introductions. Matt came forward with his right hand outstretched, but Martin's was covered with the milky paste.

"I'm afraid I can't right now," he said.

Matt smiled and offered his left.

They shook their wrong hands, a perversity that seemed to Martin almost sexual. But anything would have: a card on a tray, a name tag even. It made him nervous. With Matt looking directly into his eyes, he couldn't get steady. He started to tilt.

"Well," said Stella.

Matt turned toward the dining-room table. "Can I help you or something?"

"No, no," Martin said. "It's under control."

Stella smiled.

"We brought some flowers," said Matt. "They're just from some Moonie on the street, I'm afraid."

"Thank you. Stella, could you—a vase?" Oddly for him, he pronounced the word to rhyme with Oz. "Above the sink?"

Stella walked into the kitchen with the plastic funnel of tiny roses. "Oh, Martin," she said. "All over the floor yet!"

"I didn't wear the glove," Martin explained. "The béchamel. I forgot it would be hot."

Matt smiled a vague understanding. "You have a lovely apartment," he said. "I've never seen anything quite so orderly."

Martin moved away. He had to move away. Something was going awry in his body. Not as if he were going to faint, but as if he were going to inflate and then burst. One minute since meeting. Or maybe it was just the burn.

Matt was slim, hungry looking, not spindly like Martin. Shorter, compact. Something springy just beneath the skin. His hand had been soft, but the fingers long and intent. Martin continued to feel the lock of them in the webs of his palm. He could not dismiss the strange image, so nearly correct. What's wrong with this picture? The improper hands, matched up like gears.

It wasn't right to think this way, but as long as he looked, it was all he could think. His logical self had packed its bags, leaving behind only an insatiable eye. Matt dropped himself into a Corbusier club chair—the only modern piece in Martin's apartment—and rubbed his neck like a cat against it. A puncture at the thigh of his jeans showed red skin beneath—well, it couldn't be red, could it? Could it? His eyes were gray and tapered like minnows.

"Do you live here alone?"

"Yes. I do."

"And do you like that?"

"Yes. I mean, it's—small. For two. Not that I've ever had two. People here, I mean." He sighed. "Barely one."

"I know what you mean," said Matt, and Martin irrationally believed that he did.

"Good," he said.

A broad smile rose slowly across Matt's face, then subsided partway. "Good. How's your hand?"

"Oh. Fine," Martin stalled. "It's sort of numb." He turned toward the kitchen. "Stella," he called, "have you found a vase?"—and this time he pronounced it the other way.

"Let me see," said Matt.

"What?" said Martin.

"Your poor hand."

He held the offending item up.

"No, let me see it closer."

Martin walked toward the chair with his hand out in front of him as if to say stop.

Matt leaned forward. "I almost went to medical school. But it was too much what my family wanted. The sad thing is I would have been good. I like what doctors get to do."

"Cure people."

"Yes. And examine them."

After a moment Martin took his hand away. "Stella?" he said, uncertainly.

"Stellaaaaa!" Matt roared, sotto voce.

Water was rushing from the spigot into the vase; Stella couldn't hear them at all. They were alone. They looked at each other.

Well why not? Martin thought. Everyone else believed in love at first sight. And even if it was only lust, might he not be allowed his share of that? Despite its impermanence, despite its mess? Oh, there were a million things to be said against it, but one thing stronger to be said in its favor: It was true. He felt it—it was true.

Martin smiled openly, the first honest smile of his life, he thought.

"My girlfriend has a chair like this," said Matt. "Not as nice, though." He rubbed the arm.

Martin cocked his head away and saw his face hang in five copper pots. Spotless, he noted to himself with relief. Then he studied his dappling palm. Not spotless, he thought. Stella, returning from the kitchen in time to hear the startling news, dropped a sprig of baby's breath on the dining-room floor.

"Leather," said Matt.

Stella let out a short, stubby laugh. "Whoops," she said. "I think we've made a tiny mistake."

Martin turned smartly and dashed to the kitchen. The béchamel was crusting, blob-shaped on the floor, like a daisy decal for the bottom of a tub. So you would not slip. He took a sponge from the sink and knelt down to scrub.

Stella followed him and closed the door. "Martin. Martin. No call for anger. An honest mistake. Anyone would make it." She patted his back.

"I spent fifty dollars and a day off from work to prepare a dinner, I burnt my hand doing it, I smell like some kind of industrial accident—" He started to pant. "I told Maria I couldn't take Delia to rehearsal tomorrow, *just in case*—" He stopped to get control of his breathing. He slapped his good hand in the pool of white sauce, leaving a handprint.

Stella lifted him up by the arm. "That's enough," she said. "No use crying over spilt béchamel. Just wash your hand and let's have the soup." She straightened his shirt then looked at the stove. "*Is* there soup?"

"I can't," said Martin.

"Gandhi, Gandhi."

"I'm so ashamed."

"Ashamed? Good Lord. Whatever for?" She started to open the kitchen door. "You know, he could be nice, even so."

"I don't want him to be nice," Martin sputtered.

Stella breathed deeply, listened to the clock. "All right," she said, when ten seconds had passed.

"I can't," said Martin.

"Gandhi," she answered. She clapped her hands, then clapped them again. She opened the door. "Dinner, Matt?" she suggested brightly.

DESIRE and shame. The two elements came together like halves of a formula for glue, and stuck like it. Instantly. Permanently. Martin had never encountered one without the other crowding in. His fondest hope in sex was therefore not for happiness; happiness was impossible. Or never yet achieved, at least. But oblivion, blankness, these he had known.

To such a blank union he owed his life. Perhaps everyone did. Conception was just a chemical event, accompanied by grunting and pleasure, if lucky; by grunting and pain, if not. In any case blank. But his he believed to be blanker than that: he believed his conception had been immaculate. Not mystical, but very, very clean. There was no other way to imagine it. That conception had occurred he grudgingly admitted, on the weak evidence of his own existence. But surely his mother could not have endured the prerequisite wrangling, the damp entanglements, the inexcusable mess. And yet he knew she had. She had done it more than once. It was just another of the thousand household indiscretions a mother faced: dust, thumbprints, scraps of linguine in the sink drain trap.

But this theory failed to account for Martin's perception that his mother lacked a body. She seemed to exist where skin showed only: below the hem and white cuffs of her navy-blue dress, and above the dotted line of pearls at her neck. He never saw more. She didn't undress in front of him or even in front of his twin baby sisters—not a watch, not a ring. And undressing *them* was mostly left to Nanny.

"Nanny, change the babies."

"Nanny, see that Martin's in his pajamas by eight."

When occasionally she was forced to handle the naked skin of her children, she did it as quickly as possible. Bathing the twins once—Nanny was away—she barely touched them and did not get wet. She filled the tub with too many bubbles from the clown-shaped jar and let the girls sink in the froth. She watched them play from the toilet seat. "Look, rainbows," she said as they burst indiscriminately. Martin sat under the sink.

When it was over, she rinsed them down and squeaked their backs like dinner dishes. "Dry off now, girls," she said as she left the room. Martin watched them rise shouting from the tub, in a fairy-tale mist, attached by their upraised hands like paper dolls. They started to cry. It was cold in the house. They were too young to dry themselves, even Martin knew that. They could barely hold on to the giant plush towel.

Martin dried them instead, and was grateful for the chance. He studied their bodies intently as he rubbed and polished all the strange, doughy limbs. His own body, which he knew he must not question too closely, had, naturally enough, yielded no answers. Perhaps the twins' bodies would answer instead. But they squirmed and displayed every inch of their skin without revealing anything. Their bodies were different from his, it was true, but offered no explanations. He had a clothespin dangling below his abdomen; they had mysterious change-purse folds tucked between their legs.

But he would sit on the edge of a hotel bathtub, later that year, nine years old. Water would drip down his body from the shower and funnel across his little blue penis. He would rub his stomach, as he knew he should not, and feel at first a strange, tight pain, a steely wet blunt light. Then there would be a pop, like a hiccup, and suddenly warmth—red, rose, orange, peach— which would fade. And last a face. A face that floated up to the ceiling, that broke apart as it struck the plaster. Who? Who? Or just the moon? Amazed, Martin would open his eyes.

How could his body contain this feeling, this pop and blossom of color? How could anyone's? Even his mother, drunk from a party, had come to frightening life one night. "Undo me," she said, meaning her dress. Martin stepped up on a chair to un-thread the glass bead buttons from their loops. Very gravely, he counted them off as the black knit fabric peeled open upon her. One—*be careful*—two—*come on, now*—three—*that's good*. She tilted toward the floor and finally bent over so he could reach number eight at the small of her back.

"Thank you, Martin, now it's off with you."

She slid a shoulder out of her dress, then headed unsteadily toward her husband's voice.

Sex could make you another person, it seemed; if not a happy person, if not a warm person, then a person at least who followed voices into bedrooms. Drunk you might have to be, deranged. Horny to the point of tears. But you listened for a voice and you followed it. You were someone else.

Martin once followed a man in the Village, a man whose shirt was stripped off and hanging from the back of his waist like a horse's tail. His shorts were cut breathtakingly high on the leg. Martin could see one end of the fresh, pink tan beneath the fray of denim at his thighs; the other end was hidden, would dip, he imagined, like a valley road across his hard little stomach. Between those lines it would all be white, all glowing and im-portant, like a featured state set off on a map from the darker-colored outlands.

Martin looked, then looked away. He was late for a meeting with a director who lived on Barrow Street. But where was Barrow? None of the streets at the intersection recommended itself; they all looked the same in the Village. In each of them men like the one in shorts leaned on buildings, talked out of the sides of their mouths. The streets themselves curved quickly out of sight, or bent off improbably around triangular buildings.

Martin wondered if any of these men actually did anything. Didn't they need jobs? He studied the one in front of him, the one in the shorts. A perfect diamond of fine, straight, almost invisible golden hair shimmered above his heart. No, Martin decided, he didn't do anything: he didn't need to. He was complete just standing there, drawing life in and holding it for himself.

Only when the man suddenly smiled did Martin realize how intently he had been staring. Then he blushed, ashamed to be caught: blushed, but could not stop looking. The man's teeth were as carefully laid in as piano keys, the smile broad and inconclusive. He was absorbing Martin's admiration, sharing it with him or ridiculing him for it. Ridiculing, probably. Who am I after all, Martin thought, wearing a long-sleeve shirt at the crest of July? Carrying a briefcase of sketches to a meeting on Barrow, when men are tangled in knots on the pier?

The man walked north on Seventh Avenue, but soon glanced back. Martin, confused, glanced back, too, behind him, south, thinking there must be a fire, or a cop. Then at last he understood. When the man resumed walking, Martin followed, forever it seemed. I can't be doing this, he thought. I must be on drugs. And he continued to think these two thoughts exactly as they walked ten blocks, climbed five floors to the man's apartment, as the door locked behind, as the clothes dropped away.

"My name's Bill," said the man no longer in shorts.

"Steve," said Martin.

They were standing naked on opposite sides of the bed.

Steve—or was he Bill?—had his penis in his hand. He spit on it and rubbed it until it lit up red like a flashlight.

"Well, let's get in," said Bill—Steve—rubbing.

They did get in, and so did a fly.

A person could become someone entirely different, but that new person never stayed very long. Martin's mother, having said "Undo me," appeared the next morning at breakfast as usual, pearls already on for the day. It hadn't been *her* the night before, and *she* had not been changed. You were possessed, but the demon was fickle and afraid of the light.

Not a demon. Nothing so vivid. Just someone else. Anyone else. For Martin, it was that anyone else within him who performed the old kiss-and-rub—a substitute slipped into bed like the fly, then swatted away with a pale, sweaty hand moments later.

"HILLBILLY heaven," Stella was saying. "No, really. Morgan County right across the ridge. Oliver Springs. The poorest places you'd ever want to see. Think feuds and whiskey stills, and you've basically got the idea. *Tennessee.* Unlikely, I know. But that's where I'm from."

"I would have guessed New York," said Matt.

He had finished everything—but everything—on his plate. Nothing had failed to elicit his admiration. The apartment: so beautiful! The chicken: so tender! The béchamel better for its mishap, yes! Martin wanted to bash his face in.

"Right," said Stella. "That's because everyone in Oak Ridge was *from* New York. Or other big cities. The place had nothing in common with its surroundings at all. It was created from whole cloth and just stitched in, with barbed-wire fences. A little bit of Manhattan in the Ozarks. The part where we lived was Z-25. Not exactly Michigan Pines. But that's how I thought everyone lived."

"How bizarre," said Matt. He licked his index finger, slowly, thoughtfully. Martin stared.

"The roof of my parents' house is still green—camouflage. The checks from the bank have a mushroom-cloud design. Do you see what I mean?"

Matt nodded. "But it must have seemed normal to you. It was your life."

"Yes. It was normal. The Hatfields and the McCoys were up in the hills, but down in the valley, the Steins and the Kleins."

"And after the war—why did they stay?"

"My father always said it was the beauty of the countryside, as if he ever went to look. And it *was* beautiful. You can't imagine. But it was less the countryside itself than the fact that it had been given to them. Who ever gave them anything before? So there they remained, the Steins and the Kleins, with daughters named Mary and Melody and Rue. Because Jews always have to accommodate a little."

"Like Stella," said Matt.

"Yes. A nice Jewish name."

"Stella for star."

"But they weren't all Jews," said Martin, who had hitherto refrained from commenting.

"What?"

"They weren't all Jews. They weren't even mostly Jews, were they, Stella?" Martin was getting tired of this party piece, of the party, too. He was ready to clear the room and clean the dishes and get some sleep and go back to work. But Stella seemed to have something else in mind; she wouldn't let up. As she chattered on her tone got more brittle, spoiling for something, Martin didn't know what.

"I suppose you're right," she said. "Probably they weren't all Jews. But I really don't know. It wasn't until after I left that I understood Jews as a separate thing at all. I never even knew people hated them. In Oak Ridge, everyone was a Jew."

Martin made an impatient face.

"Metaphorically."

"And what on earth is a metaphorical Jew?"

"Well," said Stella, "*you* should know."

Martin looked down at his chocolate cup, which lay in shards on his plate. Had he eaten it? He couldn't remember what it tasted like, or the rest of the meal either.

"And where did you grow up?" Matt asked.

"Rye," said Martin. "Nothing dramatic."

Stella smiled. "Not unless you consider Tennessee Williams dramatic."

Matt didn't laugh.

"Gothic," she whispered.

Martin's hand had now come up in spots, yellow and crimson. He thought about acne, about underwear, about the hopeless battle against impurity in adolescence. He thought about the spot of blood in the occasional egg.

"Gothic?" Matt asked. "Like turrets and bats?"

"Suburban gothic," Martin replied. "Everything covered; nothing seen. The exit you take is called Playland Parkway, if you can imagine. *Playland Parkway*. With a suicide rate like Sweden. And all those beautiful lawns and trees. I found it sinister, isn't that unnatural? But then I find everything sinister there. The houses. The *birdhouses*. The hills, rolling like there's no tomorrow. The next town over was called White Plains, which I always thought referred to the people. White. Plain. They've all got lawn jockeys by their mailboxes, now painted to look Caucasian in deference to the times. You can see right through the paint, though, to the big lips and noses. The paint makes it worse. The only blacks around were maids—this actually grieved me. And all of the maids were black, except ours. It was embarrassing. I was so excited when the people next door got a maid who was white, but my mother told me she was just albino. I was so disappointed."

Matt's big eyes shone with interest, but Martin got up from the table.

"Don't be fooled," Stella said. "He's nostalgic for Rye."

"I am not."

"He voted for Reagan."

Matt looked shocked.

"No, I didn't."

"Hey, it's no shame," Stella said. "At least you voted." She looked at her watch. "Here, Matt, have my dessert." She'd eaten one bite.

For a moment the passing of plates demanded attention, then Martin could think of nothing to do.

"Coffee?" Stella prompted.

Martin left the room.

"Stella tells me you have a show in previews," said Matt.

In the kitchen, Martin closed his eyes and leaned his head against the refrigerator. It took so little to be trapped. You merely had to move an inch.

"Martin?"

The refrigerator lurched into a cooling cycle and began to shake. Martin jumped back.

"Martin?" called Stella.

Hours ago, he'd set the timer so he wouldn't have to fiddle with beans and water in the midst of dinner. Now he wished he hadn't; he wished he could say: "Go home, people, there's nothing left to see here." But the timer apparently had had no change of heart; it never did. Were Martin to have died, the coffee would still be ready at quarter to nine.

"I'm the assistant designer," Martin said, bringing the hourglass pot to the table. "We started previews yesterday."

"Two of the drops are entirely his," said Stella. "And some of the furniture. Beautiful wallpaper, too, he designed."

"My specialty. Wallpaper." He heard himself spiraling into self-deprecation, but couldn't stop. "Can you imagine?"

Stella let her coffee spoon clank in its cup. "Martin, you are the sourest person on God's green earth. What is the matter with you?"

"I'm sorry."

"Be proud of your achievements. Think better of yourself."

Matt laughed, and Stella turned on him suddenly. "What's so funny?"

"I'm sorry. I was only just thinking of that old joke," he said. "You know. The man comes to the doctor complaining of a rash, and the nurse tells him to *walk this way*? So she wiggles toward the examining room, and the man says, leering, 'If I could walk that way, I wouldn't need the doctor.' "

Martin thought for a minute and then started laughing. He looked for Stella to join him, but Stella was staring at Matt as if she had witnessed a butterfly turning back into something unpleasant.

"WE SHOULD do this again," said Matt at the door. "I mean, not burn your hand, though."

"Yes. I'd like that," Martin said.

"Maybe you could bring your girlfriend," said Stella.

"Or maybe we could go to a movie or something."

Matt put on a denim jacket, threadbare, dirty. "Do they ever let people into rehearsals? I'd really like to see one."

"You could just go stare at a tree for ten minutes, get the same effect," said Stella.

"Tomorrow's a tech," Martin said. "You could come to that. Yesterday Delia—this little girl in the show—got thrown into the wings during a set change. So we're adjusting the turntables."

"Well, I'm sure that will be fascinating," said Stella.

"There might be some light cues, too."

Stella grabbed Matt by the sleeve of his coat and dragged him into the hall. "Come on, come on, before he gets started with winches and pulleys."

"No, I'd like to come," Matt said to Martin. "Would that be all right?"

Martin just stared, a bad habit that conveyed doubt when it really reflected surprise. "Oh! Sure, yes, that would be fine."

"God knows, I hope to work in a theater someday, I mean one with real seats and ceilings and lights. Phone sales is only my hobby, you understand."

Martin laughed uncertainly and followed them out to the elevators. Phone sales? What was that exactly? He realized he had not asked Matt one question all evening—and had not paid much attention when Stella did it for him. Nor had Matt volunteered information. He had sat and listened with an eagerness that was flattering if not charming: he had been all ears.

Matt said, "So is that a problem?"

"No, please come. I mean if you like. Come around ten. It's Fiftieth Street, just west of Broadway. And ask for me at the stage door, which is closer to Eighth. Maybe you better—well, I'll tell them to expect you. I mean, if you like. Or—"

The elevator opened immediately upon Stella's touch. "He'll find it," she said. "He's a big boy now."

"Good night, good night," Matt sang in an unexpectedly high voice.

Martin waved his painted hand.

"Sleep well and when you dream—"

The elevator closed.

Martin walked slowly back to his door, which had shut behind him and was locked. Stella had the only spare key, and by now she'd be halfway across Central Park. Martin would have to ask the doorman to let him in, but it hardly seemed worth it. All that awaited him inside was hard labor. A crust of béchamel on the kitchen floor—he'd probably need a jackhammer to dislodge it. In the sink, dirty dishes would be stuck together like old candy. And even when all that was done, there was the chore of listening to himself think all night.

Stella would call at eleven: "Sorry," she'd say. "An honest mistake." It *was* an honest mistake, he'd admit, and then he'd admit that mistake or not, something had happened. A key had turned in a lock and fallen, a hinge had sprung open. A liquid had spilled. It was indefensible, and yet it was true. He was trapped again wanting something impossible. He was trapped wanting something *because* it was impossible. He would say he was wrong, wrong to feel it, wrong to say it, wrong all over.

Then Stella would say, "How do you think *I* feel about this?" For the honest mistake affected her, too. Matt was not what he seemed, what she had assumed him to be. He had a girlfriend; he therefore might just as well have had her. Why not? *The Rejection of Stella* would come alive on the phone.

Martin had a portrait, too, albeit painted on black velour: a sad, sad clown, with rubber hanky and size eighty-thousand shoes. His cheeks were completely sunken under the weight of cross-hatching, and his eyelids drooped like a bloodhound's. In the background, people were laughing, pointing, or scratching their heads in confusion. Martin called it *The Greatest Show on Earth*.

Their portraits were not so different really: they both depicted the aftermath of insufficient, imposter love. And perhaps the imposter—though it could never pass for the genuine article—was better than nothing. Perhaps the genuine article didn't even exist. Only knockoffs, always knockoffs.

So Martin would sympathize. He'd see it Stella's way. He'd realize what a blow it had been and bemoan the injustice. All this would still be a chore, but chores were how you filled the day. He would comfort her, and be comforted. They would urge each other to dreamless sleep. Finally Stella would draw the moral, which Martin would doubtfully, quickly affirm. "Don't throw good money after bad. Don't waste time on impossibilities."

It didn't seem worth disturbing the doorman just to play out this scene already known by heart. Maybe Martin could sleep in the hall, which was warm and clean. He could curl up like a baby, abandoned on his doormat, abandoned to himself.

N O, he thought in his most romantic moments, abandoned to beauty. When he was five, he had wept so hard over a Waterford vase, his mother had had to purchase it for him. From that seed, that first indulgence, the beloved monster grew. His father looked on in horror and his mother in bafflement, for it seemed the love of beauty was suspect, even in a five-year-old. In a fifteen-year-old it was downright dangerous. They sat him down and spoke vaguely against it: Art is all right in its place, you understand— On they nattered.

But Martin was already too far gone. He saw himself defending a proud tradition. What was mute and radiant perennially opposed itself to what spoke and was withholding—this was just another battle in the age-old war of art versus commerce. He would not give in. It was the strongest feeling he had ever owned and he would not relinquish it.

He got his way. He was allowed his art lessons, his white buck shoes, his new wing chair in exactly the shade of pomegranate he had chosen. There was no turning back. They could have tied him to a pencil-point bedpost and stuffed his ears with caviar: the siren call of this dangerous love would rip him away. Even now, in the apartment his disapproving father had financed, the Waterford vase stood glittering in honor, filled with a Moonie's tiny roses; his parents' dour portrait lay in a drawer, reviled.

Reviled, retained. Stella often criticized Martin's ambivalence—rightly, he thought, yet Martin persisted. He blamed his parents for what was sad in his life, even as he had to admit it was their indulgence that allowed him the things that made him happy. He disdained their intolerance, yet it was true: he was registered as a Republican and had voted for Reagan. He was glad the White House would be enjoying new china; it was an embarrassment in the world that America should be seen as a land of philistines. And if beauty opposed all the things that produced and permitted it, what could you do? Martin did not wish to be robbed of his only viable passion.

Perhaps he would not have sought beauty so assiduously if he believed he possessed it. But only once had the magic word been applied to him—and that anonymously, in seventh grade. He could not determine who had written the note, but its fifth word thrilled him as if it were obscene. When he got home from school, he hid it in his encyclopedia on the page where his own name was unbeautifully defined. *Any of several forked-tail swallows.* He folded the yellow note in quarters, held it in place over the tiny illustration, closed the book, and opened it elsewhere, many letters beyond.

The *One-Volume Illustrated Encyclopedia of the World* was his favorite book; he had memorized its pictures before he could read. The casement window, the vascular system, the shapes of the states. Everything in the universe was organized and accessible on its smooth, white, tissue-thin pages. An impressive book, with an emerald-green crown embossed on the spine, heavy and cool as luggage. The thumb indexes were leather, the letters upon them printed in gilt.

But it was not his book alone; when the twins were old enough, he had to share it with them. One of them found the note while preparing a report on the planet Mars. "Dearest Martin," she read aloud. "You have beautiful eyes. You're so smart, and you're so quiet, I like you better than the other boys." It was Kelly who read it, to judge from the huge, derisive shriek that followed.

"Beautiful!" She laughed.

Martin tore the book from her hands and then heaved it back at her. He was trying to kill her but missed. The book landed on the floor instead.

"Look what you've done!" he screamed. "Get out of my room!"

When Kelly had fled, Martin bent down to appraise the damage. The tissue-thin pages had flailed and bent, the spine was disjointed. He flattened what he could and tried to repair the rest, but the thumb-index tab for *M* had come loose and could not be found.

Kelly had been right, though, and Martin knew it. He was by no means beautiful. On the other hand, he wasn't ugly. He was what his mother would have called, if she weren't his mother, *well turned out.* Clear skin, even as a teenager, short, neat hair and clipped nails, corduroy pants, polished shoes. That's all it took to be well turned out. Beautiful was another thing, an inscrutable matter of planes and angles, of gait and proportion. Martin once asked his mother if he was beautiful and she said, "Men who are beautiful we call handsome, honey." There was an awful pause. Finally she said, yes, indeed he was handsome, or would be soon, but Martin knew it was not the same thing. His face had too many of those planes and angles; there were only supposed to be a certain number. His nose was too long, his body too thin. At fifteen, he was already more than six feet tall, with visible ribs, and hips like doorknobs. He would row crew for three years in high school to beef himself up, but you couldn't work at handsome, only well turned out. Crew was a well-turned-out thing to do, so he just became more so. Then five years later, he really *was* well turned out—by his father.

Or that's how he told the story sometimes. When he was more forgiving, he knew he had participated in the expulsion. When he was completely honest, he knew he had expelled himself. With a cab waiting in the driveway, he had assembled his parents in the living room, told them he was homosexual, and took off on the two-month European trip they had given him for graduation from college. Yes, his father had yelled something as he walked out the door, but who wouldn't? And perhaps it was only good-bye.

Stella considered the question moot. It little mattered whether Martin had been turned out by his family, or had bravely left of his own accord. It only mattered that he was past their reach—irretrievably, it now seemed. Robert Gardner had died soon thereafter. Martin was paged while deplaning at Orly after ten days in London: a phone call from his father's lawyer. *Son, I have some difficult news.* So much for Paris. Without leaving the terminal, Martin flew back home, where he found his mother completely altered. "I need you more than ever," she said, which turned out to mean she needed him to assist in the periodic administration of pills. By Labor Day he had moved into 14J.

When Martin waxed nostalgic, when he lamented his abandonment, Stella bade him remember the story of Moses, found in his cradle, floating among the reeds in the river. "He did much better with his new family," she said. "You will, too."

BUT he had not yet made that new family; no one was waiting to let him into his apartment. The eyehole stuck out from his door like the eye of a fish on ice. He peered through it, backward, at his miniaturized apartment. The Hepplewhite chairs with their blue damask seats looked like well-made toys in a dollhouse. One might have mistaken for a mushroom, he thought, the tufted gray ottoman. It was a home fit for small lives. He could imagine a frail elderly couple, who rarely went out, perching on the matchstick furnishings. She would have blue hair, he would have none. They would rattle their wee porcelain cups as they drank, and smile across the impassable postage-stamp rug.

But a couple at least was bearable. Martin had cast his image instinctively with husband and wife. No matter how pathetic the pair might be, it was preferable to living alone. Life without love was no life at all, was not a life, was lifeless, was loveless: was the subject of a million lyrics. People who lived alone were falsely cheery at best, or so they seemed in the movies. And the ones on the news—parents beware! At the first sign of trouble, they started molesting neighborhood children, who were usually found rotting beneath floorboards months later. Police would move in. A lonely man would emerge from his house into the camera light: neat but pasty, colorless of eye. He would look like an overgrown baby himself. People would say they ought to have guessed. He had the appearance of a crazy from the start, and what's more, he lived all alone.

Martin only mortified himself with this scenario when he was depressed; but to his horror, he found that in photographs he sometimes looked like such a man. The sudden light of the flash would freeze him, hands halfway up in the air, head turning, not fast enough, turning away. Even in posed graduation shots, he had the look of someone caught in the act. But what act was it? The act of existing? He had a drawer full of pictures of himself from all ages. Whether seated among classmates at a young teacher's feet or wearing a mortarboard in front of a false blue sky, he seemed more prepared for disaster than advancement.

But also in the drawer was a picture no one had seen: Martin supervising the hanging of a backdrop. In it, his head tilts up toward the flies, and what might have been a squint appears to be a smile. In one hand he holds a rolled set of plans; the other hand points up. A work light hits him accidentally like the moon, and in its glow he seems confident.

Martin called it the happy picture, but it didn't really look like him. Nevertheless, he occasionally took it from its drawer for examination, as if he might learn from it how to become the person it depicted. This person was alone like Martin, but not undone by it. He had mastered his aloneness; he looked as if he had better things to do. His job was exciting—not, like Martin's, a way to pass time. His outlook was hopeful. The most obvious difference, though, was that the man in the picture was attractive—beautiful. He looked like someone who would not lack for love.

This was the terrible paradox; Martin had seen it again and again. The most interesting people were the ones who looked as if they did not require you. If no one came along, they were willing to be alone. And yet that very self-sufficiency drew people to them in droves. How could this be studied, how achieved?

For Martin's vaunted self-sufficiency was really just withdrawal, as Stella had pointed out. Martin would copy the pose in the picture to see if it made him feel more independent. It didn't. His smile would fade back to a squint, his hand would drop. There was no life in the copy of a pose, no moonlight in the bathroom mirror.

His thinking was wrong. He was trying to become that other Martin, the one who was content to be alone, precisely in order to *avoid* being alone. He wanted to make himself appear confident so that someone would let him fall apart in their arms. *His* arms, *his* arms, might as well say it. But it would not work that way. You had to achieve your contentedness first, on its own merits. But what were the merits? Even greater loneliness? A different, fabulous variety of loneliness? What would you want to achieve it for—and how?

This was all beside the point. Matt would not be susceptible to even a radically altered Martin. He would not make a life in the miniature blue apartment, would not come to justify the letter on Martin's foot. He was just another in a very long series of beautiful impossibilities. Martin should have known better, yet he'd admitted Matt to his heart: no identification, no papers, no password. Soon he would be unable to root the stranger out. Stella was right: Don't throw good money after bad. Don't waste time on impossibilities. He should live that way, he told himself—but if he could live that way ...

He tapped the door with his forehead twice, though no one was waiting inside to answer. "Knock, knock," he said, thinking of all the tired old jokes.

II
THE
APARTMENT

Matt was leaning against the parking-lot fence. His hair, which the night before had been neatly combed in place, now stood up all over his head, in individual tufts, like flames. He was wearing the same pants and shirt he had worn, the same denim jacket, but black Chinese slippers instead of lace-up shoes. Martin imagined he hadn't slept. His eyes were closed, or hovering nearly closed, but even the lids looked bloodshot. He'd have that unbaked feeling, Martin knew, that feeling you needed more time in the oven, that the day was too bright to witness.

"Hi," Martin said from down the alley, but Matt did not respond. He was listening to a Walkman. Wires trailed down his back and into a blue nylon knapsack. As Martin approached he heard the jangly music leaking out from around Matt's ears.

"Hi," he tried again. He leaned delicately into Matt's field of view, not wanting to shock him into awareness. He had not expected him to show up at all, and now that he had, it seemed possible he might disappear if provoked.

Matt opened his eyes and smiled a crinkly oyster shell of a smile. The face transformed: grimace, wince, Mona Lisa, oblivion. He closed his eyes again and nodded in time to the music. "Hi," he barely said.

"Have you been waiting here long?" Martin asked, enunciating carefully to be understood.

Matt shook his head yes and yawned. "Oh, a few hours," he said, and Martin was surprised, for it was only now nine o'clock.

"Really?"

Matt performed his facial cabaret once more, but didn't answer. "Here, listen to this," he said. He put his earphones over Martin's head. "Philip Glass."

Martin signaled him to turn down the volume, then listened for a minute to five notes climbing over each other like very precise, very industrious insects. "It's so mechanical," he said, meaning it as a criticism, but saying it with apparent wonder, as if it implied something exotic, something beyond his ability to fathom.

Matt shrugged.

"You know, like a lovely—machine?" Martin listened dutifully for another minute, then closed his eyes. The insect sounds seemed to be opening up geometrically, their paths twining around each other like the bonds and spirals of DNA. He signaled Matt to turn the volume back up, and now it all poured over him suddenly, a wave breaking upon a child's red bucket left on the beach. Then beneath the roar, as his ears adjusted, he heard a kind of dance, a dance of the inner workings of the whole inert world around him, the vibrations of the chain-link fence, the captive atoms in a concrete alley. "Wow," he finally said, not certain how long he had gone without speaking.

"Isn't it miraculous?"

"Miraculous?" An odd word, Martin thought—a pretentious word? But no. Not when you considered the source. "Well, yes, actually," Martin said. "Miraculous, yes."

Matt's eyes were closed again and Martin took the opportunity to stare. *Miraculous* transmuted itself effortlessly into *beautiful*. And from there it echoed, lower in his body until he had to ward off an erection. He turned away.

"Beautiful. Shall we go inside? I can show you around before rehearsal begins."

Matt nodded yes.

Martin's day had only just started and already there had been hope, disappointment, pleasure, and embarrassment. The sun had come up and passed behind clouds and repeated this transit tirelessly. Even the music in his ears was receding. The insects seemed to be packing up their constructions, collapsing their spindly legs and bodies back into the holes from which they, and everything else, had come.

"Off we go then," Martin said. And off he went, or started to, not realizing he was still attached to Matt by the two rubberized wires.

■ ■ ■

"IT'S a little precarious," Martin said, sprinting fearlessly up the steps. He and Matt were climbing a staircase on the inside wall of the theater—a staircase made more of air than of iron, occasional slats crossing between beams. Below them, the stage was empty and dark except for the ghost light blaring in its cage. As usual, Martin had been the first to arrive.

Matt moved more slowly, checking his foothold, stopping every few steps to look around.

"These are the rigs," Martin said, waving his hands across a wall of bundled ropes. "They make the drops fly up and down." He pointed up. "Two of those up there are mine. Well, not really mine, exactly—"

"Which ones?"

"Third from the back and fifth from the back. They come down during—well, let's just say they come down. And then disappear."

Matt stared up.

"You can't really see them like this," Martin explained.

"Can you let one down? With one of the rigs?"

"The union would kill me. There's a fine for imagining it."

"Is anyone from the union here?"

"Well no, not yet."

Matt smiled.

"I couldn't, no. And it takes two strong men."

Matt pointed to himself and to Martin.

"Stronger than us, I'm afraid," said Martin. "And besides, my hand."

"Yes. How's the burn?"

"Oh, better, better," Martin said. He held the injured hand, which was neatly wrapped in gauze, up to the feeble light. Somehow he had managed to dress it properly, had managed to clean the kitchen, too. Nothing, not even disaster, altered the force of habit. If the world blew up, Martin sometimes thought, he would clean his kitchen of radioactive dust immediately afterward, and commiserate with Stella by phone at midnight.

"But I'm never cooking for you again," Martin continued. He had meant this as a joke, though it came out without any comic inflection. He emitted two sharp chuckles and mercifully Matt smiled.

"But I insist," Matt said. He walked ahead the last few steps, humming a complicated melody.

And now Martin could think of nothing more to say. He smiled inanely, as he had seen mute wives at cocktail parties do. When he tried to grasp a conversational hook, it trailed away without him. His mind kept emptying. Matt kept humming.

"Are you a singer?" Martin finally ventured.

"Not really."

"A musician?"

"Once."

They had climbed now to the sixth and highest level; Matt sat down and dangled his legs over the side.

"What did you play?"

"Can't you guess?"

Martin looked at his lips and guessed French horn; Matt smiled acknowledgment.

"Really? Were you any good?"

"So they said."

Martin stood still, looking down on Matt's dark hair, which was thin from this angle: delicate and mortal. Wedges of white scalp showed where the various sections started off from one another. It looked unwashed.

"I like this theater," Matt said.

"Do you?" Dimly Martin could make out the empty house, the extinguished chandelier. Using the darkness as a canvas, he tried to picture Matt in various naked poses, but the images were too vague and fleeting to give pleasure. Soon the pornographic pretzeling of limbs was supplanted by images of the limbs of chairs. Chairs never failed to hold their poses.

"Something seems to be flapping," Matt said. Indeed, a sound like a sheet being shaken had intruded upon the silence. Dust floated down from the flies.

"A bat probably. They get in through the vents and get lost. Or they're born in the theater and can't get out. They make little squeaking sounds like aliens."

"The Judy Garland story," said Matt. "Should we leave it some milk or something?"

"What a sweet thought. But I wouldn't think so."

Matt suddenly lay back over the narrow iron planks of the catwalk and sighed.

"Are you all right?" Martin asked.

"My girlfriend kicked me out last night. Otherwise I'm fine."

"Your girlfriend? The leather chair?"

"My girlfriend the leather chair. She kicked me out. That's why I was here so early."

"But why?"

"Got home too late."

Martin admired Matt's terseness, even if it was somewhat at the cost of comprehension. It made you want more. Martin himself talked until something finally stopped him. It made you want less.

"The last straw, she said. And I guess it was."

"But how can she just kick you out?"

"It's her place."

"I'm sorry."

Matt grunted.

"I mean, I'm not apologizing, I just feel bad for you. I know how much—"

Matt smiled.

"I mean, of course, I don't know anything. I've never been kicked out. I'm more the kicking-out type. Though I haven't done much of that either. I'm more the kick-myself type. How'm I doing? I'm more the—I don't know." Martin silenced himself. "What was her name?"

Downstairs, the stage door opened. Noise streamed in from the alley. After a moment, lights came up and started smoking, then dimmed a bit. Matt sat up.

"Where did you stay?"

"I shouldn't burden you with this."

"No, please. I don't feel burdened. It's a relief not to hear my own problems. I mean, I don't mean that exactly. It's not a pleasurable substitution. No. Wait. I want to hear." He sighed. "Where did you stay?"

Matt appeared to consider this, then said, "In a bar. Eating peanuts. I left when the sun came up. I thought you'd never get here. Chloe, by the way. Was her name."

The cast and crew could now be heard arriving. A high-pitched squeal announced Delia's presence as she dashed across the stage. "You're it!" she called to no one, disappearing.

"I was attempting, for the sake of someone looking in from outer space, to differentiate myself from the bums and drunks half-dead in the booths. By eating peanuts and chattering about current events with the bartender. Anything not to sleep. *I'm not here like you people.* Only maybe that's how they started, too."

Delia dashed back across the stage, heading for the door.

"Delia, no running!" Martin called suddenly over the railing. Several stories down, she stopped and looked up.

"Who said that? Who's up there?" She walked backward until she could make out Martin on the catwalk. "Oh you," she said. "Martin Martin Bo Bartin." She skipped away.

"Maybe we'd better go down," he said to Matt. "The tech will be starting soon. Only—" He stopped himself.

Matt looked up.

"I was wondering where your other friends were. Why you couldn't go stay with one of them."

Matt rubbed his fingers across the nap of his one-day beard. "Good question," he said.

"Unless they were all *her* friends," Martin ventured.

Matt closed his eyes.

"And maybe you came to New York together?"

Was Matt starting to cry? Martin backed off. "Well, anyway I'm really sorry. And maybe we should get ready for rehearsal."

Matt nodded, lifted himself up by his arms, and started slowly down the stairs. Following, Martin tried to picture him in a seedy bar near Forty-second Street, propped up on a stool, staring at himself in the corroded mirror. He would disdain to drink as he had disdained to sleep, and would try to remember that he was handsome and talented and young, still, too. That he had a family he could always return to, and skills, if necessary, to fall back upon.

But Martin's picture was made up of questionable strokes and could not be completed. Was Matt talented? he asked himself. He had no idea. Did he drink? Again no idea. Who was to say he had not been abandoned by his family as he'd been abandoned last night by Chloe? And yet, as Chloe must have once, Martin found these mysteries appealing, providing for them as he did only the most appealing solutions. Matt would prove to be sweet and loyal and responsible if trained: a companion, a comfort. If they could not be lovers, they could at least be— what? Master and dog?

Martin, appalled by his fantasy and by the speed and selfishness with which he had spun it out, erased the entire picture from his mind. He thought of chairs.

"Props!" someone yelled.

Matt turned around on the stair as they approached stage level. He looked up four steps to Martin. "I was thinking," he said, "if it isn't too much of an imposition, that maybe I could stay with you tonight."

Martin saw that Delia was watching them intently from a few feet away, her eyes unblinking as if it were a scene on TV.

AT SIX, Delia had a stronger personality than Martin believed he had at twenty-seven: stronger not just in its makeup but in its fixity. She was already a very definite human being. She had elaborate opinions and defensible tastes. She picked out clothes for her father to wear, unusual contrasts like black and jade green, which often elicited comments at cast parties. Martin had heard grown people say, "Gee, what a great combination, could you pick something out for me?" He had had the queasy sensation that they were only half kidding. "How do you do it, Delia, what's your secret?" they'd ask. But Delia refused to confide in them. She was like a fortune cookie, naive and unnerving, and impossible to leave unconsulted.

Martin admired her, half longing to exchange his childhood for hers. She certainly didn't lack for parental attention. Maria escorted her to voice class, dance class, acting class, school; David, though buried under mounds of references at the courthouse— at thirty-four, he still clerked for a judge—came up frequently enough to indulge his prerogatives as a father in the eighties. No Sunday pony ride in Central Park was missed, no creative opportunity with paper and paint skimped upon for the sake of tidiness. Delia was frankly the family's focus and master; no attempt was ever made to disguise it. When Martin was invited to join them for dinner, he found Delia's dolls and games rearranged, her crayons reheaped, but never removed.

In Martin's family's house, chairs had held steadfastly to their dimples in the rug; no childish accouterment ever disgraced a cocktail party. No child either: when visitors were expected, Martin and his sisters were exiled with Nanny to another end of the house for the evening. And the only paternal outing Martin remembered was an unavoidable father-son evening at the Science Museum. The boys had walked through a model heart.

In his real heart, Martin felt threatened and mesmerized by beautiful people: by Matt, say, by Delia. It was hard for him to tell how much was admiration and how much, the desire to change places. When he had loved beautiful men before, he had been unsettled by the creeping uncertainty of whether he wanted to possess them or *be* them—and by the suspicion that both desires were improper. With Delia, his longing to be happy and free, even at the expense of being a six-year-old girl, was some-times so intense as to fill his dreams with images of himself in tiny floral dresses and madcap sneakers.

These dreams had once mortified Martin, but after watching some afternoon television recently, he'd come to the conclusion that his perversities were mild. He had even read an article in which a prominent analyst revealed a secret desire to be Lena Horne. The desire had made its first appearance buried in dreams, the analyst reported, but once exhumed, took on a life of its own. For months he unnerved his clients by humming "Stormy Weather" when he thought they wouldn't notice. After a year, the symptoms grew worse. A drawl crept into his New York accent. One day his wife found her green satin pumps hidden behind the cans of tennis balls at the back of his closet. She insisted he seek help. Complying, Dr. X—as he called him-self in the article—tried to consult Anna Freud at a convention in New Orleans, but was rebuffed. Finally he begged to be re-analyzed by his mentor, a German, who developed a fascinating hypothesis. "Your fixation," he proposed, "is based on an overly developed identification with the housekeeper who raised you." She was a black woman named Helen—all the letters of whose name also appear in the name Lena Horne. The German be-lieved a woman named Nora or Rona had played a secret, com-plementary role, but couldn't prove it. Even so, he declared the analysis successful at the end of three years. "There's only so much you can expect from life," he told the disconsolate Dr. X. "Happiness? What is it? A monstrous riddle, an improbable an-agram! Forget it. Go home. Consider yourself cured."

Martin had been comforted by this story until he began to suspect it was a hoax. Still, when he looked at Delia, and felt himself beginning to evaporate under the light of her scrutiny, he was able to remember that evaporation wasn't the worst thing in the world, not even close.

Though Delia's talent was eerie in that child-star way—a Puccini tenor's voice imported into a Disney body—she enjoyed her childhood and was fearless. Now she was hiding under a sofa onstage, flat on the floor in a space that must have delighted her for being a space only she could occupy.

The set was slowly assembling itself, drops flying in, wagons sliding, furniture edging toward tape marks on the floor. Martin examined a breakfront as it passed, took a notepad from his jacket, and wrote down a reminder.

"The china needs to be glued in place," he explained to Matt, "or else it will fall."

"Hey, Martin," an assistant stage manager said. "What's with the carpet? Last night it got snagged in the scene change."

"I'll have a look, let me just take my friend here to a seat."

"Shouldn't you introduce us first?" Joe, who often called cues in the voice of Mae West, had bleached his hair blond and wore one immoderate earring.

"Joe, this is Matt."

"A pleasure to meet you. I work in the booth. Why don't you come up and see me sometime?"

Martin was appalled, but Matt laughed and shook the man's hand. "I'd like that," he said.

Joe had apparently taken it as his mission to bring Martin out. "You're so hopelessly stiff," he would say with a leer. One day in Philadelphia he snuck up behind him—no easy task, given Martin's antennae—and goosed him but good. Martin yelled, turned red, delivered a lecture on self-restraint. Joe laughed. "Aren't we the little martinet," he declared. And from then on whenever Martin behaved like a prig, Martinet is what he got called.

But now Joe seemed impressed with Martin. "Ooh," he said, wiggling his shoulders. "I like your friend." Then he turned around and called places for rehearsal.

The actors involved in the scene change appeared; Delia crawled out from under the sofa.

"I should take you into the audience," said Martin, and led Matt through a series of doors. A costumer passing them raised her eyebrows and smiled. Martin found himself raising his eyebrows in reply. What was he saying? Fifteen hours ago, Matt had not had a face; even now Martin knew almost nothing about him. But already it was clear he was going to be an asset. Martin deposited him in a plush seat, center.

THE STAGE turntable shifted, imperceptibly at first, so it seemed like something else moving: the theater itself, or your eyes in their sockets. Then it sped up suddenly, as it had the other day, and tossed Delia against the breakfront again. The stage manager raced out from the wings to make sure she wasn't injured, but Delia was already skipping around the apron, singing a song. The stage manager banged on the floor with her foot. "Too much, guys!" she yelled, down into the traps.

People always expected rehearsals to be thrilling in some way, when in fact they were generally just long and inconclusive: eventless save for the periodic snapping of cables and tempers. Once you got over the glamour of the machinery, there was nothing to recommend one day above the next except the complexity of the difficulties it held in store. A production became known by the sum of its disasters: the show in which the turntable broke, the show whose violist had a heart attack in the pit. Martin came to understand a play as a technical and economic event, like the introduction of a new kind of shoe. He could be proud of the proficiency of his work on the team, but never be struck by the beauty of the product. Well made or not, it was only a shoe.

But the theatrical life, before Martin entered it, had seemed capable of beauty. It would be religious, he thought, without the drawbacks of religion; profound in ritual, light in retribution. The worship of beauty would be simple, not encrusted with grotesque justifications. As Martin imagined it, the theater was like the church before it got churchified: free, communal, guiltless, magic. Didn't people speak of *the magic of theater* in the same hushed tones they employed while touring Chartres? But

Martin could no longer believe in that magic once he was permitted to participate in making it. He found you couldn't know the ropes and at the same time believe they didn't exist. Oh, there was magic in the theater, all right, but never where Martin sought it, never when he was prepared to take it in. The magic was confined to tiny moments: hard and sudden and unpreservable, like hail.

This rehearsal seemed particularly lacking in magic. The drawing-room set was fully prepared but absolutely empty; and empty it seemed for all time to come, as if evacuated of its tenants by the threat of imminent lava. From beneath the stage, the elephantine trumpeting of the malfunctioning cables grew louder and more insistent until it seemed something would certainly explode. Finally a wing chair edged forward an inch, teetering in place, and then stopped.

Martin was afraid that Matt would be bored, so he came into the audience with a set of blueprints and sat down next to him. He unfolded the trap plan and explained how the turntable worked—or, in this case, didn't. Matt was attentive, but crossed his eyes. "Wait," he said, "I'm not really getting this."

Martin started over. "Okay," he said. "Here on page twelve you see the turntable in section. This is the cable."

Matt put his hand on Martin's arm. "No," he said. "What I mean is, I'm not *capable* of getting this. I don't read plans. Anyway, please don't feel you have to entertain me. I know you've got work. I'm happy just watching. It's fascinating to watch."

"It is?"

Matt nodded, removed his hand, but Martin was sure that red ghosts of Matt's fingers were still developing there on his arm. He shut his eyes for a moment and forced a chill that was stuck in the middle of his back to climb up into his neck. He opened his eyes and tilted his head. It occurred to him that this little sensation, this little shiver and interruption of normal awareness, was all that desire meant: not so very much, not even pleasant, really. It should be easy to make it go away, if you tried. "It's really quite simple," he said stiffly, and pointed back to the plan.

A break was called on stage, and Delia came running down the aisle. "Who's he?" she asked, pointing her chin toward Matt.

"Delia, this is my friend Matt. Matt, this is Delia, the star of our show."

"I'm not really the star," she said confidentially. "But I might as well be. I'm going to be when I'm older. Everyone says so. May I join you for tea?" She jumped into the chair next to Matt and fanned her dress out. "I'm six years old and yes I know it's amazing. Two lumps please." She sipped from an imaginary teacup. She stuck out her stomach and puffed her cheeks.

"Delia," said Martin. "I was just explaining the turntable to Matt. Would you like to join in?"

"Oh, that boring stuff? I never touch it. Ta-ta, now, must run, do!" She jumped out of her chair and dashed down the aisle. The seat swung back and forth for a moment, creaking on its hinges.

"*She's* a breath of fresh air," said Matt.

Usually Delia could draw from a scene its maximum potential for embarrassment. Uncannily she'd uncover the topic most likely to turn cheeks red, then mercilessly exploit it. She had no censorship mechanism whatsoever; in fact, if anything, she had a reverse kind of censor, one that especially let pass those items considered by others unfit to be spoken. Infidelities, crushes, vendettas she'd intuited, she'd happily reveal to anyone at all. "But it's *true*," she'd protest, when someone tried to silence her. "I was told always to tell the truth."

Just now, when she had run so directly to where he and Matt were sitting, Martin had gotten the idea, looking in her quick, blue eyes, that one of her famous, embarrassing truths was about to be uttered. She had read into his thoughts, he imagined, and had found them ripe. Then, as she was about to pluck the mortifying berry, he had finessed her with his line about the turntable. *Join in.* He was surprised it had worked, but he had to remember, she was only a child. This in no way moderated the joy, however, he felt in outwitting her.

Maybe, he thought, he had outwitted himself as well in the process. Could the whole awful moment of truth be avoided if he pretended there was no awful truth to face? For he dreaded the conversation in which he would have to admit his feelings and have to have them delicately rejected. Perhaps for once he could reject his feelings and later have them delicately admitted instead—accepted because unoffered. Yes.

He flipped a page of the blueprints. "Here's a lighting plot," he said to Matt. "You'll like that better, I expect."

Delia had clambered up onto the stage by now. "Martin has a boyfriend," she chanted, lifting the hem of her skirt up and down. Out of nowhere the crew reappeared in time to watch her little dance, and laugh.

Matt looked serenely at Martin, who had covered his eyes with the palm of his good hand. He peered out from between two fingers every few seconds, waiting for the horror to end, then shut the fingers again like scissors.

"Matt and Martin, sitting in a tree," sang Delia.

TRUTH, whatever else it was, was for Delia a favorite game in which you had to answer any question she might think to ask— any embarrassing, occasionally sexual question. If you lied, or if she thought you lied, or if you failed to answer, or failed to answer in time, she hit you. Those were the rules.

Martin had discovered these rules only empirically; the first time they played, there had been no explanations. Maria had barely shut the door behind her when Delia took command. "You lie down there," she said, pointing to the couch. Then she took a chair near his head and began.

"How are babies born?" she asked.

"Maybe you should ask your mother," said Martin.

Delia hit him on the shoulder. "One point for me," she said.

"How are babies born?" she repeated. "Only this time, I'm warning you, I know the right answer, so don't try to cheat."

"If you know the right answer, why do I have to tell you?"

Delia hit him. "Two points," she said. "Because those are the rules. Is there something wrong with it or something?"

Martin did not want to be responsible for making her grow up, as he had, to feel that sex was shameful. He tried to answer. "Well," he said, "first two people love each other very much, like your mommy and daddy, and then, he, well, they, get very close and kiss and touch and say how much they love each other."

"Go on."

This was as far as he'd imagined going. This was as far, he also realized, as he had ever bothered to imagine at all. He tried now to draw the picture himself. "Well," he said, "then he, the man, he takes his penis—"

Delia shrieked and hit Martin repeatedly. "A billion points! A drillion points! You lose! You lose!"

"But I'm telling the truth."

"It's gross, I don't care! I win the game." She jumped on the couch with Martin and tickled him. "You're just silly," she said. "Silly, silly, silly. You're a very silly boy. The kind you don't bring home to mother. You don't even *have* a penis, I bet. Let's see. Let's see."

"That's enough now, Delia."

"I don't hardly think so," she said, and laughed wildly. She pretended to bite Martin's bare arm with her gums.

"Isn't it time for your bath yet?" he asked.

She stopped short. "Yes. Let's play Paint!"

An hour later, when he heard Maria's key turn in the latch, Martin panicked. Most of his clothing was dripping over a line in the kitchen; he himself was sitting on the edge of the tub, in David's bathing suit, letting Delia draw all over him with crayon soap and watercolors. "You're better than Daddy because he has all this hair and his skin is so dark," she had just finished saying, with evident approval. But Martin suddenly imagined how this scene might be taken; up until then innocent, he now felt naked and compromised. Before he could destroy any evidence, however, Maria had stopped by the door for a look.

"Oh, it's Paint," she said. "I should have warned you."

"He's great, Mom," said Delia. "He doesn't have a single hair on his body."

"High praise, indeed," said Maria.

PAINT came off, but truth—the uncanny conclusion, the letter spelled out in veins on one's foot—was indelible. Delia had not misread the scene, though she'd given it a child's happy, impossible ending. First comes love, she sang, then comes marriage, then comes baby—and here she amended the lyric to suit her—*in the baby marriage*. Well yes, thought Martin. The baby marriage.

Delia wanted a baby; everyone knew it. Maria was already three months pregnant, but the six months remaining could not pass quickly enough. She said, "Hurry it up in there," to her mother's slightly domed stomach as if her brother-to-be were hogging the bathroom. Perhaps she thought that Martin and Matt, if they started soon, could beat Maria to the wire. If only they would creep toward each other in their spindly new tree, if only they'd k-i-s-s-i-n-g. Delia, for all her precocity, misunderstood some inconvenient facts, as, for that matter, did Martin.

Martin too had believed—if briefly—that love was universal, its effects transferable. He had not comprehended that limits were drawn around affections as skin was drawn around flesh. When he was only nine, he had loved his camp counselor fiercely and sexually, without even knowing what sex might mean. It would certainly lead wherever these things led. *The baby marriage.* Dissolution and merger. He imagined they would lie close, wrapped in each other's underwear somehow, their skin eventually fusing together. He would live inside his beloved. That John was grown, male, engaged to be married: these were mere facts. Facts interfered but could be assimilated; they had no more of an absolute existence than did his body, which had none.

So the fiancée became part of what Martin loved. He would lean against the wall of lockers in the shadow of the kerosene light and dictate letters. Behind the wall, past the laundry bags and insect repellent and moldering towels, the other boys would all be sleeping. Taps would long ago have sounded.

"Dear Betsy," he tried, "no, dearest Betsy, or my beloved Betsy, maybe."

"That's the one," said John. "Beloved."

"My beloved Betsy, then."

"Let me get that down." John appraised the blank sheet of paper and started writing.

"Here under the stars I can think of nothing but you."

"Oh yes. Let me get that down."

"Nothing but you," Martin repeated.

"All right, got it."

"The world is so huge and empty without you. I must fill it up with you."

"Kiddo, you make me want to cry just listening."

John worked carefully, forming his letters full and round as if he were stitching them into the page.

"Can I sit on your bed?" Martin asked.

John smiled and rose, picked Martin up by the waist, turned him upside down until his pajama top fell over his head, righted him, held him, hummed in his ear, finally lowered him onto the bed. "Of course," he said.

John played the bass fiddle; he was as tall as one, too. He had a soft, drawling voice and honey-colored hair cut regulation length, with cowlicks sprouting at every corner. His face was square and his eyes pale gray. Maybe none of this was true, maybe he was short and dark, but Martin was only nine years old. What he remembered with certainty was being lifted up and held. When John held him, he felt he could hear those deep beautiful notes groaning and singing from within him, as if he, Martin, were the strings, and he, John, were bowing him with his mighty arm.

"Okay, go on." John sat back down.

"Where were we?"

"World huge and empty. Must fill it up with you."

A photograph of Betsy was propped up on the peeling windowsill, just inches from John's blue pillow. Her shiny black hair fell down in swoops until it fell out of the picture entirely. John had told Martin she was even more beautiful than a photograph could capture, even more perfect. She made him feel beautiful and perfect himself. Martin could not understand why John needed such assurance, but looking at Betsy's face in the picture, he saw that she offered it anyway. Her eyes were bright and calm, as if to say she knew and loved him, and always had, and always would.

"I know and love you, and always have, and—"

John looked up from the letter. "Isn't that too corny?"

Martin reconsidered. He knew the kind of thing John wanted and had no trouble producing it. "The sky is black and the lake is black and the other cabins are dark and sleeping. The woods are black, too, and filled with emptiness. The noise of the trees—"

"Hold on. I'm not as fast as you." John reached to the bed and opened Martin's eyes with his thumbs. He held one hand on Martin's cheek.

"Your face in my dreams is like a beautiful moon," Martin went on, regardless. "Your face is like—"

"Wait, I haven't got the other stuff yet." He turned back to the letter. "The sky is black and the lake is black," he said. "And what?"

"The other cabins—"

"Oh yes. The other cabins. Who would think of that but you?"

Martin shook his head and yawned. He lay down on the black-and-blue blanket, which he already knew was a Black Watch plaid. He looked at the picture of Betsy and then back at John. Maybe they would get married, he thought; and he could be their son. Maybe he could lie between them, holding on to John, and John hold on, behind his back, to Betsy.

He yawned again. This pillow smells so sweet, he thought, so sweet.

"Almost there, kiddo," said John. "The noise of the trees is what did you say?"

Martin's eyes started to close. "Like the moon."

John married Betsy and had kids of his own. This Martin discovered when he wrote John, years later. A kind but characterless letter came back, relating the facts, nothing but the facts. He remembered Martin, yes indeed, didn't he play the clarinet? John wished him well.

BODIES were needed for the technical run-through, now that the cast had been dismissed. At Martin's suggestion, Matt volunteered. In various scenes, he stood in for actors, entering, crossing, doing whatever the stage manager commanded. Martin had thought he would enjoy the exposure, but he didn't look very happy up there. The lights produced a palpable heat, and Matt was sweating profusely. Carpenters had been at work, dust was everywhere; whenever a drop or curtain flew in, Matt could be heard coughing behind it.

Martin had noticed a similar phenomenon at the openings he attended with Stella. Artists other than those whose work was on display were always quite miserable. They scowled at the paintings, snorted during toasts. Martin found this behavior unforgivable, but Stella defended it. "How would you feel?" she asked. "To be so close to achievement, in the very arena of achievement, and not have it yourself? I sympathize."

"But surely everything rises to its proper level. They'll get what's coming, don't you think?"

"Oh Martin, that doesn't even deserve an answer. The artists whose work you see on display are in no way superior—not artistically, morally, intellectually, not even commercially—to the would-be's. Choices are utterly random; I know. *I* make them."

Martin nodded. Stella's arguments were always convincing in their élan, at least. But he had no sympathy for the feelings she described. Envy was, mercifully, a vice beyond his grasp. The success of others seemed a result of their natural superiority.

He had therefore not wasted much time agonizing over his own descent from painting to drawing to graphic design, or over the even bigger move down the scale, as he saw it, to scenic production. If he went low enough, he'd eventually stabilize, and that's all he wanted. His training—at Rhode Island School of Design—had been unbearable: the weekly critiques by doctrinaire professors, the daily backbiting competition, the momentary swings from despair to exaltation. Much as he had attempted to acquire it, he did not have the artist's temperament. He lacked that hunger for intensity, that comfort with change, that pride in defying timetables and fashion. The closer he came to a nine-to-five job in a three-piece suit—the closer, that is, to his father's example—the safer he felt.

Stella was always trying to push him more toward the avant-garde: to wear black sheaths nearly indistinguishable from her own, to design for street mimes and performing attics. But neither the clothes nor the arty milieu became him. Even as a child he had refused to finger-paint: too messy. He was too well turned out; his conventionality—despite the one glaring exception— was written all over his body. The *M*, he sometimes thought, stood for *moyen*. He liked middle floors of buildings, not too low, not too high. Theater belonged where it was, he believed, not upstairs in performing attics, and not on the street in the mystifying hands of mimes. Theater took place in between, in the middle. Theaters knew what they were about. How had they reached this state of beauty—for the Hellinger was a beautiful theater, it could not be denied—if they weren't right?

"We're talking to a man," Stella said when Martin started expounding these views at a party, "who voted for Reagan."

She always did this. It was the worst thing, apparently, to be said about someone.

"It isn't true," Martin said.

Stella laughed. "And Hoover, too."

If he was stiff, slow to respond to trends in the arts and in his own feeling, he had the unusual merit of stability. He had come down the ladder enough by now to have no fears of falling off it. Whatever was asked of him he could do proficiently, if not always with brio. And most important, the uniform fit: the chinos, the loafers, the pale oxford shirts. They made him feel ordinary, religious, clean. When occasionally he desired ornamentation, he could clip his tape measure to a belt loop, or a wrench on its rubber corkscrew cord to his pocket.

The actors he knew enjoyed their trappings as much as he enjoyed his. The trappings need not even be their own. Any stage they could get themselves onto, they held to the point of unseemliness. They appraised Martin's sets when they came to visit with the boundless eye of a pioneer. "I will take this land," they seemed to say. "It is my manifest destiny to have it all, stage left to stage right."

But Matt's eye was timid. Perhaps, like Stella's artists, he was too pained by what he had not yet inhabited to feel any pleasure in visiting it. Perhaps it was a rule among ordinary humans that you could never enjoy what has once rejected you, no matter how much you continued to desire it, no matter how long you lived in its presence.

Or perhaps Matt was merely sick from lack of sleep. And sad at his loss—which Martin could not help but see as a gain. In any case, the rehearsal ended: the flies flew up, the furniture retreated. "Thanks, you're excused," the stage manager said.

"For what?" Matt said, under his breath.

■ ■ ■

THE WALLS of the restaurant where Martin and Matt had dinner that evening were papered with the names of a thousand actors. Some were famous, some vaguely familiar, but most were the kind to strain the memory of even an enthusiast.

Martin was uncommonly antic. He read names aloud. "Starry Madderlake. Monica van Meehan. Who are these people? It's so pathetic! Ruta Alter? What is that, a tuber? Burke Alexander. They sound so fake!"

"They are," said Matt.

"But why don't they choose names that sound *real*?"

"Because then you wouldn't notice them."

Indeed Martin had skipped right past the Mary Jameses and Peter Carsons and had settled on names like Starry Madderlake instead. "Well, maybe you're right. But I don't think names should draw attention to themselves."

"How about this one? Inkaysa Chokin."

"Who? Where? You've got to be kidding."

"No, look. Right over there. Inkaysa Chokin."

Martin followed Matt's glance to the sign explaining the Heimlich maneuver. "Very funny," he said, approvingly.

"Didn't she star in *Projectile Vomit*?"

Many of the names were of people now dead, but a worse fate than death was available here. You could have a new name pasted over your own. At least a hundred actors had suffered this indignity, had been replaced by slightly more timely ephemeralities. And though the job was done crassly, it was complete. Not even the shadow of the old names bled through.

"It's a tough business," said Martin.

Matt made a face that combined several expressions into one illegible mask.

"No, I think of even Patricia Allen." Her name had been pointed out on the wall. "Now *that's* a real name. I did a show with her. *Hedda Gabler*."

Matt nodded.

"Did you see it?"

"Yes."

"In New York? Or—"

"Was it Washington maybe? I'm not sure."

"Baltimore?"

"That's it, Baltimore. With, um—"

"Ted Lazarus."

"Yes," said Matt. "*She* was wonderful."

"Didn't you think? He, of course—"

"Left something to be desired."

"Well, then you know. It was a trauma for her. I mean an established star. It was pre-Broadway, but we had long stops in several cities, so I got to know her a bit. She was really kind. And surprisingly frail. Considering her power onstage."

"Yes. I met her once. It was quite a surprise."

"Did you really? Well, then you know. I didn't notice it so much at first. We started in New Haven. But by the time we got to Philadelphia she just seemed defeated. Disappointed with Lazarus, with herself, even, I think. Though she was great, as you know."

"Her hands—"

"God yes, her hands. They're actually very small, you know. It's just the way she uses them. You'd think her fingers were ten feet long. She uses makeup to extend the line back behind her knuckles. She's the old school. Any trick that helps. Any port in a storm."

Matt smiled.

"Anyway, she missed her house in Putnam County terribly. She didn't like to be away from home so long, from her garden. She hadn't done a tour in years. But she remembered what they were like, and was dreading the succession of anonymous dressing rooms. I mean you would think her contract would have stipulated— But no. The old school. You're there to act. There was nothing prima donna about her. Get the work done. Like plumbing, she said."

Martin studied her name on the wall before continuing.

"Anyway, the rooms were so depressing. Even in the most beautiful theaters. Just cement-block cells really, with noisy radiators, if they worked, and views of alleys through windows that barely opened. There'd be a vinyl couch maybe. A bare bulb."

"I get the picture."

"So. I don't know, I like going to flea markets, and there wasn't always that much to do, so one day she comes in at seven for her call, and there's been this transformation. I'd gotten these cheap batik sheets and hung them from the ceilings, and a fake coromandel screen in front of the radiator, and a really bad gramophone that didn't play, but with a pile of old records anyway, and a quilt on the couch, and pillows, like that. A Japanese lantern over the bulb, which I changed to pink. I mean a bit like a brothel, but warm at least. And she said, 'This is absolutely the nicest thing anyone has ever done for me,' and she hugged me and cried and kept looking around at this absolutely mad jumble that cost me a hundred dollars, tops."

"Still, a hundred dollars more than anyone else spent."

"And it made me feel a little self-conscious. But it was worth it for that look on her face."

Whether purposefully or not, Matt made a face much like the one Martin was remembering.

"Anyway, the set was on its feet by now, so when the show left Philadelphia for Boston, they sent me back to New York. I told her, 'Everything is yours to keep so you'll have a home with you wherever you go.' One of the costume girls agreed to help set it up and take it down and pack it after Boston. So for the next five months she carted this collection of junk from theater to theater, and it grew, because one of the hairdressers or someone would add something new in every city. I know because I saw it when the show came into New York. They had made a crate for it. But the dressing rooms here are even smaller than on the road, so she had to donate half the stuff to other actors. When she finally left the show, she bequeathed what was left to her replacement. The only things she kept were the gramophone and its pile of unplayable lacquer records."

"And did you ever hear from her?"

Martin sat with this question a moment and said, "No."

"One never does." Matt said this with unexpected sadness, and Martin looked at him curiously.

"I mean you spend so much energy on a person and they barely remember you."

"Well, after all, why should she? You can't blame her. That's just how it goes."

Martin looked at his watch and saw they had been sitting an hour since the waiter came by unasked with the check. The last of their ice cream had melted and congealed. Outside, the street was the color of salmon from the sodium streetlights, and an after-theater crowd was lined up at the door. They stared angrily at the table that would not leave.

"I guess we should go."

"On principle," Matt said, "we should stay and torment them. But in fact I'm tired."

Martin took the check.

"No, I want to split it," said Matt.

It had not been Martin's intention to do otherwise, but now he waved Matt off.

"No, really."

"Come on, it's on me." He opened his wallet and withdrew a credit card. "Anyway, I mean, well—"

"I have money."

"No, I mean—"

"I actually *do* have money," Matt said, lightly. "I may not have a gold card, but I do have some cash."

"I'm sorry, I just thought, you know, with what's happened, I'd just, you know, treat you—"

Matt looked down. "Thank you," he said.

"May I?"

"Yes. If you'd like."

The gold card glistened as the waiter bore it off on his salver. "In fact," Matt went on, "my money is in Chloe's account. Well, some of it anyway." He raised his eyebrows significantly. "But let me leave the tip at least."

"What?"

"Nicer to leave the tip in cash." He dug some bills from his pocket and stood. "Shall we go?" he said.

When the waiter returned and the paperwork was done, Martin folded his receipt neatly. He placed it and the credit card in their particular places—everything in his wallet had a particular place. He put on his jacket and, while Matt wasn't looking, added several quarters to the insufficient tip.

MARTIN had once thought nothing of sleeping with men he knew practically nothing about, but taking a man home *not* to sleep with him felt peculiar, almost dangerous. Isn't this how people get murdered in bed? he thought. Or worse yet, robbed? It was a relief then when Matt suggested they make the long walk home instead of taking a taxi: Martin could use the time to get information. But how ask questions without seeming to interview? Unable to resolve this dilemma, Martin kept quiet and looked in store windows. There was something chilling and romantic about them at night, something never adequately reproduced on stage. But then anything too literal looked fake in the theater; it had to be fudged to look real.

"Penny for your thoughts," Matt said eventually.

"Where are you from?"

"Buffalo. Why?"

"I just wondered. I know nothing about you."

Matt sighed. "Oh, you want the story then. Well: Buffalo. Suburb. Lower middle class, I guess you'd say. Parents teachers. Even now. Scrimped and saved—you know the story. True-life saints." He stopped to yawn. "They moved into the good neighborhood, though they couldn't afford it, so we could go to the good public school. That is, my brother and I. Older: three years.

Let's see, what else? Junior year of high school abroad. France. College at SUNY, communications. Also wrestling squad. And Little Theater, as it was called. After college, worked in a local TV station. Moved to New York. Met Stella. Met you."

"You forgot French horn."

"If you like. Though none of this is quite real to me."

"What is real, then?"

"Everything else I haven't said. There's this woman in France—my year abroad—my French mother. Have you ever been?"

"No. Almost, once."

"We were very close. I called her Maman. Then there's these people I worked for a while back, husband and wife. They own a club downtown. They were nice to me."

"What did you do for them?"

"This and that. Mostly that. What about your parents?"

"My father's dead."

"I'm sorry."

"Don't be."

"You shouldn't talk that way. How did he die?"

Martin started laughing. "Massive heart failure!"

"I'm not sure I get what's so funny about that."

Martin declined to explain. "My mother flipped out. She was always a little on the edge, I guess. Now she goes to groups. Self-centering I think it's called. I believe she's found religion, too. Perhaps she found the one I lost."

"You're Jewish?"

"Lord no. Why did you think?"

"I just like Jews."

Martin blushed. "No, not Jewish. Not Jewish at all."

"You're being mysterious."

"I don't mean to be." But Martin liked the attribution and declined to name his poison.

In fact he wasn't sure what religion he was. His mother had originally been Catholic and his father some sort of generic

Christian. But Martin and the twins had been raised as nothing. They never went to church, and they'd learned no prayers. What imperfect impression of the Bible Martin had, had come from Nanny, whose retelling of the parables was generously laced with Irish folklore and spinster's venom.

One thing he was fairly certain of: The Bible advocated hospitality. And so, halfway home at Fifty-ninth and Third, he felt somewhat pious. He had satisfied himself that he would not be murdered, and satisfied himself more generally as well. He was content. In the window of Bloomingdale's, reflected amidst mannequins all a-scowl, there was his face: long, angular, and smiling.

And there was Matt, admiring a suit. "You could wear that," he said. "It'd look good on you."

"You've got to be kidding." The suit was sharkskin, big in the shoulders, narrowing down to nothing at the ankles. "*Are* you kidding?"

"Live it up," said Matt. "There's more to life than navy-blue blazers."

The navy-blue blazer Martin was wearing was insufficient to the cool April night; he had not expected to be walking home so long past dusk. Wind rushed down the avenue in bursts, tossing wrappers and circulars before it. It silenced him for several blocks. He bent his head into it. "Aren't you cold?" he eventually asked, hugging himself at a DON'T WALK sign.

"No," said Matt. He took Martin's good hand between his two and rubbed furiously as if starting a Boy Scout fire with sticks. "Better?" he said.

In fact it only made Martin shiver more, and seemed to dislodge a thought from his mouth. "I only have the one bed," he said. "You saw."

"Is that a problem?"

"I thought it might be a problem for you."

"No problem," said Matt. "I had a brother, remember."

Martin tried to look straight into Matt's eyes for some acknowledgment that this was indeed an odd situation, a delicate moment, but Matt just smiled pleasantly. "Hey, why did the chicken cross the road?" he said.

"Oh, I don't know, why?"

"I don't know either. How about you cross and let me know?"

Martin's building stood opposite, the friendly doorman reading the next day's paper at his post.

"Well, that's a first," Martin said brightly. "Me the straight man." And they dashed across the street together.

LATER, while Matt was in the bathroom, washing his face, Martin sat on the bed changing slowly and out of the light. He pulled off his pants painstakingly leg by leg without getting up, then left them in a neat figure eight on the floor. The quarter-inch hairs upon his legs arose curiously, seeming to peer around for something to look at. He took off his shirt and handed it, too, to the floor. His heart beat faster, exposed; his chest flushed red. He knew what the night would be: the brush of Matt's arm, the brush of his breath. This was the most that could be. He'd have to draw an imaginary line down the center of the bed and observe it. If Matt should roll toward him, the line would roll, too. Martin would watch him sleep; he would not sleep himself. He would lean on his elbow and his arm would fall asleep. But he would not sleep.

Not to sleep. Martin could flip through the files of his life and see a hundred nights of wakefulness. There he was on his elbow or on his side, X or Y or Z on his back: asleep, content, dreaming. When people were awake and you asked them, searchingly, what they were thinking as they stared away, they answered, "Oh, it's that ficus tree, a leaf's turned brown." At least when they were asleep, they made no answer. It was safe to ask anything. Do you love me? you could ask. Is there even the threat of the possibility of love?

A brigade of armed sentries would pour forth from Martin's hollow eyes. The body next to him, sleeping like a French mountain town during war, would not notice as his troops clambered out. It would not feel them take their positions on every side— at the pillow, at the bed table, at the sheet wrapped over to expose a warm leg. These troops would watch for any sign of compliance, any sign of attention. They were instructed to be kind but unflinching, to stand their nighttime ground, to mark it out with tiny sharp standards that would prick into the depth of sleep. The mountain would heave and alter during the night, moving but not shaking its colony of spies; and there, nearby, Martin would lie, an empty barracks with open doors till morning.

But as yet Matt was only in the bathroom, brushing his teeth with Martin's brush. The windy sound of the water started up. Matt said, through toothpaste foam, "This *mirror.*"

"Yes," said Martin, knowing what he meant. The mirror was dark and had an imperfection running up its left side. As you crossed it, reaching for a bar of soap or a towel, your image rippled slightly. You could watch as a wave of something moved across your face. You could imagine that this was what an emotion looked like: a slow, glassy disfigurement that passes.

Martin wondered how many mirrors Matt had looked in while brushing his teeth for a night of sleep in strange apartments. How many shower curtains had he seen in reflection: stripes, jungle scenes, distorted world maps that merged India with Brazil? What was it like, never having a mirror to call your own? Always seeing differently warped images of yourself, never one you recognized? Martin had seen himself with a warp up the left side of his face for six years now; when he saw himself elsewhere, in storefront windows or dressing-room mirrors, his face looked thinner, not like his own. But Matt would look to himself however he looked at the moment, and being Matt, that would always be good.

Surely everyone desired Matt. Surely every girl wanted to kiss him, if not every boy. Martin would not be the first, he told himself, and yet it would be no less painful for that. He had tried to avoid it, he had honestly tried; why was this effort not sufficient to spare him his punishment? For he felt the punishment coming soon, tonight, perhaps, a day or two down the line, absolutely, arriving like pain within seconds of a burn.

Martin changed into a T-shirt and running shorts that had never once been used for running. Matt came kicking his clothes from the bathroom. The pale blue briefs he wore, lodged so perfectly under his hipbones, seemed part of the same skin that emerged from under them, a suggestive though featureless continuation of his body, an arousing, neutering integument. Martin tried to remember where he was supposed to look, tried to see the faces of boys in gym when those naked dripping figures lumbered from the showers, swinging so entirely without shame it made for him its own kind of obscenity. Where would *they* have looked? At the floor? At themselves? Martin ended up eyeing the top of Matt's right shoulder.

"Are you tired?" he asked.

"Exhausted. Which side shall I take?"

"Which do you usually take?"

"Usually? I'm not sure there's a usually."

"Then take the right, I guess. I'll stay near the clock."

Matt slid into bed almost without disturbing the sheets. He turned once and lay flat on his stomach. "Good night," he said.

Martin sat down and set the alarm, but the next day was Saturday. He disengaged the ringer. "Matt, I think I should say something," he whispered.

"No need."

"About what Delia said. Sang."

"It's all right."

"But I think I should say—"

"Better not to say." He touched the back of Martin's neck. "Better not to say."

The hand dropped down Martin's spine, lingered, withdrew. For a moment there was silence. Then Matt started snoring.

■ ■ ■

O N E of the boys, the tall one, the one who had been left behind several years, stood a few feet from Martin and said in a quiet, toneless voice, "You're a faggot, aren't you?" He held out his penis and wound it with his fingers, deliberately, methodically, like a much-loved watch. "You'd like to suck my dick, wouldn't you?" he said. "You'd like to suck my balls."

Martin continued to remove his gym shorts, sliding them down his legs to the floor, stepping back through them awkwardly because of his sneakers. He looked straight ahead, at his open locker, at his regular clothes neatly folded within it, at his books and his can of deodorant. Another boy said, "Faggot," and then two more chirped in, randomly.

The boy holding his penis in his hands came closer to Martin. "Tell them you're a faggot," he said.

Martin reached slowly forward into his locker to get his pants, but just as he could feel the heat of them beneath his hand, someone from behind put a foot on his back and launched him onto the floor. A few of the boys laughed. "Faggot," the first one said.

Martin reached toward his locker again and touched the pants tentatively. He waited for a moment in this position and then removed them from the stack of clothes. Very evenly, as if in slow motion, he lifted himself off the floor with his legs and free arm, backing up until he was seated again on the bench. He flattened the pants in his lap for a moment and waited. Peripherally he could see the boy's penis expanding, suddenly poking out from the ring of his thumb and forefinger like the head of a burrowing animal. It turned purple at the end as he continued to twist it. "Say you're a faggot," he said again.

Martin carefully unfolded his pants, first from quarters into halves on his lap, then from halves all the way open. He let the legs drop to the floor and, sensing no reaction, decided to continue. He grasped the tabs of the waistband on either side of the fly, opening the waist into a circle. Change shifted in one of the pockets. He extended his left leg.

"Faggot," someone said: two quick syllables, a transmission in code. Another boy echoed the first. "Faggot."

Martin tried to concentrate, not to let his breath give way, not to spin into a faint. Still grasping the waist of the pants, he dropped them down toward his extended leg, shaking open the leg hole. He had almost got his foot in place when another shove from behind tumbled him onto the floor.

The first boy let go of his penis and pulled Martin up by the neck of his T-shirt. "Say you're a faggot," he said. Martin looked into his eyes, wondering what back there so required this admission.

"No."

Next Martin was falling back onto the bench, then off behind it, his legs splayed up in the air. The boy who had kicked him was now standing above, leaning down, grinning blankly like the moon. He emitted a thread of spit from his kiss-shaped lips, letting it drop in stages onto Martin's face. Martin rolled onto his knees and tried to scramble from the room, but the three remaining boys closed ranks to block him.

The first boy had gathered up Martin's pants and was using them now as a whip. Quarters flew out of the pockets and sprayed around the room. "It's a little faggot dog now, isn't it?" he said.

Martin stood up, one piece of a limb at a time, touching nothing. The boy with the pants, varying the formula, said, "Say you're a faggot, faggot." He circled Martin's neck in the crotch of the pants and crossed the legs tight around the front to make a noose. He pulled Martin back down to the bench. "Sit, dog, sit," he said. His penis now swung back and forth between his thighs, unattended, like the clapper of a ringing bell. He pulled the legs of the pants into a tighter X. "Faggot," he said. "Say you're a faggot."

Someone behind Martin took the legs of the pants from the first boy, wrapping them once more around and pulling. Martin's head lifted back and his mouth opened. He breathed narrow raspy breaths. Around his temples and ears, a clamp seemed to be tightening.

The first boy took his penis in hand again and this time stretched it out longitudinally, away from his body and back again toward it, seeming to peel it off like money. "Say you're a faggot or I'll come in your face," he said. "I'll do it in your mouth." He moved a step closer.

The boy was wearing only a T-shirt, yellowed under the arms. He had thin, colorless lips and long bleachy hair parted in the center. Not ugly, not beautiful. Ordinary. Martin was looking directly up his nostrils, which against the pink of his face were utterly, unnaturally black.

A drop of liquid appeared at the end of the boy's penis, and soon, from the action of his hand, was spread across the length of it. His pace quickened. Martin began to whimper.

"Shut up," someone said, pulling harder on the noose. The first boy looked annoyed. He interrupted himself long enough to take Martin's face in his hands and lower it back to the level he seemed to require.

Martin could breathe more easily now, and from the new angle watched the boy masturbate. It was the first close view he had ever had of anyone's genitals, even his own, which he touched only at night without looking. Now he had no choice but to look. The penis appeared and disappeared in the blur of the boy's moving hand. His scrotum expanded, seemed to breathe open, the little transparent hairs dancing upon it, then suddenly contracted and hardened between his legs. It looked like a turtle shell, but mauve. To his shame, Martin felt himself becoming aroused. Tears ran out of the corners of his eyes, trailing backward until they fell into his ears.

The boy's own eyes were closed and twitching. "Say you're a faggot or I'll come in your mouth," he said, clenching his teeth.

But Martin said nothing.

He had been called a faggot for as long as he could remember. In third grade, before he or anyone knew what it was, boys used the word to describe him in the schoolyard. He knew it had something to do with the way he looked, or walked, or spoke. It had something to do with being good in art class, and not being good in gym. But what did it mean? What did the word actually say about Martin? *The Illustrated One-Volume Encyclopedia of the World* persisted in defining it as a bundle of sticks, which Martin found reasonable but somehow incomplete.

Later, boys had scratched the word with ballpoint pens into bathroom stalls and chanted it from the backs of buses. By ninth grade, even some girls called him faggot: pretty girls in tartan skirts who congregated around the water fountain. With time it had mysteriously come clear to everyone exactly what it meant. They used the word not randomly, not opportunistically as the first insult that came to mind, but precisely. It was the particular insult that would fit Martin better than any other. They seemed to have read into his oldest secret thoughts, his love for his counselor John at camp, his fascination with the cartoon *Eighth Man*, and now his desire to be touched by even the boys who beat him up. They seemed to know what he thought about them in their maroon-and-gray crew clothes, that he imagined what they would look like undressed, what their clothes would smell like, how their hair would taste. It was true, it was all true, everything they said, everything they thought, more true than they meant; true even then when they didn't know what they were saying, true still now.

Though he had heard it over and over for years, he had managed never to speak the word: not aloud, not even to himself. If he never said it, he thought, it might yet turn out not to be true. Books he looked in were always warning that most boys pass through such a phase—though Martin never saw evidence of it in anyone else. Nevertheless, the books said, such boys should be discouraged from deciding one way or another, lest their lives be labeled indelibly.

There were hundreds of things it was better not to say, or even think, lest they come true. "Don't even say such a thing," people said, because words had the full power of deeds. Words were actual presences, not representations. The Tropic of Cancer was not a region of earth near the equator but a dotted line you must not cross. If you did, you would contract the disease itself.

"Say it," said the boy, his back arching, his legs beginning to tremble. There was a point of inevitability, Martin knew, when the boy would come whether he wanted to or not. It appeared that point had been passed already, so Martin said nothing. He looked directly ahead into his locker, at the can of deodorant, at his geometry book. In complete silence except for the distant thud of basketballs in the gym, the boy finished off. He spattered himself on the bench a little, then most on the floor, then finally, making a special effort to hit somewhere near his mark, on Martin's clean white underwear. Martin did not move it out of the way, but noted only that he would have to destroy it, lest the spots be discovered on Thursday in the wash.

THE UNDERWEAR was incinerated in a trash can behind the potting shed, but the spots stayed in his memory, reappearing from time to time as pimples, as blood, as blisters on a hand burned by béchamel sauce. Was shame, Martin wondered, the pulsing, indefatigable engine of his soul? Was his martyrdom to lie next to but not above, below, or within the object of his desire?

Which *snored*?

Martin groaned as if this were yet another in a life's worth of grievances against Matt. He found himself thinking: On top of everything, he has to snore. But on top of what? he wondered.

The snore, though, as he listened, was not so terrible. It was an airy, hoarse sound like the sound of furniture being pushed along the floor of a distant apartment. It was peaceful and domestic, just another sound of the building. When the refrigerator cycled in the kitchen, it seemed to be speaking in kind, and Martin noticed that Matt was smiling as the sound whistled past his lips.

He had always considered snoring slightly disgusting, slightly shameful: a bodily function you should really be able to control if you tried. It was something poor people did, and drunks in cartoons. Martin imagined tubercular bums, asleep in alleys, thin and unshaven, as Matt was now. People who snored were potentially dangerous, and led unsavory lives.

Martin resented the upbringing that had given him such a preposterous image of the poor. If they weren't dying, they were dangerous; if not snoring, licentious. His parents had made them out to be exotic instead of pitiful, even in their potential evil. If you didn't watch out, they would seduce you into poverty and degradation. Artists were somehow lumped in, too. Martin's father had warned him against the allure of bohemianism, the empty luxuriance of the counterculture. Martin imagined a dirty saloon, a beatnik hideout in Greenwich Village, with boarded doors beneath street level. It was dangerous, of course, but all the more exciting for the danger. Poor people would be there, unshaven artists, slightly rank but captivating men sitting at the counter and touching legs beneath it. That was the counter culture. It wouldn't sparkle like the counter in his mother's kitchen, but sex would be there, which was certainly nowhere else.

So Martin had ended up dreaming of sex with unshaven artists. He mooned after black-jeaned, stiff-haired, sleepy-eyed men, the ones who fell asleep standing up on the subway. They were immediately identifiable by the fine layer of silvery bed sweat that had settled over their skin, making it glitter like mica. They smiled easily and talked about anything. By comparison, Martin was barely a boy, trying to infiltrate the real life of men. Sex still made him blush, but they wore their sex, the fact that they *did* it, like flags, painted on the purple fields of their eyelids, run up on the stubble around their purple lips.

Dirt was the common thread. Sex was a stain. The men Martin desired were as much to be avoided for their affront to cleanliness as for the germs of some dread new disease they might bear. They would ruin Martin's health, turn into monsters, rob him, hit him, leave him for dead. He would suffer for involving himself in an *inexcusable mess*.

So Martin longed for sweat and alcohol breath and dirt, but slept only with the cleanest possible men, men who wore bow ties to the opera, whose skin was bright, whose hair was neatly parted. They didn't interest him, but at least he didn't worry where he put his wallet. He would lie in bed, not sleeping when sex was done, and watch the light bounce off the perfectly shaved face on the adjacent pillow. He would listen for sound, sniff for smells, but there were none, not from himself or from the other, just cleanliness and silence, and no snores.

Now had come Matt, both snoring and safe. The terms of Martin's impossible equation were merged in him, but not by him: the merger was Martin's own doing, achieved in his mind and doomed to remain there. The impossible equation had produced what it could: an impossible solution. Matt's body lay on the bed, but he himself lay elsewhere; this body rising and falling only a monument to him, a representation, carved in beautiful skin. Only the snore suggested a real existence, real though unreachable and uninterpretable.

MARTIN sat up in a panic at midnight: he couldn't remember Matt's last name. Had Stella even told him? He must know at once.

Quietly he rose and walked around the bed; Matt's black jeans lay on the floor. No change rattled as he lifted them up. They were stiff, held their shape, as if Matt were still inside them. But Matt was snoring, inches away.

From the back right pocket, Martin removed a battered wallet; surely he could find Matt's name on a driver's license or library card. But the folio of acetate leaves was empty. Martin fished around in one of the wallet's inner compartments and felt something sharp: a business card? He moved into the starlight at the

window to see. He felt guilty—and a little sick—to find a con-
dom in its foil package.

Still, he had come this far and might as well finish. He fished
again and came up with the prize: a partially filled-in ID card.
No address listed, no person to contact in case of trouble. But
the name was there: Matt Melodondri. Which, if Martin's high-
school Latin served, meant something like honey hair. Or perhaps apple tree.

Martin stared at the card and memorized the spelling. Surely
he would have remembered the beautiful, unlikely name if Stella
had mentioned it.

He put the card back into the wallet exactly as he had found
it, then slipped the wallet into the pocket and arranged the jeans
on the floor by the bed. He went to the kitchen and telephoned
Stella.

"Can't really talk," she said instantly.

"Oh. All right."

"What's the matter? Just a minute." She could be heard rearranging something, perhaps a man's limbs. Then she came
back on. "What's the matter?"

"Nothing's the matter, just calling."

"Are you alone?"

"Am I ever."

"Okay, so, fine, I've got to go. You're okay?"

"Fine. Just bored. Matt Melodondri's sleeping over."

"Is that his name?"

"Apparently. Good night."

"He's *sleeping over*?"

"Yes. Nice chatting."

"Martin, not really? I don't understand. You *boys*. But then I
never understand." Fierce giggling ensued. "Well, I've got to go.
Tell me tomorrow."

"Why do you got to go?"

"I wouldn't want to be late for some crushing insult," she
said. "Painters, you know."

"Well," said Martin. "The course of true love—"

"Never did run."

"Right."

"Right, doll." Stella hung up.

Martin knew there was no point in returning to bed with his mind spinning as hard as it was. He considered warming some milk to drink, but couldn't face the ill-starred saucepan. He was in no mood to read a cookbook either. He turned instead to the television, and made a tour of the midnight airwaves.

An actress he remembered fondly was weeping on Channel 11. Years ago she had played the girlfriend on a situation comedy, dippy and hilarious, minding everyone's business. When the concept of the show was altered, however, the girlfriend was suddenly transported to Belize. Not long after that, the actress herself disappeared, leaving a trail of tabloid rumors behind her. She was said to have joined a mystical sect; she supposedly bore someone's love child. Wherever she had been, whatever the true story, she was now back on television, but fat and puffy and middle-aged. Her trademark voice, shrill but somehow musical, too, had cracked and sunk in the intervening years. She sounded desperate. A tear guttered down the side of her face. Martin lowered the volume at once.

"These kids are the most beautiful kids in the world," she said, pointing to a claque of brown children behind her. "They ask for so little, they love so much."

The camera fixed on a small naked boy. Two flies orbited his head.

Each week the actress appeared in a different impoverished nation with a slightly different shade of undernourished child. "These are the most beautiful kids in the world," she'd invariably say. Sometimes she'd pick one out of the huddle, lift it up, and press it to her enormous face. The child would look directly at the camera, or at the actress's white ear, impassively, without curiosity. "Aren't kids what the world is all about?" she'd ask.

Yes, the world was all about children, but was this as it should be? Always children; children first? Politicians were forever promising to change the world for the sake of the children, but for whomever's sake, they never succeeded. Martin couldn't help feeling the world's focus was misplaced, or displaced rather, not to something completely irrelevant but to something purposely beside the point. A child in need could always bring tears to your eyes, and teary eyes see poorly. What was it you weren't meant to see?

The actress's voice rose. "Shoes! Food! Medicine!" she implored. Martin quickly flipped the dial. On another channel, a man who looked like a turtle was divulging real-estate secrets that could make a tycoon of anyone. "Little or nothing down," he said, stretching out his neck.

But Martin returned to the actress. Like everyone else, he was a slave to the image of children. He mistrusted them and was drawn to them anyway, a W. C. Fields and a Mary Poppins by turns. In one incarnation he would avert his eyes from their smeary faces; in another, look wistfully as they were swept by, sleeping in prams. In either case he doubted he would ever have any of his own. There seemed no good reason to take on the awful burden. When he thought of other people's reasons, he just couldn't sympathize. Doctrine, custom—these were unimpressive arguments. So was biology. There was a lot of talk about improving the gene pool, but Martin suspected his kind of genes were not the kind desired.

If not for eugenics, if not for the sake of conformity or piety, what reason was left? Martin's mother had recommended plaintively the sense of fulfillment only a child could bring, but Martin knew, from her own example, that there was no fulfillment to be found in making a child and sending it out into its own unhappiness.

There were already too many children in the world. People replenished themselves for none of the exemplary reasons they cited. At bottom, as far as Martin could see, they only had children to help dissolve the rock of the pain of mortality in their hearts, to create for themselves the caretakers of their dying years, caretakers who would then grow old themselves and face no nicer a fate than their own.

But the children on television were real living beings. However unsound their parents' reasoning, the children had been born and were now faced with life. The actress stood bravely among them, holding back tears. They joined hands in a circle and listlessly danced about her. "Aren't they worth saving?" she implored. "Couldn't you just call us now?"

A toll-free number flashed on the screen, barely brightening and then dimming Martin's kitchen. If only to stop her crying, he thought, reaching for the phone.

THE NEXT morning, as he stretched his freshly showered self, Matt spotted a couple in the building across the street, on the same floor in their building as Martin was in his. They, too, were stretching, naked, in front of their window, and looking out at the day. Matt did not hide from them, or cover his waist with the towel at his feet. Instead he continued his calisthenics, tilting to the right and then to the left with his arms fully extended as if transmitting signals in semaphore. He gestured for Martin to come have a look, but Martin dared not go. From the bed he could make them out quite sufficiently. The familiar man faced a woman in the sun—the woman to whom he spent nights writing letters? She had long, wavy, wet-looking hair, as if she had swum through the dark to find him.

"Come on," said Matt. "Come say hello."

"You're shameless."

"I have nothing to hide."

Martin slowly got out of bed, straightened his shorts, and walked to the window. He stood a few feet from Matt, whose body was so clean and bright with the sun it seemed like something you must not approach too closely. But Matt urged him closer anyway, that he might be seen. He lifted Martin's right hand and started it going. "Live it up, brother."

They stood there like royalty on a balcony, waving—a king and a queen, Martin thought. But he waved and smiled anyway, full of hope for the future of his people, whoever they might be. The thought pleased him, that he had no specific people—certainly not family—just a random cross section of the city, a group who had nothing in common but the particular floor they lived on in various buildings, the elevation they shared by chance. Anyone waving in a window could be royalty, and anyone else in other windows could be, at least for a moment, their people.

"They don't see us," Matt said, resuming his calisthenics. He snapped his torso down to his legs as if he were a pocketknife retracting. Then he sprang up and repeated the movement. "Come on," he said. "You try this, too."

Martin bent down as Matt instructed, then creakily returned to his unbearable height. It made him dizzy. "Oh," he said, but Matt was looking out the window, where the couple had finally noticed them and were waving happily back.

"Oh," he repeated. He hated to be seen.

Matt must have gotten a glimpse of his face, for he put his hand out to hold him just as Martin started to fall.

HIS MOTHER said he was delicate, his father said fainthearted. Fainthearted had the merit of economy. Delicate made him sound like a teacup.

He fainted first when he was eight years old. He could feel it coming. He was standing at the window where he knew he should not be. He should have been back at his desk already; everyone else was. He was thinking of nothing. Miss Allen said, "Martin, come away from the window, it's time for show-and-tell." But he could not move.

He saw himself in the window, how he wasn't moving. Then the room twisted, and instead of beside, he was above himself in the glass. Here was *I*, calm and alert, and there was *me*, below, dead, almost hollow. Not quite hollow. Inside the hollow was another *me*, and inside that another. "Martin, Martin, Martin,"

Miss Allen called. He could hear her, but could not get his selves to respond.

He saw all his bodies below him stiffen as his heads went dizzy. He thought he was a fleet of boats, then a carnival full of Ferris wheels, then finally a forest of bent old trees. His heads were birds in the branches of those trees, about to take off. A hot wind was circling up inside; a bicycle blew by. "The twister is coming," he whispered. He saw himself thrashing around in its eye.

"What are you doing?" Miss Allen demanded. The other students giggled at their desks. Martin could hear them amidst the bells and wind. Miss Allen approached. "Martin, Martin, Martin!" she was yelling. His name, repeated, meant almost nothing, then nearly nothing, then just about completely nothing. Random sound, two syllables in a seamless band of abstract noise, distant and threatening, but beautiful, too. Like Saturn's rings must seem to someone on Saturn, Martin thought.

He had done Saturn for his planets report. Saturn, Saturn, second largest of all the planets, sixth from the sun ...

And then he was on the floor, cool against the green-veined linoleum. "Martin?" asked Miss Allen, leaning over him like an anesthetist. "Martin? Martin? Martin?"

There was the fainting and then there was the stomach. His childhood had passed, it sometimes seemed, between one and the other, in bathroom and bed. Of the two, fainting was better. The stomach was like a faint that persisted without the gift of obliteration.

He did not travel well, for one thing; that's what his mother said. She meant he got sick or cranky in the car. But at other times, Martin noticed, she used the same phrase in reference to cheese. "That Camembert won't travel well. Get the Muenster instead," she'd say. Now she meant something that lost value when moved, something that, when you got it there, was spoiled.

He was spoiled, too. That was his father's version of *does not travel well*. And old Dr. Einhorn seemed to agree. He examined

Martin as carefully as a half-blind man could. He certainly touched every piece of Martin's skin, and embarrassed him by saying, "Let's have a look at the waterworks now." He poked around for the longest time, but concluded suggestively that nothing was wrong. "Just a frail constitution," he told Mrs. Gardner, who seemed almost overjoyed to hear it.

And so he was frail: frail is what he decided to be. It drew his mother so close, gave them something to share. Luckily, she could not tell the real from the fake. Oh, maybe the first few times it was real, but later—well. It had gotten to the point that Martin could not tell the difference himself. *Was* there a difference? Either way, it was what he did. He would feel a stippling of heat, or a snake coiling up the inside of his throat, and just let it happen. It was absurdly easy to do; he did so now. He looked at Matt and remembered the procedure. You just had to fall. And people believed anything.

III

BELIEVE

At Bergdorf's, Stella eyed the salesclerks as if they might be armed. She moved ungracefully and started to perspire. Thin as she was, she still dreaded shopping as if she were fat. "They play on your insecurities," she told Martin. "Some of them know me from before the change and they make me feel like I'm five years old." Occasionally she tested clerks by asking if they thought she'd look good in some big floral muu-muu. If they said yes, she sent them away.

Martin had gone shopping with Stella before. It wasn't that she needed his advice; he served more as a chaperon than a consultant. He ran interference. The salesclerks seemed awed by his height; they did not hover as close as they otherwise would. They smiled deferentially. When he'd return all ten outfits from the dressing room for Stella, they did not scowl, but said "Thank you, sir," instead.

It was late enough on Saturday afternoon that the store was no longer terribly crowded. As Stella and Martin got out of the elevator on the second floor, several hawkish women circled at a distance. "Just looking," Martin said to keep them at bay; then Stella dragged him over to the black cocktail dresses.

"Are you wearing a tux or a suit?" she asked.

"Suit, I think."

"And now tell me about last night, if you please." She flipped through a rack of skimpy size fours. "Omit nothing."

Martin obeyed, delighting in Stella's amazed reactions. She took particular interest in the physical details: exactly how long did his hand linger, what did he look like in his underwear? Martin answered as truthfully as possible, and found himself in the retelling, thrilled.

"Well, is he a closet case, do you think?" asked Stella.

"No, of course not. He's just comfortable with who he is and unthreatened by me." This sounded a little too pat, even to Martin.

"And you find him attractive?"

Martin nodded vigorously.

"Then how can you stand it?"

"I don't know. There's something nice about not having to have sex."

"But not being *allowed* to? Martin, this is strange. Well, at least it was just for the night."

Martin cleared his throat.

"It *was* just for the night, wasn't it?"

"I said he could stay till he found his own place."

"Oh, my God. You made an extra key."

"This morning."

"You didn't."

"Well, *you* have one. I'd let *you* stay over if you needed to."

"Would you, Martin?" she said suspiciously. "Not for long."

"This isn't for long either. And I like him. I had a good time. Is that somehow wrong?"

"I don't know, it gives me the creeps. It sounds too easy."

"I'm sure it's not how he'd prefer it," said Martin.

"I mean for you. Too easy for you."

Stella gave up on the cocktail dresses: they were almost identical in cut and color to four she already owned. "Maybe a suit," she said doubtfully, leading Martin to another room. "We can both go in suits."

"We can all three go. I'm getting an extra ticket for Matt."

Stella stopped and said to a mannequin, "Well, that settles the problem then."

"What problem?"

"The clothing problem. Don't bother with the extra ticket. Give him mine."

"But why?"

"I don't want to go. I'm busy anyway." She headed for the elevator.

"But I want you to go."

"You say that now. But really I think you should take Matt

instead—that's what you want. As I always tell you: misogyny loves company." When crossed, Stella reflectively jumped to such accusations.

"Don't be like that," Martin said.

"Be like what? If you have someone to go with, you don't need me. That makes sense, doesn't it? And I have plenty of work to do, honestly." She pressed the down button.

"You're punishing me because something nice happened to me."

Stella thought for a moment. "No, I'm punishing you because something nice didn't happen to me."

And Martin remembered the man in the background on the phone the night before. "How was your date?"

"Don't we have anything better in life to discuss than romantic entanglements? What about the boat people? What about the Afghans?"

"And by that do you mean blankets or hounds?"

Before they could get into the elevator when it opened, a woman lunged forward with a giant flagon of perfume in her hands. "Volcane d'Amore," she said. "An eruption of love." She aimed it at them and smiled maniacally.

"If you spray us with that stuff, I'll break your fucking nose," said Stella. Then she buried her face in Martin's insufficiently sheltering chest.

MARTIN came home to a touching, preposterous meal prepared by Matt. It incorporated yogurt, rice, potatoes, canned peas: whatever had been sitting around the kitchen. "Poor man's porridge," Matt called it as he served. "No béchamel, but I did what I could."

Afterward, while Matt watched television, Martin closed the bedroom door and undressed to take a bath. He studied the things Matt had brought that day from Chloe's: no more than a foot's worth of clothing in the closet, one suitcase, some books, a clock, a fountain pen. In the bathroom were some unusual soap—amber, European—and a tube of natural toothpaste. Martin looked for more. By the right side of the bed was a picture in a small pewter frame: a beautiful blonde with a forties haircut, dramatically lit. It must have been Maman.

Martin thought of his own mother, living by herself; the twins were at college. She was dangerous for him and yet he missed her. It touched him that Matt missed a mother, too, even if it wasn't his real one.

He sympathized with the lonely gaze in the photo, and with his mother's empty nest. He had lived so long that way himself. And then he realized, stepping into the bath, he would live that way again quite soon. But if I could live that way ...

Martin smiled at his joke, while the unbearable water inched up his endless legs.

D E L I A loved Martin's sharkskin suit; once she said so, everyone else professed to love it, too. Even Martin thought he looked good in it; Joe, the campy assistant stage manager, was over the moon. "Martin," he said, shouting over the band, "between you and your friend I don't know what I'll do!"

Of course Joe was drunk—nearly everyone was—and high even without the liquor. The early *Times* review was borderline positive; the television critics gave *Jet Set* raves. Among the revelers at the opening-night party only Maria seemed equivocal. "Well it's a trifle, isn't it," she said to well-wishers. "If a pleasant one." But Delia and David were ecstatic enough to balance the family. Delia had been called "preternaturally gifted" in one of the papers, and while that was clearly true, she was not so preternaturally gifted that she could pronounce the compliment. Her father did it for her instead. Repeatedly.

Matt was more at his ease than Martin had expected. He did not need an escort. At one point, when Martin came back from the bathroom, he found Matt engaged in conversation with the female star, a haughty woman Martin did not like. Soon she was taking him to meet someone else; hands were shaken and faces kissed. As Martin approached he could hear that Matt was talking in French—an achievement that made Martin feel irrationally proud, as if he had been Matt's teacher. A woman listening with vivid interest began talking in French as well, but when they reverted to English, it turned out she had a British accent.

Martin did not cut in. He took Matt's example instead, and started mingling. He spoke into the ears of people he would not otherwise have bothered to address; they responded with delight and giddy conversation. They introduced their spouses, their lovers, people standing near them whose names they didn't know. When they realized Martin's relationship to the show, they exclaimed over his fabulous contributions. Even the director, Peter White, a man Martin had previously found difficult to approach, welcomed him exuberantly. He nudged his big pink head into Martin's armpit, wept and kissed him, then hugged him harder and kissed him again. "That skyline!" he exclaimed. "That wallpaper! Martin!" This might have gone on for minutes if Matt hadn't come by and introduced himself.

"A friend of Martin's is a friend of mine," White shouted, and hugged Matt, too.

After a fanfare, the band launched into a rendition of the lilting, melancholic "eleventh hour" ballad—eleventh hour because it came just before the show's grand finale. People sighed and dashed to the dance floor, leaned into each other's ears and hummed. The ballroom droned with all the humming, like a field of poppies. All kinds of unlikely couples rocked in place as the lights dimmed low: black with white, tall with short, men and women in all the possible pairings. There was even a knot of three by the bandstand.

Martin often disparaged his profession, but one good feature of the theatrical world was its tolerance. He could have danced with Matt if he liked; no one would have thought anything but pleasant thoughts about it. In the theater, every Jack Sprat was allowed his symbiotic spouse, no matter what an odd pair they made; he lean, she fat, they would get together and have marbled children. But Martin didn't like to dance, and anyway, the Englishwoman had taken Matt by the hand.

Martin moved to the side of the room and found Maria, who was sipping cranberry juice.

"Is there any food?" she asked. "I'm a little sick." She held her stomach, which was not yet visibly larger than usual.

"Soon," Martin said. "Now that the reviews are good, I expect they'll feed us."

They watched the dancing. Delia was flitting from couple to couple, shaking her behind, lifting her arms, then moving on. David chased after her, weaving among the dancers, taking movies with his video camera.

"Well?" said Martin, over the din.

"He's nice," said Maria.

"Is that all?"

Maria nodded, then yawned. "What more should he be? *He's a genius, Martin.* Don't let the Russians get him."

"Good-looking, yes?"

"Do you need me to say so?"

She would not give an inch, she was so unindulgent. If it wasn't for her influence, Delia would surely have turned out a brat. But Maria balanced David's obsequiousness, and managed to keep Delia secure while keeping her in line. Where had she acquired her unerring good sense? In Maine, she said, in a town called Gray; people there weren't impressed with frills. They liked what was solid and true and unremarked.

But Maria made exceptions: she seemed to like Martin. And when Matt came by to ask her to dance, she put down her glass of cranberry juice and spun onto the floor with the assurance of a showgirl. After a minute Martin saw her smile. Another minute later she was laughing out loud, doing florid dips, grasping Matt's shoulder with one hand and holding her stomach lightly with the other. No matter where you were born, Martin thought, the touch of a handsome man was impressive enough.

■ ■ ■

MATT found a cheap share with two graduate students in the Village; he wrote the address on a torn piece of paper and put it in Martin's wallet. There was no phone, but it hardly mattered: Matt stayed at Martin's. He gave out Martin's number to the phone sales people, who called him at odd hours when there was work to be had. He typed the number on his résumé, too, but got no calls from that.

Martin did not inquire too closely into the phone sales job; Matt seemed embarrassed by it and rarely brought it up. One thing Martin discovered for himself was that a supervisor named Kim had taken a more than supervisory interest in Matt. She called occasionally, and then more often, staying on the line longer than business could possibly demand. Martin did not ask too much about her, either.

And he did not ask about money. He did not want money. Still, he was delighted to open his wallet one day and find a hundred-dollar bill nestling there behind the twenties. Had Matt made so much money so quickly? Or settled things with Chloe? Martin acknowledged receipt with a smile, but did not ask.

A week past opening night, Matt showed no signs of wanting things to change. As far as Martin could determine, the newest key on Matt's key ring had never been tried. "It's simply more comfortable here," Matt said one night in bed. "The other place is tiny and dirty. The bathroom's disgusting, I can hardly use it." Matt had surprisingly finicky tastes, and Martin kept his bathroom immaculate. "But it's there if I need it," Matt added.

"Well, you don't," said Martin.

"And I thank you for that." Matt touched Martin's arm good night, turned over on his stomach, and fell asleep at once.

Stella was right, of course: this was very odd. No recourse to high ideals, no notions of fraternity, could make it make sense. Eventually, they would have to discuss it. But if Martin was loath to question Matt's work, to question his finances, to question his acquaintance, he was utterly unwilling to question his sleep. He turned over, too. And did not sleep.

■ ■ ■

MARTIN stared for too long and then got confused. Minutes after everyone else had already gotten a rough form on paper, he was still trying to determine where to make his first mark. Then, when he started, he drew so frantically, he couldn't control the shape at all. He had to start over.

"Calm," he told himself.

With *Jet Set* off the ground and no compelling jobs in sight, Martin had taken Matt's suggestion and enrolled in a ten-week class at the Y. Advanced Life Drawing, the catalog called it. And the life now posing in front of him was nothing if not advanced.

The model was reclining at the center of a ring of students. He supported his chest on big arms thrown back like buttresses. His head was hanging back between his shoulder blades, and the weight of it pulled his mouth slightly ajar. Martin could see the wave of his breath beneath the lowest, fingerlike ribs, but other than that the model was still. His eyes were closed, his long hair pointed straight down behind him without shaking. A warm pin light splashed on his side.

On his second try, Martin worked more carefully. He got an outline and then set about filling it in. His fingers grew dark with graphite. He was attempting to render the skin's pearlescence. It was grainy with light like a photograph, and yet perfectly smooth as well. It's a technical problem, he kept telling himself. He smudged the lines of musculature with the side of his thumb, drew them back in, then smudged them again. Too much shading? Not quite enough? He lifted up a patch of gray with his twisted eraser, but the nose came up with it. He drew the nose back in. He sighed. He tried cross-hatching, then stippling with dots. He started again.

Back in art school, teachers were always telling Martin he wasn't enough engaged in what he was drawing. That wasn't the problem now. He was fully engaged, more engaged than he intended. The skin excited him all he could wish. He recognized it as beautiful, certainly. It covers his entire body, he said to himself. It encloses all of him. It stretches completely around his thighs, around the underside of his chin. It folds so lightly into the ridges of his ear: does it never end?

He started again.

No one else seemed to be having this problem. They produced their images from the movements of their hands alone, it seemed, without the eye or mind interfering. One student, a regal middle-aged woman, was making broad swipes with a nugget of char-coal, barely stopping to consider the result. Another was whisking the paper with his crayon, frothing it up like eggs. They all knew something Martin did not. Their heads bobbed up and down happily, like seals at Marineland.

When the hour was done, they taped their drawings to the classroom wall. Martin was ashamed. The other students had produced voluptuous flesh, tangible volume; his looked like a cookie cut from dough, a naked gingerbread man. The teacher studied it a minute and said, "You certainly have a fine eye for outline," then moved on to somebody else.

Martin took this as a criticism, but Matt suggested it might be praise. He stuck the drawing to the refrigerator with a strawberry-shaped magnet. "Maybe you'd like to draw me," he said. "I've modeled, you know. I can stay very still."

But Martin had already drawn him a dozen times at least— from memory, if not from life. The drawings emphasized the tight little bundles of muscle and flesh, so strictly bounded and so discrete. He depicted them in almost inhuman extremes of flexion. He might have been drawing the wood figurine he kept on his drafting table, its limbs all articulate and infinitely ad-justable. However preposterously you arranged it, there it stayed. And however you touched it, it responded.

All his life, Martin had wondered how people came to have the bodies they did. It seemed utterly random. Why shouldn't he have those divisions and bundles instead of a flat, unwritten page? But high-protein diets, thousands of push-ups, even his three years of crew had failed to change him. It must be genetic, he told himself—and thus had the pleasure of blaming his parents.

Even so, he belonged to a gym, though the little good it seemed to accomplish was insufficient reward for the agony it entailed. No one showed him what he ought to be doing and he was too proud to ask, so he spied on the confident men around him and tried to copy their routines. This usually resulted in pain and embarrassment: weights dropping down suddenly with a great clatter from great heights, or trapping him against the upholstered benches. Then there were the showers—just impossible—with the scowl-faced preening and disowned glances. Martin stopped going within weeks of joining, though the squat, beefy manager, who looked like a pre-Columbian artifact, had managed to rope him into a three-year contract.

Matt noticed the laminated membership card in Martin's wallet while paying for a delivery one day. "You never go, do you?" he asked.

"I'm no good at it, it makes no difference, and I don't like the people," Martin explained.

"Excuses, excuses. Why don't you take me as a guest and I'll show you what to do."

Declining hastily, Martin busied himself with the Chinese food. "But you go if you like. You can go as me."

Matt put his hand on Martin's shoulder. "I think it would be good for you," he said, starting to squeeze and palp the flesh as if appraising a mattress.

Later that week, with a new athletic wardrobe for each of them, Matt and Martin showed up at the gym. Matt was as good as his word: he took Martin to each of the workout stations, first demonstrating the machine himself, then supervising Martin's exertions. He seemed to have an inexhaustible supply of encouraging catchphrases, picked up from years on wrestling squads, each locution more ludicrous than the one before. "Live life large," he said while Martin grunted under the weight of a bench press.

"If I could live that way . . ."

"Come on, lift it."

"I can't."

"You can."

"No, you don't understand," Martin said hotly. "I literally am unable to lift it. It's a physical fact. It simply cannot be lifted by me."

"Conceive, believe, achieve," said Matt.

Martin groaned. "Who was your wrestling coach—Jesse Jackson?"

"Come on: conceive. Imagine the action. See yourself lifting the weight."

"Yes, well, that part I can do."

"All right, now believe. Believe you can do it."

"But I *can't* do it."

"Believe."

"But I don't."

"Then lie! Tell yourself you believe you can do it."

"All right," said Martin sarcastically, "I believe I can do it. I believe I can do it. I believe—"

"Now achieve," said Matt. "Lift that thing."

And Martin, much to his own surprise, did.

"Good," said Matt matter-of-factly. "Now five more."

When he was done, Martin rose unsteadily from the bench, then stood holding on to it, blinking and swallowing. By breathing slowly he managed to divert the dizzy sensation that might, in other situations, have led him to the floor. But he did not wish to faint, he realized, and so he did not faint.

Meanwhile Matt, having increased the number of bars on the stack, slithered into position. Before Martin could even say "believe," the load—more than Matt's own body weight—was lifted. Then it came down, clicked smartly against the stack, and rose again. Matt stuck his jaw out; he made explosive little noises like a sneezing dog. He repeated the exercise eight times grimly, his eyes focused—Martin followed his stare to determine—on a sprinkler knob protruding from the ceiling.

Martin did not tend to sweat very much, but Matt's gray T-shirt, by the end of the hour, was almost black. "Let's get in the whirlpool," he said, not giving Martin a chance to say no.

Two women were already enjoying the water. "It's a little hot at first," one of them warned. Martin toed the surface and withdrew from it quickly. "It gets better fast," the other one said.

Matt stepped in. Rather shyly he smiled at the women and told them his name. Martin still stood at the edge of the pool, miserable in his dilemma. To enter entailed making some sort of spectacle; remaining outside left his stupid white body completely exposed. He compromised, and sat on the edge of the pool with his calves submerged.

The water surged and eddied. A conversation ensued, completely forgettable, but animated and pleasant. The women, it turned out, were not there together as Martin had assumed; one was a lawyer, the other an actress. They each seemed curious about these two nice men, until Matt referred to Martin, amazingly, as his roommate.

"Oh!" said the lawyer; the actress smiled.

"We've been living together a few weeks," Matt said.

Martin involuntarily shivered.

"That's nice," said the lawyer, as if it were not.

The actress, who was wearing a leopard-print maillot, hoped to dissociate herself from the lawyer's apparently intolerant attitude. "It's nice that you two work out together. A lot of couples don't like to do that. Competitive, I guess."

"Oh, we're not a couple," Matt said. "Just living together. He's gay and I'm straight."

And now even the actress seemed out of her depth.

Martin thought he should be mortified, but laughed instead.

What had Matt done but told the truth simply? Was there any-thing wrong with telling the truth? "I'm so gay I'm festive," Martin said, then waggled his eyes.

The lawyer had had enough of this nonsense; she got out of the whirlpool and Martin got in. For the next ten minutes he listened to Matt and the actress chattering slyly until their fin-gers and toes were ribbed like corduroy. They were engaged in some kind of ritual work, but their performances were a little off. Each kept veering away from the other's direct questions; it was all very friendly, like amateur bridge, but the bids were read according to different conventions and in the end no con-tract was made.

Matt tried one more time as they emerged from the water and dripped on the deck. "So, where do you live?" he asked. His body came up gooseflesh.

"Oh, you know, around," the actress answered.

Matt said, "I love that neighborhood," and waved one mini-mal wave good-bye. "Time to get out of the water, Martin."

Martin obeyed, his foreshortened legs getting longer and lon-ger, until finally the whirlpool had nothing to kick around but itself anymore.

Later, in the locker room, Martin watched surreptitiously as Matt got dressed. At home, Matt paid no attention to his nudity, and willed Martin not to either. Here, he seemed to suspect he was being watched closely, as indeed he was. And not just by Martin. A few men made paltry attempts to cover their interest, staring into the air as if pondering a philosophical question; but it was not hard to see through such ruses. And one not poorly built man gazed quite openly. Responding, Matt stood a little more upright, giving his body a more definitive outline, and walked more deliberately, as a dancer might. He dried himself painstakingly—under his arms, inside his thighs—and adjusted his underwear, when he finally put it on, with uncommon pre-cision.

The anonymous approval he seemed to enjoy, but when Martin let himself be caught staring, too, Matt said, "What?" in a slightly annoyed tone.

"What does your work entail?" Martin asked—the first acceptable question that came into his mind.

Matt told him while combing his hair. "I sell something called the *American Family Learning Book* to people who can't afford it," he said.

The book, Matt explained, was actually a series of volumes, twenty in all, that purported to be not just an encyclopedia, but a curriculum as well. Matt and the other sales representatives called people all over the country. Sometimes they got farmers whose farms were in hock, or laid-off auto workers in Detroit, but the company had scripts to cover such occasions. Matt paraphrased instructions from the manual. "Encourage the client to consider, instead of the *costs*, the long-term monetary *benefits* from his/her child's enhanced education. Ask the client if he/she has thought about his/her obligation to his/her child's/children's future."

Matt was one of dozens who sat in a giant room talking to strangers through space-age headsets. He had heard of the job through some actors he knew, and indeed the workroom, filled with handsome young men and women with good teeth, looked like a cattle call. On a bulletin board were taped the eight-by-ten glossies of former salespeople who had made it into shows and commercials. Often they returned after two or three months; actors, the employer let it be known, were always welcome. They were prized for their ability to mimic regional accents, to change identity without confusion. On the other hand they were mistrusted for their tendency to sympathize with the destitute and to call friends long distance. So supervisors listened in from a booth up above. One of the supervisors was Kim.

On this point, Matt concluded his presentation. He opened his new gym bag and dropped into it his sweaty clothes, his towel, his comb, his antiperspirant, his shampoo, his powder, and his bar of amber soap.

M A T T and Kim started sleeping together—having sex, that is. In fact Matt still came home to Martin, however late, and slept next to him. "I don't feel comfortable in her apartment," he explained. "It's sort of a mess." Other nights he showed up in time for dinner, perhaps bringing Kim, or friends from phone sales, or other seemingly random acquaintances. Martin did not in general like them, but they never made more than one appearance. Stella attended occasionally, too, sometimes with a sullen painter in tow. Martin was the only constant, checking his watch, checking the oven. He might not know until seven o'clock who, if anyone, would be dining that night. As a result he came to think of it as the spring of covered dishes: casseroles and stews were the safest things to make. Rice got bought in five-pound sacks. But such was Matt's appetite that nothing was ever left over for long. Even when Matt skipped a meal, the cold ragout would not last the night. Martin would find the plastic container sitting in the sink when he woke up at seven, and a tomato crust on Matt's upper lip when he went into the bedroom to wake him soon thereafter.

Martin checked in on *Jet Set* once in a while, and Matt had his fitful work, but many days they had nothing to do between the time the *Times* was perused in the morning and the time Ted Koppel signed off at night—for Matt liked only the highest-minded television. Similarly, in a somewhat empty display of discipline, he preferred to be out of the apartment during the day, even if it meant walking purposelessly, or going to see the exhibit of Delft at the Cooper-Hewitt Museum again. Martin would have been content some days just to eat in bed, read a mystery, clean the already immaculate kitchen—as his mother had done all the days of his youth but could no longer, so manic she'd become. Matt, however, dragged him forth, and barring bad weather, they often wound up shopping.

People naturally assumed they were lovers; neither Martin nor Matt did anything to discourage the assumption. Pushing a cart haphazardly together, arguing the merits of orange-juice brands, they got knowing smiles or smirks from other shoppers. Clever salesmen always asked Martin's opinion of the clothes Matt tried on, saying, "He seems to like it, but you don't look thrilled." Then the two men would discuss the matter, Matt pretending not to care, Martin earnest, as if an important problem needed solving. If, in the end, Martin found he didn't dislike the shirt, the sweater, or the jacket too much, he would take out his gold card and buy the item while Matt got changed in the dressing room.

He was not Martin's lover, but he had seen Martin's bankbook, as no lover had. If the balances fazed him, Matt did not let on. This was a more intimate relation than sex. Sex after all required grueling concentration on things that had no outside existence—a spark in your head—and was thus always solitary. But money only existed in relation to the outside. It was always communal. Matt opened bills when they arrived in the mail, marked with a red pen expenses he had incurred. Some of these he would attempt to pay back. Others, Martin insisted—most of them—were gifts.

One March evening, Martin was in bed with a stomach flu; his doctor, over the phone, prescribed an expensive antibiotic. Martin gave Matt his bank machine card and told him his identification code: the single letter he could never forget. This was, perhaps, his most intimate secret; it both thrilled and frightened him to reveal it. After all, the teller had said *tell no one your code*, as if some dread fate awaited those who blabbed. But Matt came back a half hour later with a bottle of pills, a carton of soup, and accurate change from one hundred dollars.

Matt nursed him through this embarrassing sickness, with magazines and juice and extra blankets from the closet. He did not disdain to sleep in his usual place on the right side of the bed. When Martin emerged after two days from his ills, he felt as if the recovery had been some sort of consummation. They were not lovers—indeed Matt already had a lover—but Martin began to feel loved nonetheless.

Even Stella began to think so. "You're keeping something from me, Martin. He's your lover, isn't that right?" She said this jokingly over the phone but kept at it longer than the joke seemed to warrant. "He's your lover and now you're trying to protect me, isn't that it? Well, I give you permission. I give you my blessing. So let's just hear it."

"No," said Martin.

"Well, he might as well be, the time you spend!"

Martin sighed. "Maybe so. Might as well, but not."

"Then why bother? Bark up another tree if this one hasn't got fruit in it. Is that the right metaphor?"

"Am I a dog then?"

Martin could not speak the truth, which Stella would find demeaning and insufficient. Whatever else he didn't provide, Matt was there, night after night, untouchable but warm. If they weren't technically lovers, it *was* a relationship, and come to think of it, the best one Martin had ever had. It was everything he had dreamed of: a devoted partner, someone to wake up with, someone to cook for, someone to dress. It was a Hollywood movie from the 1950s, the sex edited out by the Hays Commission. What was sex anyway? An *inexcusable mess*. A variant of love that burned itself out.

And yet he wanted it.

For a prude he was developing an impressive masturbatorial repertoire. He made love to himself—as he ironically phrased it—in dangerous, semipublic venues. In the back of a crosstown bus at night, under a book. On the empty stage at the Mark Hellinger Theater. In bed, on his side, while Matt slept on.

It mortified him to recall these scenes and yet the mortification almost instantly transformed itself back into lust, as if the blood in his cheeks were the same as the blood alive in his groin—and of course it was. He could not get over how arousing the thought of his own warm flesh could be, out of context. In the shower, of course, or in a bathing suit, it meant nothing. Plastic, cold. But exposed to the improper air of the world, un-coiled from its nest of elastic restraint, it made his breath gutter. And the more he indulged himself, the more it seemed his hopes of actual sex receded. This was a mercy. Perhaps the *M* on his foot stood for Martin.

''W O W,'' said Stella. "Check out those manly, manly arms." She felt Martin's biceps and made him feel hers. "Pretty impressive," she said, "don't you think? But I have to admit it looks like you win. Of course you're a boy."

"Thank you," said Martin.

"A big boy now."

His thrice-weekly trips to the gym under Matt's supervision had, by Memorial Day, begun to produce visible changes in Martin's physique. He was wearing a new short-sleeve shirt as he cooked, in hopes it would elicit exactly such a comment from Stella.

"And your chest," she said. "It's like one of those, what do you call them, those cones of meat."

Martin had no idea what she meant, but beamed. Live life large, he thought. Conceive, believe, achieve.

Matt set the table, with a finicky attention to utensil align-ment he had at first ridiculed and then copied from Martin.

Stella patted his behind. "You look as fit as ever, Matt. Who's that letter on the bureau from? With all the stamps."

Matt put a fork down and then stood still.

"From France," she added.

"Stella, really," Martin said.

"What is it, top-secret diplomatic business? I can't even ask?"

Martin looked at Matt, who nodded reluctantly. "It's from Maman," Martin said.

"Who?"

Matt finished setting the table and sat down. "The woman I stayed with for a year in France," he said. "Junior year of high school." His face went soft. "We were very close. She was like a mother to me—I mean, one's own mother can never be that, can she? *Like* a mother. She can only be your actual one. Maman was like all the *ideas* you have about mothers."

"Manipulative, hysterical, jealous?" Stella ventured.

"Well, maybe she was that way to her actual son. But not to me. Her actual son was in college and had no time for her. So we became close."

Stella considered. "I think, at age eighteen," she said, "everyone should switch to a new set of parents."

Martin brought forth a big yellow bowl filled with corkscrew pasta. "What did she have to say?" he asked. He had not felt comfortable inquiring before, but now that Stella had opened the issue, what was the harm? "If you don't mind telling," he added nervously.

Matt didn't answer.

"Oh come on, this isn't a Bergman movie," Stella said.

Matt relented. "Well, if you must know, she's sick and would like to see me. She says she's dying. Of course she's said that before, but still. I guess I'll have to tell her I can't."

"No!" said Stella. "You should go."

"I can't afford it. It'd take me forever to save the money, although—" He stopped. "She says she's leaving me something in her will."

"She said this?"

"Yes. And a ring I loved."

"A ring?" asked Stella. "What kind of ring?"

"A big sapphire. The size of my thumbnail."

Martin stopped eating and threw a look at Stella, who grabbed Matt's hand and examined it as if with a loupe. "She was wealthy, then?"

Matt hesitated but eventually said, "Yes. She several times mentioned her intention to leave me something, but I told her not to talk that way. I said it was morbid—and inappropriate. Now I think she must have been telling the truth when she said she was dying. Only she didn't know when. I shouldn't have kept shooing the subject away, making a joke. 'You'll outlive us all,' I said. We'd be walking around the gardens. 'You'll be cutting the roses for *my* grave,' I said."

"And her son? Do you know him?"

"Yes. I'm afraid he's jealous of my relationship with her, though he never did anything to improve his own. He called her by her first name—disrespectfully, I thought. I called her Maman—what she told me to call her. Is it my fault? I don't think he'd be happy, though, if she left me any money."

"She's not thinking of leaving it *all* to you, is she?"

"I really don't know."

"Well, I think you should go in any case," said Stella. "Don't you, Martin? Think he should go?"

"Maybe he should write first."

"No, no, he should get himself over there."

"But I can't afford it!"

Stella widened her eyes just slightly, but Martin knew what she was trying to communicate. "I could lend you the money, if you wanted," he said.

Stella nodded. "It would just be an advance, really—not to sound too cold about it."

Matt looked pained. "Can we talk about it later? I want to enjoy this delicious pasta thing Martin made."

Martin did an imitation of a wife blushing prettily. "And how was work today, dear?"

"I thought only of you."

"What is it exactly you do anyway?" asked Stella. "Sell phones or something?"

Matt, alternately embarrassed and defiant, explained.

"And you use a different name every day?"

"No. I vary the name to suit the locale. This afternoon I was Malcolm Morris, calling from Atlanta," Matt said. "I always use my own initials. Marvin Moss when I call Westchester. Mike

Mahoney for Boston. It preserves a scrap of identity at least. Anyway, Kim gave me some likelies today—cards from good suburban area codes—and I made six sales. We get paid by the sale."

Stella looked astounded. "This has to be the single most objectionable job I have ever heard of. Selling useless crap to people who don't know better. Playing on their insecurities. How do you stand it?"

"I don't know, Stella, how do *you*?"

She leaned back in her chair and then laughed. "Touché," she said. "But *my* dupes are rich."

Martin had a big smile on his face. He sat at these dinners as he had once been encouraged by his father to sit at tennis matches: not completely interested in the details, but glad for the distraction of the game. He rarely intervened except to suggest possible new subjects and to clear off old ones—a ballboy, as it were.

"And Stella? How was work today, dear?"

"Actually, you know, I got a strange phone call. I picked up the phone and said, 'Imago Gallery, Stella speaking,' and this man said, 'Stella?'

"I said, 'This is she.'

" 'How are you, Stella?' the man said.

" 'Fine,' I said. 'How are you?'

" 'Fine, fine. How's the gallery going?'

" 'Oh, terrific, fine,' I said, trying desperately to place the voice. Finally I just said, 'Look, do I know you?'

" 'Of course,' he said. 'Don't you recognize me?'

" 'Is this Matt?' I asked. 'Do you have a cold?'

" 'Yes,' he said. 'I caught a bug out in the rain this weekend.' "

Martin looked at Matt, who seemed perplexed.

"So I said, 'Oh, Matt, hi, how's Martin doing?' and he said, 'Fine.' And I said, 'I'm looking forward to seeing you tonight, is Kim coming with you?' and he said, 'I'm not really sure,' and then he just stopped and I heard him breathing.

" 'So can I help you with something?' I asked. 'Are you up at work?'

" 'No, I took the day off,' he said. 'And I was thinking of you. I couldn't remember—when was the last time we saw each other?'

" 'I don't know,' I said, 'two weeks ago? With Kim and Alex at Martin's?'

" 'Yes, that's right,' he said, 'two weeks ago. With Kim and Alex. You looked so great.' "

Stella paused and made a self-deprecatory face. "This was really strange," she went on. "I mean, it had to be you, Matt, but you didn't sound normal."

"Wait," said Martin. "I don't understand."

"Just a minute," said Stella. "So I said, 'How *is* Kim?' and he said, 'Actually, I'm through with Kim, and I'm feeling blue.'

" 'Gee, I'm sorry to hear that,' I said, 'but unfortunately I'm in a terrible rush right now. A shipment's just come in,' This was a bit of a lie, but, you know. 'Can we postpone this till tonight?' I said. 'Or is there something I can do?'

"There was this long pause and then he said, pathetically, I thought, 'Stella, do you like me?'

" 'Of course I do,' I said. 'Who chatted you up at the gallery? Who introduced you to Martin?'

" 'That's true,' he said. 'But do you really *like* me? Enough to make out with me over the phone?'

"I laughed. 'What is this,' I said, 'some kind of safe-sex joke?'

" 'No joke,' he said. 'I'm really hot for you. Would you like to get off on the phone with me?'

"This was getting creepy. 'I'd like to get off *of* the phone,' I said.

" 'But what if I say I'm licking your nipple right now,' he said. 'What if I say you're rubbing my dick in your hand? What if I say you're sucking out under my skin?'

"I listened to this for a minute, because it was all very interesting, you know, until finally I realized what was going on and I said, 'What if I say I'm kicking you in the balls, you little

pervert?' And as I hung up I could swear I heard him moaning."
She sipped her water. "Some people!"

"Wait," said Martin. "How did he—"

"Don't you get it? See, I fed him all the information and he
just fed it back to me. He added a few innocuous details I couldn't
even prove or disprove. Or know I needed to. So I convinced
myself it was you, Matt, I mean I never even doubted it was
you until the end. Even then, for a minute, I thought, gee, he's
broken up with Kim and he's temporarily deranged."

"Then what convinced you it wasn't me?"

Stella arched her eyebrows.

"No, tell me."

"I took 'skin' to mean foreskin, isn't that the lingo?"

Martin blushed for real this time.

"And a little birdie tells me—"

"Lord, Stella, please, that's enough."

"I tell this story for its psychological significance. It was like
a Chinese finger torture. The more I struggled, the more I was
stuck. Only of course I didn't know that till later. I didn't even
know I was struggling—I mean, I knew I was struggling, but
with the wrong thing. It was quite amazing."

"Well," said Martin, "I don't know what I would have done
in that situation."

"Stayed on," said Matt.

"There's only one thing to do," Stella said, "and it's what I
always tell you, Martin."

"And what is that?"

"Only disconnect," she said.

ONLY disconnect. "There's too much togetherness in this world,"
Stella would say, "too much unnatural obligation. Why do they
need to provide the greeting cards if people innately feel the
bond? *To My Darling Stepson's Wife?* Come on. It's a racket,
Martin. Disconnect."

It was not so easy, now that his father was dead. Martin often replayed their last conversation—the fatal conversation, as he called it—and each time found his behavior more obscene. He realized he could not have goaded the man more if he'd poked him repeatedly with a pointy stick. It made him almost queasy to remember his father saying, without malice or pity, in his ever-mild voice: "You are a stranger."

His father had often amused himself, if no one else, with the claim that his son was adopted. Indeed Martin looked nothing like Robert Gardner. Getting an occasional glimpse of his father's sandy eyes, Martin could find nothing of himself in them, no speck in the iris that meant *You come from me*. But why would one hope for it? What he saw in his mother's eyes was only depressing. It was a bird-shaped patch of brown set in amidst the green. It meant fearfulness, and he recognized it as his own.

Other than that, he looked nothing like his family. They were all fair and slight; the girls redheads, and tiny like terriers. Martin's hair was as black as tar. At his great height, he stood out in family photos like the proverbial sore thumb. And the *M* on his foot: perhaps he really *was* adopted, and this was the brand of his original owner. He was a Medici, a Mountbatten. Or maybe a Martian.

Certainly the girls treated him like an alien who had landed in their house, never suspecting that he'd been there first. It didn't anger him. He could not take them seriously. Their being twins made them somehow four times as inane. They were the television twins across the hall, with their coordinating but not identical clothes, their green and pink headbands. They were two, and he was one, and all were nothing. He was less than one.

Eventually the girls came up with biological evidence to support their father's jocular contention. In fifth grade they did a science-fair project called "An Experiment on Inherited Traits." Their thesis suggested that Martin should be able to roll his tongue in the shape of a *U*; the ability is passed in the genes, they had read, and everyone else in the family could do it. "And we mean everyone!" Kelly had said in a threatening manner one night at dinner. Two different branches of cousins had been tested: parents, toddlers, grandparents even. All had succeeded and Martin had not.

"He's ruining our project," Kelly said.

"Make him stop," said Jane.

Martin stuck out his tongue and pressed it along his lower lip, trying to make it curl, but he only managed to drool on his plate. His mother said, "Martin, please," and his father made the usual joke.

"Well, girls," he said, "like I've always told you—"

"Like adopted?" asked Jane. "Do you mean it, Dad, really?"

They considered this a happy possibility, as it would save their thesis if it turned out to be true. But Martin sat in his room all evening with a straw and a mirror and bent paper clips. At ten he emerged. "Loolk," he cried. The girls came running. "Loolk, I kuh dloo id!"

Half-relieved, they tore up their refutation of Mendel's theory. Their project was saved. But later they won a certificate they could not successfully split.

Perhaps, Martin thought, he'd have had an easier time of it if his father's joke were literally true. Certainly he flirted with that possibility. At airports and stations, when he got detached from his parents, he selected new ones by accident. He'd go up to men in nice-looking suits, men whose cuffs were turned up in the same way his father's were, and say, "Daddy, will we be there today?" The man would turn around, gently, and perhaps crouch down to Martin's level. "And whose little boy are we?" he might say. Martin would stare and say nothing. Soon the wife would turn around, too. "Who's this handsome little boy you've found? I bet his own mommy and daddy are eager to have him back."

Martin already recognized the irony of this statement, but kept his mouth shut.

The new couple's children would get involved, sometimes walking right up to him as if he were a puppy they hoped they could keep. Other times they wrinkled up their noses and tried to pull their parents away. In either case, Martin's own family was eventually found, and his mother would grasp his hand more firmly. Martin would watch the new family thread itself back into the intertwining crowd and would feel as if he were looking at them from the wrong side of a mirror, as if they were real, and he should be with them instead of here in this unreality.

Embarrassing though it was, Martin did it over and over, latching onto alternative families, losing himself in airports and stations. Embarrassment wasn't the worst thing in life. The worst thing in life was feeling nothing about the impossible condition you were in. At least embarrassment manufactured feelings on the subject, and brought you pity, if only your own.

But the night he left for Europe, he felt neither embarrassment nor pity. *You are a stranger,* his father had said. Martin laughed to hear the old joke again, the old joke come true. If he was a stranger, at least he was free to be strange. And free to leave. He stood there elated; he, so tall, his father nothing more than a mouse in an armchair. I could kill this man, Martin realized. And I don't have to. Outside, the taxi was honking; inside, silence. No one moved until his mother suddenly fled to the kitchen. When Martin followed her there, he found her bent over the dishwasher, fiddling with dials.

Alas, the novelty of orphanhood wore off at his father's grave. Had Robert Gardner lived a bit longer, it might have been easier for Martin to disconnect. As it was, he felt more in common with the man now dead than he ever did with the man he knew. And though the girls were never important to him, his mother was still alive in his heart. She alone kept in touch, hesitantly it was true, but with some pathetic regularity when she came to the city.

Stella believed these visits were dangerous, that Martin owed it to himself to forbid them. The idea seemed cruel, yet it was Stella's knowledge and acceptance of cruelty that made her sympathetic to Martin's condition. Only she among Martin's circle could accept the existence of a family disaster that was not mixed picturesquely with success.

When at camp one day it had been announced during lineup that Martin's father, tragically, had died, Martin had packed his bags calmly and waited in his bunk. Only later that morning was it revealed that a different Martin was the one bereaved. Martin *Gardner* would get to remain at camp. John, his counselor, sat with him and held him tightly, thinking no doubt what an awful injustice had just been done. Well, the embrace was lovely, and Martin wept obligingly, but for the rest of the summer the false death of his father was his greatest, wickedest disappointment.

Though it would later come to haunt Martin, Stella found this story deeply satisfying. She bore no particular hatred toward her parents, but she understood its flavor at once. Her own bond was as blank, if not as twisted. She had no intention of returning to Tennessee and didn't particularly care if her parents visited her in New York. These were not the important figures in her life anymore.

But Martin had not the strength of Stella's certainty. He was not so sure he was new and improved, not so sure his mother was irrelevant. And so when she called to announce an upcoming excursion to what she referred to as Bloomingdale's Country, Martin equivocally invited her to lunch.

"Oh, Martin," Stella said when he told her during salad, "how disappointing. Now I'll have to get nurses and defibrillators ready."

"It's not for two weeks."

"I'll just have time."

He had completely expected this disapproval; what he didn't

expect was Matt's comment, whispered as he brought dishes to Martin at the sink, that Stella's disapproval was an excellent reason to be confirmed in his course.

T H E Y walked Stella to the elevator, which opened at her touch as usual, making the leave-taking awkward. "When will we see you next?" Martin asked, uncomfortably recalling the way guests escaping from his parents' endless barbecues were detained by the very same question.

"In your dreams," said Stella as the doors slid shut.

"In *your* dreams," said Matt.

They walked back down the hall in silence.

"Are you angry at her?" Martin finally asked.

"No, not particularly. Weird of her to tell that story, though. Don't you think weird?"

"I think it would have been weird of her not to."

"And I don't like talking about Maman just because Stella has to know every last detail of everything on earth."

"You could have said no."

Matt considered this. "She put her hand on my butt."

"Who wouldn't?" Martin smiled. He had seen the gesture, had judged it harmless, but now he wondered exactly what it meant. And what was Matt implying it meant?

Matt shrugged as if withholding an obvious answer. Martin moved ahead to the kitchen.

They were comfortable now in their routines. Dishes done at night by Martin would be dried by Matt—and evaporation—in the morning. In the meantime, Matt got in bed or watched TV in the living room. If there was a documentary on nuclear war and destruction, as there usually was on Channel 13, so much the better. Matt watched documentaries religiously, and suffered bad dreams.

Martin admired his toleration of horror—his fascination with it—but could not tolerate the horror himself. He drew no satisfaction from knowing the worst. "I've been there," he'd say.

The Channel 13 documentary of his life would detail the ravages of the nuclear *family*: a bomb, like its namesake, that depended upon the quick degradation of fused materials. Matt, Martin thought, must have had solider ground in his upbringing to stand upon, so willing was he to risk it all now with stories of holocaust and Hiroshima. But he couldn't find out, as Matt refused to talk about his family. Only Maman—and Maman only sporadically.

Matt had turned off whatever he was watching and come to bed by the time Martin emerged from the bathroom in a nightshirt. Though Matt had progressed in comfort to the point where he slept with no clothes, Martin had taken a step or two back and modestly changed when Matt couldn't see him. It was embarrassing, but Matt was kind and said nothing about it. He turned over when Martin got into the bed, faced away, and dropped off at once. Martin habitually stared at his back, ridged and tapered as an arrowhead, for several minutes before flipping onto his stomach for sleep.

Sometime later, Matt turned over and touched Martin's forehead. "Would you really be willing to lend me the money?"

"Yes," said Martin. "I'd give it to you."

"That's nice," Matt said, "but I really don't need it. I made that up about Maman being sick."

JET SET, to Martin's surprise, was still running after almost three months. The good reviews had been bolstered by a blitz of ads featuring ordinary people who loved the show saying how much they'd love to see it again. In fact these ordinary people were shills. The ad agency had given out-of-work actors free seats for a Tuesday performance and tempted them with AFTRA scale if afterward they enthused viably for the camera. Martin knew but could not disapprove of the ruse because Matt was one of the actors chosen. "The juiciest night on Broadway," he said, and received nine hundred dollars for saying it.

Martin had gotten him the job, but it was Matt who had to

find something to say. He planned the line well in advance of the actual taping, testing alternatives on Martin at dinner. "The costumes! The sets!" was rejected as too technical; "I'm truly moved," as too unlikely. "People want to know that something has flavor," Martin said, and so Matt developed the idea that the show could be juicy. In fact, he quite rightly found it insipid. Cynical as this was, he would not have won a prize for it. One woman caused herself to weep for the camera. "Better than *Cats*," she managed to utter, and these were words of genius.

The show's success was like the proverbial high tide that lifts all boats. Martin found himself vaguely respected. Hadn't he been involved with *Jet Set*? people asked at parties. "Well, yes," he would start, but before he could get his demurrers out, a look of approval would glaze the faces of all who listened. He stopped demurring.

The sensation was novel but pleasurable. Success, no matter how little one contributed to it, was easy to accept. Even the people who had known him all through it, employers and co-workers, heartily credited the value of his work. This, Martin knew, was a form of self-congratulation, but no less welcome for that. His Manhattan skyline had made the show, one of the producers said in a moment of exuberance, meaning nothing but that the producer was richer for it.

Soon the director, Peter White, was hard at work on another project. He was putting the finishing touches, he told Martin, on a script he hoped to produce for the fall. It was to be a break-through: a serious musical from a classic drama that would treat the audience as if it had a brain in its body.

They were meeting in the top-floor office of White's posh brownstone on East Forty-fourth. Rain was hitting the glass wall and ceiling like artillery fire. The computer screen glowed amber on White's desk, the cursor flashing at a word left incomplete.

"It's called *Six*," White said, raising his eyebrows as if to say, "Get it?"

Martin worked his way through the possibilities but could not determine what White had in mind.

"After Pirandello," he said. "Picture it with music. Isn't it thrilling?"

Martin did indeed feel thrilled, if not by the subject then at least by White's enthusiasm.

"And the score is priceless. Really classic. And I have ideas for the visual production—well, you know me."

Martin laughed loudly if uncertainly.

"So," White continued. "Are you interested?"

Martin said, "Sure, yes," completely unaware of what White intended. Only a half hour later did he realize he had just been asked to design the whole show. Before he could start to panic, however, the meeting was over. White hugged him good-bye and said, "Welcome aboard. I'll have a script sent around as soon as it's done. And my secretary will send contracts around to your agent."

Martin didn't have an agent, and could only wonder how he would get one. From the subway station he called Stella to ask her opinion.

"Martin, honey, think about it," she said, and then laughed. "You're essentially offering someone a ten-percent fee for a job you already got for yourself. It's a free ride. You can pick who you want." And so Martin stepped aboard a 6 train transfixed by pleasure.

The car was filled, as it usually was, with people notable to Martin for their strangeness. No one looks like me, he thought. They all wore mismatched clothes, and had crazy, unconsidered hair. He felt he had only the most tenuous connection to any of them, but today this sensation was welcome. They were reading tabloids and trashy novels; *he* was now a Broadway designer. With a chill he realized he had reached the top of his field— the top, the top, the top of something! And here was a man with walnut-red skin and small blue eyes who was tall and hairy;

where on earth was *he* from? Martin wondered. What is he doing, rattling through Manhattan, a little square children's book on his lap? Was he learning to read? At the bottom of the page his enormous hand had stopped at a line that asked in italics *Do you want to fetch the bucket right now? If so, turn to page 77. If you want to wait, turn one page ahead.* The man, apparently, could not decide. He was stumped in time, a dinosaur.

But then the train stopped in between stops, the lights went out, and Martin knew he was no different from anyone else. One moment of achievement had made him a fascist. In the darkness, Martin considered his miserable propensity for the tiniest pride, and doubted the source of his whole life's sadness. Was it not pride, too, to believe oneself egregiously unhappy? Select among the multitude for injury and shame?

And he *wasn't* unhappy. If only he could remember that.

When power was restored, Martin read headlines from someone else's tabloid. It was penance, he told himself, for his unwarranted pride, but even this formulation was prideful. No, he corrected himself, this is nothing but curiosity—a truth that delighted him almost as much as the knowledge that aliens had robbed Dolly Parton.

IT WAS NOW in Martin's power to help Matt get auditions, but not in his power to make him attend them. The prospect of reciting a two-minute monologue to a bored casting agent understandably filled Matt with dread. Upon close questioning, Martin discovered he had never had eight-by-ten glossies made up. He believed he could get away without them, if necessary.

Still, Martin persevered. He was flush with success and could not be completely safe in the feeling until those around him were flush with it, too. Stella he needn't worry about. She was moving her gallery to SoHo that summer; the East Village was dead, but Imago was not. The new space would be larger, with double-height ceilings—perfect for the very large paintings she was certain would be in vogue by fall.

But Matt no longer had even the big, sterile room of thirty salesmen and a hundred names to report to. He no longer hawked *American Learning*. Kim, apparently, had succumbed at last to the whispers and smirks of her coworkers and friends. They said eleven years was too large a gap; men at twenty-five were really just boys. This she had dutifully reported to Matt at dinner one night, in Martin's apartment.

"I have covered for you enough," she said, throwing her napkin onto the carpet. "I give you the likeliest cards, and I mark you down on time when you're late, and what do I get?"

"I never asked you to cover for me."

"Two nights. Two lousy nights. I'm supposed to feel grateful?"

"I'm not asking you to feel anything," Matt said.

Even Martin found this a cruel response, but under the circumstances he didn't object. He merely shifted in his seat as if to rise.

"Stay where you are," Matt said in even tones.

Kim eyed him malevolently. Her blond hair, knotted up on her head, reflected light like a honeyed roll. Her clothes—boots, jeans, a man's T-shirt—were tight with reproach. "Well, I think we know the real story here," she said syllable by syllable, leaving Martin perplexed.

"Oh, do we!" Matt said.

Much to Martin's vicarious mortification, Kim had now to make her exit through a door whose lock she could not unlatch. "Damn it," she yelled, yanking at the knob. "And you're fired, by the way. That's not just from me!" She slammed the door so hard it bounced back open. Martin and Matt stayed in their seats.

She had dressed up for this encounter, she had chosen clothes both defensive and sexy. Now she'd go home and rip the boots and jeans off her legs in disgust. She would throw herself down on the bed in her underwear and cry. Later she would quit her job and tell her friends she was making a change.

"I must say I sympathize with her," Martin said when Kim had escaped.

"Don't *you* start now."

"Only that you do seem to—" he hesitated. "You know, let people wonder. What you want."

"What do *you* want? Do you want me to leave? I can go to the Village." He pulled from his pocket a set of keys.

Martin looked down at his lap as if he had been caught in a lie. "Let's just drop it."

Matt ostentatiously transferred Kim's uneaten roast beef to his own plate and ate it. "I know another place I can work," he said. "Selling toner to confused secretaries. 'Hi there, Michael Madison speaking. Mr. Ferguson said you needed more toner. Ferguson over in your other office. Last week, he called. He didn't tell you?' "

He looked as if he might start to cry, but bit his lip and then resumed eating. After a while he said, "She was so pushy." Martin made a sympathetic, noncommittal face; he was afraid to do more lest some basic fact, like Maman's illness, be suddenly swept out from under him. *Her name wasn't Kim, by the way. It was Maureen. And—she was black!* Martin somehow felt this kind of bombshell coming, and so sought to duck. What was the perfectly innocuous thing to say? "Looks like rain," he ventured.

Matt kept eating and didn't look up. After dessert, he left the room quickly.

Kim probably *was* a little too pushy, Martin thought while washing the dishes. And not a good match for Matt even without that. But who was? Matt had a low tolerance for interference, and perhaps there was no one unpushy enough. Even Gandhi, though passive, resisted, and made a holy show of it, too. No one came with no strings attached, though the strings might be invisible at first.

Matt kept looking, though. Even before Kim's departure, he had spoken approvingly of the Englishwoman he'd met at the *Jet Set* opening-night party. She was powerful, almost arrogant, and frank to a fault—Matt liked that. You had the feeling, he said, that she conducted relationships in a businesslike manner, without obscure expectations or hidden agendas. The agenda would be spelled out in detail in her eyes, or on her hand as it made its way toward you. Martin had the feeling this woman was waiting in the wings somewhere, listening for her cue.

A ghastly sound interrupted these speculations. Martin put down the plate he was washing and ran to the bathroom, where Matt was kneeling in front of the toilet, throwing up. The noise was horrible—it sounded more like heavy machinery than a human cry—and the back of Matt's shirt was completely soaked from the racking and heaving. It was too much to watch, but Martin was able to master his own nausea as it rose within him. He sat on the edge of the tub and found he was permitted to pat Matt's neck. He cooled Matt's forehead with a dampened washcloth.

When it was over, Matt flushed the toilet but did not rise. He covered his face with the palms of his hands. Martin kept patting.

"What a night," said Matt.

"Maybe it's good."

"Good? How?"

"Well, you could kind of have a vacation from it."

"It meaning what?"

"You know, involvement. Maybe you need some time by yourself to get to know what you want."

"Are you sure you mean by myself?" And he made a face suggesting, kindly, that the motivation behind Martin's advice was jealousy.

It was true, in part, but only in part. Equally salient was his real concern for Matt's happiness, a happiness that seemed unattainable by current methods. And there was also the disturbing sensation that he, Martin, was complicit in the events he complained of. Chloe, he remembered, had cast Matt out when he came home late from dinner at Martin's. He never met her. Kim got further, to the table at least, but seemed suspicious of Martin's role.

Was something wrong with the food he was serving? Or was he being used to help precipitate reactions that otherwise might take weeks of unpleasantness? Martin could see Matt as an element that easily combined but that needed assistance in breaking bonds. And he could see himself with no trouble at all as the secret catalyst, useful but unheralded, consumed by the reaction.

Still, Matt was here, rising slowly, putting his arm around Martin's waist to be walked to the bed. Martin undressed him, tucked him into the covers, then padded shoeless down the hall to the laundry room. Washing Matt's soiled clothing, he thought: Somehow there must be more I can do.

MARIA was speaking from her experience with Delia, taking her around to auditions, trying to treat them casually. "Make it light," she said. "Don't get caught up. Treat it as nothing. The worst thing is to make it seem that this one matters more than another. There's *always* another. It's got to be seen as a game or it's deadly."

"That's easy when you're six," said Martin. "Matt is twenty-five."

"I'm not really talking about him. I'm talking about you. The toll I'm concerned about is the one *you* pay. And you're, what, thirty?"

"Twenty-seven."

"Oh, sorry. But *I'm* thirty-six." She looked down as if involuntarily to her slightly swollen stomach. "Hear that in there? Stefan? Hear that?"

The child had long since been sexed and named. It only remained to enroll it in daycare.

"I appreciate your concern for me, but I'm concerned more with how Matt does."

"Look, Martin, is he talented or what? Is this a pastime or is it for real?"

"I don't know. I've never seen him perform, except in that commercial. He's certainly good-looking enough."

"That's true."

"And charming and intelligent."

Maria said, "Hmm."

Martin had managed to get Matt an audition for the summer theater at Williamstown, Massachusetts. "They do classics there," he'd explained in bed. "Ibsen, Chekhov, they're really good. And they have this second company that does modern and slightly avant-garde stuff. This woman I know knows the casting director. I think you could try."

To Martin's surprise, Matt had said yes. He worked up monologues from Shakespeare and Shepard, and allowed Martin to arrange for pictures. These came out beautifully—everyone said so—and earned Matt a chance to read for a part. But now Martin had a sinking feeling that he'd invested his hopes imprudently. The Shepard was at least convincingly rageful but the Shakespeare—Hotspur—made no sense.

Now, the evening before the dreaded audition, Maria's advice was too late coming. Martin had already made it such a big deal that Matt refused to eat home that night. He made a date instead with the Englishwoman and left Martin stranded with a quiche in the oven. He'd taken it over to share with Maria.

She was alone that evening, too. David and Delia were both at work. Stefan, in the womb, was for the moment undemanding. The apartment was clean.

"Come look at something," Maria said. She led Martin into Delia's room. "Look, here. A picture of you."

Delia had pinned a Polaroid photo of Martin backstage on her bulletin board.

"You know she loves you, Martin. I think it's important for you to know."

"I knew she liked me—"

"And look, over here," Maria went on, by now distracted. "Her first pair of shoes. It almost makes me cry to see them. So *small*, Martin. Can you believe so small?"

She sorted through a trunk of clothes at the foot of Delia's bed. "Say, these aren't too bad. Do you think Stefan can wear them? No one cares anymore about pink and blue, do they?"

"I should think they do," Martin said.

MARTIN removed a new sheet of scalloped gray stationery from its drawer and then returned it: too fancy. He tore a piece of paper from a legal pad, but this was too plain. He crumpled it up. Finally he settled on the simple white Crane's with his name engraved in black at the top: a gift from his mother. He felt like Goldilocks. This was just right.

Dear Nana, he wrote, and his pen blotched the comma. He tore up the sheet.

Dear Nana, he tried again, on a fresh piece of paper. This time he lifted the pen directly away, at a ninety-degree angle, as he had learned to do so long ago in drafting. "There, that looks good," he said upon examining it.

Dear Nana, he said to himself. What have I to say to you?

The folder had come in the mail weeks ago. It explained the overall goal of the program: to save earth's most precious natural resource, its children. The sponsor's tax-deductible donation would help sustain a specifically selected child in a prechosen country. "This is no abstract charity, but one-on-one," said the folder. "A particular human life will thrive on your concern, a life that otherwise would languish." And the sponsor would benefit, too, it said, from the wonderful knowledge he was helping improve the world.

For that reason, the sponsor was encouraged to write his "spiritual child" and hear firsthand what his generosity had accomplished. These children *always*—the folder insisted in ominous italics—responded gratefully if contacted by their sponsor. And several testimonials described the satisfaction derived from such correspondence. One woman said she received mail almost every week of the year from one or another of her dozen sponsored children. *"It's like a family," says happy sponsor* was the caption beneath a sepia picture. The woman displayed several envelopes and photographs.

Inserted into four tiny cuts on the inside of the folder was a picture of the girl Martin had been assigned. Her name was Nana Obeng. A brief description below the picture said she was nine years old and lived in Accra, "the capital city of the African country of Ghana." Her mother worked in the Makola markets, whatever they were, and Nana assisted. She received no schooling and was undernourished. With Martin's help she'd be able to attend a girls' academy outside the city. There she would get proper medical attention, a uniform, good food, and books to learn from. When she grew up, she might not have to work among the muddy, hectic stalls of the market, but might be a nurse, the folder suggested, a teacher, or even an engineer. Her own children might know a better life.

Nana's face was absolutely round, and reflected the flash of the camera. She wore a white T-shirt from which her thin arms emerged like links of sausage, constricted at the elbow. It appeared she was standing between two other children, but they had been cropped from the sides of the picture. She smiled with her mouth closed.

So perfectly needy, so picturesquely poor: Could she, too, have been a shill? Was she actually a child actress, like Delia, in New York? Was she paid to look sincere, like Matt in the commercial? Martin had checked off, when given the option, the box marked *Wherever my help is needed most.* But Washington Heights?

Yes, Martin thought, even Washington Heights.

Now he reviewed his letter so far. *Dear Nana,* it said. The paper was much too large, he realized; he'd never be able to fill a whole sheet. Nevertheless, he picked up his rapidograph. *My name is Martin,* he wrote, feelingly.

IT WAS eleven o'clock when Martin heard his door thump shut, heard keys drop onto the hallway table, the refrigerator drone upon being opened. That would be Matt taking his nightly swig of milk from the bottle, or rather—bottles being a thing of the dim, suburban past—from the paper container that folded out a diamond.

He was earlier coming home than expected, but Martin, not letting himself wait up, had already gotten ready for bed. He was reading a cookbook: a dessert recipe that seemed to require a structural engineer for final assembly. He glanced up to find Matt at the edge of the room, facing away. Something was wrong. Usually he'd have come to the bed, grasped Martin's foot through the blanket, and talked. Instead he now paced a corridor bounded by the Sheetrock wall and the ring of Martin's lamp. A few stray lumens picked out a semicircle of white above his lips as he glided in the shadows. Martin felt like an astronomer. He was tracking the milk star.

"How was your date?" The Englishwoman, whose name Martin still did not know, had made her entrance not two days after Kim made her exit. She turned out to be some kind of international securities dealer; negotiations with Matt were quick and businesslike.

He smiled recalcitrantly. "She wore a green silk dress, very tight. Her hair was done up kind of Grecian. No jewelry except very large earrings, which kept slipping off. She won't pierce her ears. Barbaric, she says. Finally she unclipped them, these two gold doubloons, and put them near her plate, like a tip."

The sentences were emerging blank and uniform, expression canceled out, like news bulletins. Martin mimed changing the channel by remote control.

"She ordered our meal so assertively that the waiter got confused. She put her finger through my belt loop."

"That *does* seem confusing."

"And now, if this interrogation is over, would you turn off the light?"

Martin did so, wondering why. It was not a typical request from Matt, and anyway had little effect. The room was not much darker than it had been before. Moonlight and streetlight washed across the room, softening all edges and colors in its path.

Matt faced into a corner and took off his clothes. His back glistened with points of perspiration like an overwhelming summer night sky. He closed the blinds.

"What are you doing?" Martin asked.

"Stop watching me."

"Are you nervous about tomorrow?"

"Stop watching me."

He turned around and Martin could plainly see the problem. Oh, is that all, he thought, and laughed to think it.

Matt threw his pants at Martin and hit him. They stared at each other.

"What do you want from me?" Matt snapped. "Can't you leave me alone for one minute? This has nothing to do with you. This is *my* life. *My* life, yes?" He was accenting syllables almost randomly, Martin thought, like bad pop music. "I see the way you look at me. Don't think I don't. And I don't say anything. But whatever I have—not much, I grant you—is mine, not yours. You cannot have it. Don't you have enough already? Don't you have enough?"

The wind picked up in Martin's ears and his heart lurched into action, skipping beats, shutting down, surging on. He felt something like mercury rise up within him, as if he were the thermometer tube and his head would burst as the temperature climbed. He couldn't breathe—this time for real.

"Help," he gasped.

"Are you all right? Martin? Martin?" Matt came over to the bed and grabbed his shoulder.

"Yes," he said. The mercury receded. Was it for real?

"You should see a doctor about that, you know."

"I did. He said there was no physical reason."

"Then maybe you should see a shrink instead."

There the conversation foundered, but Martin had scared himself. What if something really was wrong? Immediately he suspected his heart. His father had died of a massive coronary, with no warning, at age forty-eight. And that basketball player who just keeled over—hadn't the papers made a big deal about his height?

How much of your life, Martin wondered, was based on concepts you could not verify? He had made himself frail in obedience to an incompetent doctor's failure to diagnose. His mother participated in the fraud; for years she argued leniency and indulgence on the basis of Martin's "delicacy." But the delicacy all along might have been something much more straightforward. Perhaps even treatable. A hole or a tear, a faulty valve. He would look it up. He would consult Stella's medical dictionary. He would . . .

In the darkness, time disappeared. Martin assumed Matt was still standing near him, but he suddenly felt the bed sink at his side. He's next to me again, he thought.

"Good night," said Matt, the anger gone from his voice.

Was the incident over? It hadn't been so bad. A spat as any two people might have. In a way, a good sign, demonstrating loyalty. After all, Matt was still here, though Martin dared not yet look to see. Fights between other people sometimes ended in gunshot or chase. This had ended with sleep, like a marriage.

The angry man who was not your lover, standing there in his insufficient briefs, his skin alive, even if not alive for you: How could anything so beautiful be bad? Did you have to touch everything you loved to love it?

Nana Obeng, for instance, he might never even meet—was that not good? A child without the *inexcusable mess*?

He was filled once again with affection for Matt, who was on his side, curled into the bed, sniffling like mad.

"You're crying," said Martin.

"No, I'm not."

"It's all right. I like you to cry."

"But I'm not," said Matt.

The denial was all right, too, Martin thought. Matt was a law unto himself.

The sea-blue blanket was pulled off to his waist. The form of his legs beneath it merged in the shadow like a mermaid's tail. The shallow bowls of his chest hunched together against the sheet. His head lay taut upon the pillow, his mouth just open. Whistling noises and gusts of low sound emerged. He was trying to talk, or trying to learn to talk. He was evolving from the homogeneous sea. What was he saying? What was he trying to learn to say?

MARTIN slid silently out of bed and stationed himself at the window. Behind the lifted corner of a blind he saw the man across the way alone in his yellow light. His bed was closed. His fingers manipulated the top of his head as if attempting to dislodge it. Martin leaned further toward the window. On the street, a woman struggled to get out of a cab. Will she be visiting my friend? he wondered. With her wide-brimmed hat and voluminous raincoat, she resembled from above the concentric circles of an archery target. The target moved.

Matt had ceased to make any noise, and now lay in state like Tut. In the corner where he dropped them, his clothes still huddled, dead to the eye but alive with cologne. Martin picked them up. The jeans he smoothed along the top of his dresser, the shirt he brought to his face and shamelessly inhaled. Then he hung it on the back of a chair, where it shrugged at itself, like a comic, in the mirror. Inside Matt's shoes, which Martin had bought, something was glinting. Change it was. Quarters and dimes.

If there are moments of realization, Martin thought, they may as well come like this. A quarter sequestered in a Cole-Haan shoe. Matt will never be mine, it said. Like reports of starvation in Africa, this was a much-repeated headline, but one that failed to convince completely without the eloquent illustration. Money withheld in expensive shoes. Martin tapped them into proper alignment—he believed there was a proper alignment even for shoes.

There were rules for such things: how pictures should hang, where cuffs should break. These rules need not mean anything deeply—how could they?—as long as the consistency of the surface was upheld. This is how Martin lived. I am neat, he told himself, not sanitary—for he cared more about the chrome on the refrigerator than he cared about the crumbs behind it. Correct, not good. Attractive, not functional. This is enough, because this is what I am.

In the living room he stood and watched: the heavy draperies swagged back in iron catches, candles in brass sticks snuffed out in midburn. It looked as if a party recently in progress would be continuing momentarily. And yet, by all signs, the interruption had lasted several centuries already. Still the furniture stood poised, alert. On a table, miniature statuary waited to be admired. Venus, Hadrian, *Le Baiser*, considered each other warily across the ages. On either side of the window, backs high, two prize Chippendales guarded the view. They sniffed out human presence like overbred dogs, poodles with pompadours.

Martin was filled with love for this room he'd invented, but its beauty, he knew, came to nothing, as did he. Beneath the ornament it asserted itself as the primal white Manhattan box. Despite Venus, despite *Le Baiser*.

We devote ourselves to beauty, he thought, but what has beauty ever done for us? It pleases the eye, but to what end? What's the use? What's the *use*? It replicates and eats itself up. Like people, he thought. Like *some* people, anyway. People with children.

Attractive, not functional: Is that what it finally meant to be gay? Like the chairs, like the paint, to mean nothing? To be a witty accouterment of history? An ornament, not the thing, an appendage, not the body? Chippable, lost, repeatedly made anew, but never reproducing because decorative?

Bureaus, beds, pots exist in all ages unchanged in concept.

They have use and the use can be named. *Holds things, sleeps things, cooks things.* But decoration is designed and discarded. The craze, the rage, the norm, the quaint, the antiquated, the lost. The what-could-they-possibly-*have*-been-thinking? The trendsetters and the left-behind. The hairdressers to the stars and wallpaperers of Broadway. Are we the ball and claw, Martin asked, the green silk tassel on moiré drapes? Are we the broken Roman nose, the sad arm of Venus, raised but detached?

Oblivion was the answer, he decided. Matt was indelibly marked in his heart, and on his foot, but he need not read the marking obsessively. He would be more austere. There is a safety, he told himself, a safety in numbness.

THE AUDITION, as Matt described it in the cab, struck Martin as irregular. He tried to keep this thought to himself. His new austerity demanded the same tolerance for self-deception by others he hoped those others would manifest toward him. And Matt was so excited to have gotten a part. Still, it was hard not to raise an eyebrow at the scene Matt took naively for granted.

"The show," he explained, "takes place in a brothel. It's about exploitation."

"I'll say," said Martin. His new resolve was failing already.

"But there's no actual sex on stage. Just simulated, whatever that means."

"I think that means a lot of people in the audience are going to put on their glasses. Are you sure this was the *Williamstown* audition?"

"Yes, Martin, don't be so cynical. They're doing a festival of avant-garde works on their second stage. This is by a playwright from Brazil. I'm not going to be pretentious and say a *famous* playwright from Brazil because I never heard of him. But that's what *they* said."

"And what's it called?"

"They don't know. It's so avant-garde it isn't titled yet."

"Is it so avant-garde it isn't *written* yet?"

Matt took a script from his knapsack and brandished it. "O ye of little faith," he said. Then he put the script back in.

"But why did you have to take your clothes off?"

"Not all my clothes. You say that as if they made me jerk off. They wanted to see my body is all. The part is for a certain kind of guy and they wanted to see if I would look right. Hey, look, it wasn't a problem. I actually felt freer to perform."

"Perform what?"

"The actions of the scene."

"And they were what?"

"Sitting, standing, walking around. Saying a line. Look, I don't need to convince *you*. They wouldn't be doing it if it weren't worth doing. These were smart, nice people. They weren't there to cop a feel."

"And your monologues?"

Matt tapped his elbow impatiently. "I didn't do them."

Martin let this go. "Well, nevertheless, congratulations." This seemed grudging, so he added a phrase that came out sounding like his mother lying. "I think it's grand."

"Well, so do I."

"Grand, grand, grand."

"That's enough."

The cab turned onto Wooster Street and stopped. Martin paid. "What's this guy's name?" Matt asked, climbing out.

"I don't remember."

The gallery was not yet open to the public; its streetfront glass was still soaped over. The word IM appeared in gilt on the door. Presumably the letterer had left off for the day, and AGO would appear tomorrow. Martin buzzed, and the door buzzed back.

Stella was standing at the far end of an enormous room, directing the hanging of a canvas. She consulted with a man who could only have been the artist: he had round-rimmed glasses and paint on his jeans. He ran one hand through his glistening crew cut and said uncertainly, "Higher? Lower?"

A man on a ladder with a hammer and nails said, "I can't tell."

Stella considered and announced her decision. "Higher." Then she turned. "Hello, boys. Come meet Chris. Chris, this is Martin. Martin, Chris. Chris, Matt. Matt, Chris. Eddie," she said, indicating the man on the ladder, "these are Matt and Martin, my friends. Martin, Eddie. Matt, Eddie."

"Well, you've certainly got introductions down," said Chris as everyone shook hands or nodded hello.

"Is this your first show?" Matt asked him.

"No," he said, "but it may be my last."

He gestured toward the very large painting now being hung. In it, two men held hands while they walked down a lurid city street at dusk. The taller one, bearded and ethereal, wore a business suit and carried a briefcase. The shorter one, almost a boy, really, was packed into shorts and an armless T-shirt that spelled *love* upon it in the shape of a cube. He stared adoringly at the older man, who in turn was caught staring at the turbulent sky, which Chris had spiked with bits of green and violet.

"He calls it *Jesus Loves the Prostitute, Too*," Stella said.

Matt laughed, but Martin found the title apt. The painting was religious and yet profane. It was hard to resist.

"Actually, I've changed it back to *Untitled*."

"We'll talk," said Stella.

Martin broke from the spell of the painting. "Matt has some untitled news as well."

Matt explained that he'd gotten the part, and everyone toasted him with pantomime glasses.

"Here's to good flesh," Stella said.

Later, when he had her alone in the office, Martin told her how Chris had surprised them. "We'd expected one of your sexual psychopaths."

"First of all, he plays on your team, not mine, which should have been obvious. And do you think I sleep with all my artists?

Really, Martin, give me some credit. Don't believe everything everyone says. Especially me."

Martin sighed. "Well, I like the paintings. The ones I've seen. He's good, isn't he?"

"Yes." She smiled. "I think *very*. I even had my Dolly Levi hat on. What do you think?"

"I think you should take it off," said Martin. He knocked on a wall to see if it was plaster. "And his skin is so bad."

Stella did not look up from the phone, upon which she dialed at least twenty digits. "Shoot him," she said.

THE PAINTINGS, as was almost certainly intended, provoked in Martin uncomfortable questions. He thought of his roommate Cary from college, a devout boy from North Dakota, who had come to Rhode Island all unsuspecting. He was kind and virtuous, took sandwiches to Harold the homeless man, and even had a highly ironic and touching imperfection: he lisped like crazy. Despite all this, it was hard to warm up to a person who told you you would definitely burn in hell someday. Still, Martin chose to room with him, every year.

For graduation, Cary gave Martin a King James Bible, and wrote a poem on the inside cover. "Worldly love, love of God, can go together, it's not so odd." He cited, beneath this, in his spindly, laborious hand, appropriate passages he hoped Martin would read. He seemed to want them read on the spot.

Martin flipped through the pages, with their bloodred edges. "It's beautiful," he made himself say, "very nice design and type." The chapters were synopsized in italic phrases that read like Cliff Notes. *Job Muses on the Brevity of Life. The Good Man Longs to Dwell in God's House.* Martin kept flipping. The prophets appeared, made their prophecies, went heeded or unheeded. What difference did it make?

Martin mused on the brevity of life and continued to flip. At the end of the Old Testament, as a kind of divider, the publisher had provided blank pages for the listing of marriages and births.

Both words were lettered in *New York Times* Gothic. But Martin knew he would never have reason to write on those pages. There was no space for lovers or colleagues or friends, no space for favorite paintings or foods. Marriage and birth; that was it. You were in or out.

"Ignore that part," Cary said. "It's not canonical."

"Oh, good," said Martin, turning the pages. The New Testament began with Matthew.

AT NINE O'CLOCK on the morning of the New York primary, Martin was awakened by a messenger bearing the preliminary script of *Six*. He signed unsteadily; he was tired and a little alarmed because Matt had not come home the night before. He made himself coffee and toast and juice, and set this all out on his breakfast table with the unopened package. Then, when enough food and coffee had cleared his head, he slit the envelope.

The script featured seven major characters, an innovation Martin could not begin to fathom. There was also a chorus, commenting on the action from above, holding signs and tendentious Brechtian banners. Martin had never gone in for this sort of thing, but more disconcerting, from a professional point of view, was this direction at the top of page one: "The musical is played on a completely bare stage."

Now his sudden promotion by Peter White made sense. White's regular designer—the elderly Russian—had obviously turned the project down. As who would not? What could be more unfulfilling than this? Life itself?

But even a blank stage needs designing, Martin thought, and maybe there would be a projection or drop. Anyway, the money was good. The credit, too. To say no would be suicide. And maybe the next show would be something better.

In this way he managed to calm himself down, but when he later went to cast his vote, he pulled the lever, as he'd sworn he would not, angrily, again, for Ronald Reagan.

■ ■ ■

MATT was watching television and eating a loaf of semolina bread when Martin returned that morning from the polls.

"The prodigal returns," Martin said wearily.

Matt and the Englishwoman had been seeing each other almost every night since that first encounter with the earrings and the belt loop. Still, Matt had not previously stayed over with her; this seemed to be part of their explicit arrangement. Normally he'd return to Martin's, perhaps not until three in the morning, wired and hungry. He would wake Martin up unintentionally as he got into bed, and then answer questions with a matter-of-fact recital of names familiar from the gossip pages.

"Yes. Tama was there. She's actually charming. Some artist—what's his name, with the pots—Stella talks about him. Cornelia Guest. That guy from the *Voice*."

And then he'd oversleep in the morning and have to call his temp agency to say he couldn't work until noon.

Today he clearly wouldn't work at all. His eyes were bloodshot and his nose was red and he sat with a box of tissues as he ate. A wastepaper basket filled up at his feet.

"I didn't feel like coming home," he said. "I just walked around for a while."

"All night? You caught a cold."

Matt shrugged. "Or something."

Martin sat next to him and looked at the television. A man was describing a day he had spent with a woman chosen for him by a studio audience. The host of the show interrupted his narrative with suggestive comments. Had they made a love connection? he asked in a plummy, prurient voice. They had indeed.

Martin burst out laughing. "God, am I depressed," he said, when the joke wore off.

"Why, little Marty?"

Martin handed Matt the script of *Six*, holding it open so he could read the relevant stage direction. Then they sat without moving or talking.

"Have you heard of Xtasy?" Matt said eventually.

"What, as a concept?"

"No, as a drug."

"Is this a metaphor?"

"No, a drug. That's what it's called. Spelled with an *X*."

Martin curled up his nose.

"It's totally safe. It just makes you feel good."

"Have you done it?" Martin asked.

"Yes. Twice."

"You have?"

Matt dug a white gelatin capsule from his pants pocket. "It's the best feeling I've ever had."

Martin had never taken a drug before; he rarely used aspirin. In college he'd been regarded as an insufferable prude because he wouldn't join in when drugs were passed around. He hated the smell of marijuana and would wave his hands about him when he entered a room beclouded with its smoke. Stoned, people would talk with an intensity that suggested erudition and clarity when in fact they were frightful, mystifying bores.

Martin had been utterly incurious about the land of drugs, perhaps because he did not like the partisans. Since college, though, he had softened on the subject. Stella, he knew, had done a number of things—just part of her need to know everything. Even Martin's mother purchased her share of equanimity at the drugstore, abetted by her ancient doctor. And here was Matt vouching for the high.

"Do you see funny colors?" Martin asked.

"No. Just weird monsters and evil demons." Matt put the capsule back in his pocket. "But people like you probably shouldn't do it anyway. I just thought it might take you out of yourself." He got up.

"People like me?"

As if in answer, Matt held his hand out to the impeccable apartment. "Come on, let's go to the gym or something."

"Where did you get it?"

Matt would not say.

Martin asked a dozen more questions—What would happen? How long would it last?—before telling Matt he wanted to try it.

"Are you sure?"

Martin nodded vehemently, as if afraid he might change his mind. Matt broke the capsule open and poured half its contents onto Martin's tongue, the other half onto his own.

"Nothing's happening," Martin said, the minute he swallowed the bitter powder.

"Give it time."

And in a half hour there came over him the most hideous wave of white anxiety he had ever experienced. His jaw tightened to the point he could almost not open it to speak. His heart started racing; he thought he might faint. "Hold my hand," he commanded Matt, and Matt complied, though the hand was clammy and difficult to unlatch. Martin thought this must be what it was like to take off in a rocket. They were flying to the moon against impossible opposition in an inadequate vessel. The skin of the ship would surely burst.

But soon the tightness drained away and Martin felt—what? It was a vaguely familiar sensation, there was a word for it, too, if only he could remember it— Happy! He looked at Matt, who was smiling quite simply, as one might smile while watching a baby. Or if one *were* a baby. "Let's go somewhere," Matt said.

They drank several bottles of water as they walked. "Where should we go?" they kept asking each other. At eleven-thirty they found themselves leaning against the chain-link fence of Delia's school, waiting for recess.

"Hey, Delia!" Martin shouted when the children came pouring out of the building. She ran to the fence.

"You remember Matt," he said.

" 'The juiciest night on Broadway,' " said Delia.

Matt laughed so hard he started to cough, and then to sneeze. The tissue he took from his pocket was stained with blood.

"Why are you here?" Delia asked.

"Just came to see you."

She glanced over her shoulder at the other kids arranging themselves into groups for games of jump rope and hopscotch and tag. "The one in the purple socks is Mercedes," she said. "She's my best friend."

"Do you want to go play?"

"Maybe in a minute." She put a finger through the fence and poked Martin in the stomach. "Hello," she said. "Earth to Martin. Come in please. Where are you?"

"In ecstasy," he said.

"What's that?"

"Bliss," said Matt.

"Great happiness," said Martin. He put a finger through the fence and poked Delia back. "I love you, you know."

She stared at him, then glanced over her shoulder again. "Uh-oh," she said. "Here comes stupid Mr. Jalapeño. It's really Mr. Hall but we call him that because he's such a pain."

And over walked a thin man with gray-shot hair and tortoise-shell glasses. He put his hand on Delia's head in a manner Martin was sure she would hate, but which she actually appeared not to mind.

"Are these gentlemen friends of yours?" he asked her.

"Him, not him," Delia answered, pointing in turn to Martin and Matt.

Matt produced a thin, indifferent smile.

"You understand, fellas, we have to be careful."

"Absolutely," Martin said. "We understand. There's so much going on these days, you can't be too careful. We were just saying hi. I work with Delia. In the show, you know. *Jet Set.* I'm a friend of her mother. And this is just my friend. We were enjoying the day." He couldn't seem to stop himself talking, and then he started to laugh.

"Well then, gentlemen."

They walked to the lake at Central Park, but Martin refused

to get in a rowboat. He didn't like natural bodies of water—you never knew what you might find at the bottom. They walked through the Ramble. They lay in the Sheep Meadow, head to head, their bodies stretched out in opposite directions. Only the tips of their scalps touched each other, and that was enough. Martin felt forks of blue lightning branch out from the point of tangency; one moved through his forehead to his sinuses, another down his temples to his eardrums, another behind his head to the permanent knot at the base of his neck. Had any more of their bodies been touching, Martin would have exploded, he felt. As it was, he could barely contain himself. His whole body had become genital, his skin everywhere overwhelmed with sensation. Brushing a fly from his shirt, he swept his fingers past his hard left nipple and almost flew up into the grass-scented air. When he had quelled, with great effort, the sensation of impending orgasm, he looked about him. Other couples lay in the meadow, making out, making love; he and Matt were making whatever it was they could.

By the time the sun fell behind the West Side towers, the bliss was subsiding; Martin became obsessed with regaining it. "Can I have any more?" he importuned Matt. "How long do you have to wait before you can take it again? Can I take it tomorrow before my mother comes over? Do you think I should?"

Matt was reluctant, but gave Martin three more capsules from his pocket. "You're a big boy now, decide for yourself."

"How much does it cost? Should I pay you something?"

"This is on me."

But that night Maria called, with an edge in her voice. "I want to talk to you about today," she said. "I'm very concerned. Delia says she saw you at school and you acted crazy."

"She does? I did? I was just having fun."

"Fun indeed. You were not being careful, which isn't like you. You scared her half to death."

Martin believed this was an exaggeration, but even if he had scared her only a little, he was sorry. "I don't know what to say," he said.

"Say it won't happen again," said Maria.

"No, of course, it won't. I promise. I'm so sorry. You know how I feel about Delia. Please——" He started to cry.

"It just isn't like you," Maria said flatly.

"That's enough, Moonface," David said. Martin hadn't even realized David was on the line. "We all make mistakes."

They said their good-byes, and David hung up, but Maria couldn't help singing one more refrain. "Not like you at all," she said, and Martin knew what she was getting at.

He took the remaining Xtasy in his palm. Such happiness he'd felt. If only he could live that way! But it must get expensive, he found himself thinking as he walked to the bathroom and flushed the capsules down the toilet. Expensive and false. Let the fish be happy.

MARTIN examined the wonderful colors of the salmon omelet he had prepared for his mother's lunch. "What would you think of this shade for the drapes?" he asked her, pointing to the food. "It would certainly go with the carpet in the hall."

"Oh no, dear, no. That carpet's been changed." She took a swatch from her purse and held it up to the omelet sadly. "No," she said, "I was hoping for something more in the purple family."

Martin smirked. He knew she could not prevent herself from mentioning family one way or another. They had gotten through the perfunctory discussion of his work, and the endless announcements of the weddings and births now prevalent among his former classmates. She'd asked, as she had during several previous lunches, if he'd heard the news about Lisa Worbal: that she'd had a baby, but the baby was born with only four toes on each of its feet. Yes, Martin nodded, and quoted its name.

"Your father would so much have loved a grandson."

"Mother, please."

"I'm telling the truth."

"I'm sure you are." He was willing to talk about her feelings if she wanted, but not the feelings of her late husband. It was too painful, too macabre. Unfortunately, her feelings were completely restricted to and subsumed in him. In the six years since the funeral, Martin had watched his mother squander the little determination left her and shrink away under the cloak of her husband's memory. She ventured forth now like an orphan in Dickens, soon to be returned to the orphanage, half-grateful.

In order to see Martin at all, she felt compelled to concoct an alibi; this was the real motive behind her decision to redecorate. Only stores in the city would do, she told herself; the ones in the suburbs were too provincial. And perhaps it was true. In any case, she wandered from showroom to showroom, touching tiles and rugs, buying a heap of pillows on one visit, returning half the heap on the next. At this rate the project would take up years, and perhaps that was her hope. But a day would come when the job was complete: every wall prepared without a bubble, every window fetchingly redraped. The home from which Martin had once removed himself would no longer exist; no return could be made to it.

"The girls ask for you," she said between bites.

"They must be in college by now," said Martin, wiping his plate with a round of French bread.

"You know very well. I wish you wouldn't play this game."

"Perhaps if they'd write me or call me once, my memory would improve. As it is, I don't see why I should take an interest."

"They're very busy at school, you know. They're both in the chorus. You remember what college is like. And anyway, they are your sisters."

"And I'm their brother, what does that mean? Why do you always excuse their behavior?"

"What else can I do?"

"Not excuse it."

She stared at the porcelain saltshaker still in her hand. "It's not so easy," she started to say before her voice faltered. "It's not so easy."

"I suppose."

She salted her omelet again and then coughed. "They've put a light at the intersection, you know."

She was referring to the intersection where Martin had been involved in an accident. "It's only been ten years," he said.

"Poor Paula Hayes."

"Paula Hayes? Poor Paula Hayes?"

Her son, Eric, was the boy responsible; he'd driven his car straight through a stop sign. Striking the wheel, he'd gone into a coma and never recovered. The mother and daughter in the other car had died instantly. The blood could be seen on the street for weeks.

Only Martin, in the passenger seat, was left uninjured. When the noise had ended, and the car had stopped flipping, he'd found himself upside down, strapped tight in his seat belt, his book bag on the ceiling beneath him. He stayed there, hanging, until the ambulance came. His seat belt would not unlock.

Mrs. Gardner had sent a turkey to the man who lost his wife and child. "It's a miracle," she said. "It might just as easily have been you who died." Martin had not been able to see how you could judge that a miracle; it seemed more a matter of odds to him. "One out of four," was all he could say. "One out of four."

It disgusted him now that his mother's sympathy was drawn to Paula Hayes and not to the man whose wife and child had died. But then, of course, the man was from Yonkers, a plumber it turned out, and Hispanic, too. The Hayeses belonged to the country club.

"Paula's son is a vegetable," she said. "Of course it was terrible for the man as well, but he remarried, don't forget—and moved into Rye on the jury's award."

"So his pain doesn't count?"

"Things aren't so simple as you seem to think. Paula Hayes has nothing. She goes and talks to Eric in that hospital that's really just milking them, and she prays for him to wake up, but if he ever *did* wake up, she'd hate him for what he did to her life. *And* to that man's."

"Does Eric age, do you think? Does he know inside him what he's done?"

"Let's not discuss it further, darling." She salted her omelet again and tried the salad. "What's that, chicory?"

"Endive."

"Well, it's yummy."

Martin was silent.

"Honey," his mother suddenly implored. "How's that lovely friend of yours? That Stella."

"Fine. Why?"

"I think Daddy would have liked her, don't you? Let's have her up to dinner sometime, up at the house. Doesn't she do furniture? We could go to Gulliver's. Remember Gulliver's?" She started to laugh. "Wasn't that a happy time?"

"Gulliver's? Are you kidding?"

"Well, anywhere then. I'd like to see her."

"I don't think so."

"But why not, Martin? Aren't you friends?"

Martin looked down. "Mom," he said, "I live with a man. His name is Matt. He has a toothbrush he keeps here permanently. He has his soap in a soap dish on the sink. This is his home."

It thrilled Martin to say this, despite the false impression it gave. "Do you understand what I'm telling you?" he asked.

She nodded and held up her hand as if to say: "That's enough, that's all I can take."

But Martin went on, surprising even himself in his cruelty. "He is my lover, as you were Daddy's. Except I don't think we'll be having children."

She half got up from the table. Weight on her feet, torso lifted forward, she seemed suspended there for a moment, as if waking suddenly with no comprehension of where she was or how she came to be there. Her eyes, magnified by tears, seemed large with terror, distended and clear, as eyes often do when seen underwater. Then she stood up. "Excuse me," she whispered reflexively, hurrying out of the room.

Martin tapped his foot slowly and steadily. He heard his mother turn on the water to disguise any sounds she might be making. She was as fastidious as ever about things that came from the body—even words, even tears—only now she was not so imposing with her fastidiousness as she used to be. At one time it had been the very emblem and repository of her strength. Now it seemed an emblem of her frailty instead. In obeisance to it she did ridiculous things. She refolded her napkin in restaurants when she finished a meal so as to hide any smudges she might have left upon the cloth. She sprayed her mouth with breath freshener at every opportunity. What had happened to that impeccable woman, who if cold was never embarrassing? Strong people have strong faults, Martin recalled having read, while the faults of the weak are weakly.

He once had thought she would just go on forever unchanged, mastering every situation as it must be mastered. Like her own mother before her, he had imagined, she would narrow her scope of activity but not her competence within it. Expertly she would tend her prize damask roses, snipping off imperfect flowers without hesitation. She would acquire a collection of dignified black dresses for the funerals she would stand through without quaking. And though her face might soften from age while her hair, from spray, might harden, she would never lose her grasp on the things that mattered: decorum, cleanliness, tact. She might grow short, Martin thought, but never small.

Now he was faced instead with a woman who repeatedly salted her food without noticing, who ran from rooms in tears. Where would she go from there? Racing through the backyards of Rye, her nightgown flying open? Pilfering panty hose from displays at malls? There would be no dignified role for her. The dream of damask roses was shattered; she was too nervous now to tend them. She'd cut off all their heads indiscriminately or let them blight on the trellis if she tried.

The usual suburban cures were unavailable to her. Affairs were out of the question. Therapy was just as tawdry. Even discussing the problem with her son was apparently more than she could muster. No, everything had to be fixed, it seemed, by the brute will of denial. *There was no problem:* that was the family's traditional solution. But this was a tradition Martin could not uphold. Not that he didn't want to; he tried. But he was unable to master the absolute silence, to accept the full implication of the vow you took when willing a problem into the void: that it should never arise again, in any form or translation. If he could have asked his mother, she might have been able to teach him the trick, but he couldn't ask. Even when her purse would fall open while she fumbled for taxi fare, and Martin would see the collection of pills and prescriptions inside it, their eyes would meet only for an instant and then move right past each other in different directions. "Let's go, Martin," she would say, clicking shut the purse and stepping out of the taxi directly.

She had been a woman meant for mastery, but the uprisings of her life had proved unmasterable, and so had overthrown her. Was it Martin's fault? Was it her husband's fault? Or was it just life, a ramshackle car, out of control at an intersection? This was an issue no jury would decide. Even if it did, what justice could be done? Martin felt that his mother was dead already, as if she had been killed in a crash that he survived; and he hated her, with all his feeble, toe-tapping anger, for leaving him there in the car alive, strapped inside his seat belt, dangling upside down.

THEY DINED at Gulliver's religiously, on Sundays, for seven years. They sat at a beet-red table in a padded booth near the back of the room. Martin's mother was slightly embarrassed to be there at all, it was déclassé, but what could she do? Nanny was off, and where else in Rye could you go with the youngsters? Apparently other families had the same idea, for the place was busy from late afternoon.

There were four or five or six people per family. The fours had it best: plenty of space on both sides of the booth. The sixes were crowded however they arranged it. And sometimes an infant got attached to the table in its torn vinyl space chair.

Martin's family was a party of five, which meant that one side was crowded and the other was not. The girls were big enough to matter. While Martin sat with his mother on one bench, the girls sat opposite, framing their father. They reached and ducked repeatedly under the table, met and whispered and giggled in his lap. He'd tickle one or the other of them until a pile of red curly hair popped up. A barrette might go flying. "Girls, please!" Martin's mother would warn, and sooner or later the barrette would be retrieved.

Things were considerably more grave on her side. She and Martin would sit in identical postures of probity. She would study again the familiar menu and keep an eye on the condiment center, lest one of the girls get it into her head to pour sugar in her water glass, or water in the sugar.

Martin's eye would rove. Waitresses glided around in their yellow uniforms with white collars. They passed through narrows of customers unfazed, cargo stuck to their trays as if with gum. Between his body and his mother's there was a space a waitress could get through, he thought, were it not for the swatch of reflected light that sat there.

Martin would excuse himself before the meal was ordered. He'd head down a corridor past the pay phone and janitor's closet to the bathroom. The wallpaper there was pebbly and yellow, smudged brown with fingerprints, at least so he hoped. There was a disagreeable odor that excited him. He'd take his pants down as little as possible and search the wall for new commentary. There was rarely anything he hadn't seen before. After what he imagined was the correct amount of time, he closed up his pants and emerged from the stall. Very seriously he pumped green liquid into his palms to wash his hands. The metal blower churned out air laboriously to dry them, and after moments of failure, succeeded.

He'd return to the table by a different route. He'd pass the kitchen, bravely daring to glance through the portholes centered like eyes in the brown swinging doors. Through them he saw the busy cooks, hurtling through steam. They wore white hats and T-shirts with V-shaped necks that showed the hair in profusion on their chests. They moved without hesitation among rows of silver stoves.

Continuing back to the table, he passed the cashier's desk and the cloakroom lady. At the front of the restaurant, revolving doors admitted triangles of fresh air at intervals with new customers. Everyone seemed to know his place and also seemed to know that he did.

Back at Martin's table, the girls might be playing tic-tac-toe on their father's place mat. He'd have his arms spread out along the back of the booth, where the vinyl was tacked with brass-colored nails to the wood. He'd have half a smile on his face; unlike his wife, he liked to be seen here.

One of the girls would win the game, and the other would scribble over it to prevent this from being true. The winner would attempt to foil this desperate move, but Martin's mother would say *Girls!* and they'd subside into the space beneath their father's arms.

They had always been called the girls, though Martin, being singular, was called by name. It was hard to think of them as individuals. Even strangers said they looked like two of a set, which somehow led Martin to the horrible conclusion that there might be more coming, like anniversary gifts. They were so much alike it was hard to take them seriously. Could anything worthwhile be so perfectly duplicable?

This was not merely an accident of nature, but something they worked on. They wore their barrettes on opposite sides of their heads so that a magnetic impulse seemed to pull them together in the observer's eye. They were both ambidextrous, and on nights like this would eat with different hands.

Now the waitress arrived with her pad, but the family ignored her. Martin's mother would still be consulting the girls about their choice of drinks. The waitress would wait. She held her head slightly to the side, emphasizing the blunt, uneven cut of her hair. It fell from a part at the middle of her scalp in lackluster blond panels. Her skin looked soft but indefinite; the color orange, or yellow, or white. She looked bored. She seemed to be playing a game that required her not to blink. Instead her gray eyes enlarged and contracted.

Of course she was bored: Martin's mother would still be deciding. Though this did not seem to bother her, Martin looked up and smiled apologetically. She took this in and continued tapping her foot at a speed too slow for any song Martin knew. She paused in her waiting to look without expression at whoever was not looking up at her. She knew this family; she'd served them before.

The stubby yellow pencil, a half inch above her pad, would make preliminary little scratches in the air. At some indeterminate point it would start to write, just as, without looking up, Martin's mother would begin to recite the girls' orders. The orders seemed to go directly to the pencil, bypassing the waitress. She finished writing before her customer finished speaking. Then she swiveled her head a few inches to take in the girls staring fixedly at their mother, proud that they had entered into such a decision, and ready to correct any mistakes she might make. But there weren't any. There never were.

She ordered for everyone until one day she said that Martin was old enough to take care of himself. He was thirteen.

"But what about Dad? You order for him and he's over forty!"

"Daddy's exempt because he pays for the meal."

"When *you* pay for a meal," his father said, "you can have the pleasure of someone else ordering. In the meantime, it's a

perfect opportunity to develop social skills that will become necessary later on."

His father winked, a gesture toward intimacy that never failed
to fail.

Martin felt as if he were on a date. The girls leered and buried
themselves in their father's side to giggle. Martin looked up at
the waitress and hesitated. He started his order, the pencil
jumped, and soon enough she turned to face him. He smiled
apologetically again. He tried to interest her. He spoke of the
quality of doneness he desired in his hamburger as if she would
be flattered by his attention to things of her world. But she
merely wrote. Martin wanted to leave her time, but he left more
time than she required. It had taken only eight strokes to record
Medium Well. *M W*. He was caught looking up.

"Coke?" she demanded, mildly.

The date was a failure. "Thank you," he offered as she receded.

Dinner was eaten slowly and in silence. They were only halfway through the meal when other children, locked by adults in
the interiors of their booths, began to be sprung like corks from
bottles. Their tables were cleared and quickly reset. Groups of
two came to occupy them.

The crowd turned over. Martin took it painfully that his was
the only family left. His mother insisted they chew each bite
forty times for digestion—a directive his father clearly found
silly but saw no pressing reason to challenge. And so they took
forever to finish. The girls were only just polishing off their
sundaes, their faces smeared with tarry chocolate, when the clock
on the wall rang an ominous eight. Martin's mother took them
away to get clean, and his father decided to wash up as well. He
handed Martin his wallet and said, "Why don't you pay the
waitress when she comes."

At a table where a family of six had been seated there now
sat a spare young couple. They had scooted themselves all the
way into the depths of the booth, leaning forward across the
table as if to kiss above the ketchup. They barely noticed when

the waitress brought them their cups of black coffee. Why should they notice? The woman was beautiful, and smoking. Puffs of her smoke obliterated the face of the man from time to time. She leaned into the wall as if listening to it. He took her long hand in his longer hand. He leaned further into her cloud. The little silver milk pitcher twirled.

Martin's view was obstructed by the appearance of the waitress, calculating the bill. She saw him fidget with the wallet, turning it over and over at right angles. "Paying tonight?" she asked. Her voice was surprisingly musical, but cruel, too. With one eye she looked over her pad at Martin, and half a smile crept past the side.

"Yes," he replied.

But his father returned in time to take care of the check himself. He left two damp bills beneath his saucer and then loped off after the girls. They had run from the bathroom unimpeded, eager to dizzy themselves in the revolving door. Martin stayed behind to help his mother with her coat.

The tip, he thought, was insufficient. He realized the waitress had been callous and unconcerned, but he couldn't stand to see her mistreated. Perhaps that's how she'd gotten that way?

His mother arrived and said his name softly. He got up, stood behind her, and lifted the sleeves of her coat onto her arms. She walked straight ahead to the door. At the other table the couple were now chattering lightly and eating pie à la mode. Where was the smoke? How could people change so quickly, like slides?

He took two quarters from his pocket and placed them under the saucer. Twin Washingtons peered up over the rim, an apologetic smile, it seemed, on their faces. When Martin looked back from the door, he could see the waitress finding them there. She touched, with her pale hands and peach nails, his quarters. She swept them into her apron, like crumbs.

MATT would be leaving for Williamstown in the middle of June. For more than two months he would be away. It was nearly as long as they'd been together, if together was what they were. Martin panicked. He took Matt to Botega Veneta and bought him a portfolio to use at auditions. Even in the midst of doing it, he heard the parsimonious voice in his head: Pandering! Buying affection! His own portfolio, the voice noted stingily, was the laminated cardboard one he'd had since college, with one zipper torn and the other one tearing.

But affection bought was still affection. Climbing down the stairs to the subway, Matt stopped Martin with a tap on the shoulder. He reached out an arm and then embraced him, keeping him a step beneath, at a manageable height and supervising the warmth. He kissed Martin on the forehead. People passed, scowling or smiling, within inches of their contingent faces. "I love you," he said, and Martin felt as if he would fall the rest of the way down the stairs.

"They're watching, Matt."

"I could care less."

But after a moment Martin had to release himself from the long-desired, unbearable embrace. "I realize I'm irresistible," he said, "but if you stand here hugging me, we'll miss our train." He employed a voice he hoped would be comic but wasn't.

"All right, the train," Matt said.

As they ran down the platform Martin mentally smote his forehead. Life didn't offer many moments like this, and he had wasted this one—not just for himself. It had taken Matt a long time to say those words. And Martin never had.

Martin didn't know what his own love would even consist of. Was what he felt for Matt the genuine article? Though it matched all the movie images point by point—longing, impossibility, high-mindedness, chastity—it did not seem as real as what Matt offered him. Trips to the gym. Walks to the subway. Orange juice when there was none in the fridge. News of the world, if mainly bad. Laundry to do that wasn't his own.

And flowers, too. Matt often missed dinner, but when he

showed up, he always had flowers. Who would have thought? The oldest cliché of romance come true. Oh, they were waxy and tired, wrapped in sticky cellophane, purchased prearranged by exhausted Koreans. But they sat in the water of Martin's vase and twitched and opened. What else should flowers do but that?

And then they got better. Overpowering narcissus, genital anthurium. Better, yes, but Martin grew to hate them. They were flowers of gratitude, not of love, not *that* kind of love, at any rate. They were like violets brought obediently to a grave, or grotesque garlands sent only to impress. Martin was moved, and cowed as well, by the deathly touch of condescension. For this he hated Matt's good heart, and his own broken one, too.

And the flowers cost money. Where did it come from? And how could he go patronize the fancy places the Englishwoman took him to with only the casual clothing he owned? But when you looked like Matt, Martin supposed, it didn't matter. People in thousand-dollar suits would feel preposterously overdressed in his presence, unless they themselves were beautiful, too. Or maybe the woman had bought him some thousand-dollar suits of his own. They might hang in a corner of her Park Avenue closet, as jeans and Arrow shirts hung in Martin's.

In any case, Martin suspected, the Englishwoman would not last long. Matt already seemed to be souring on her. She had not put emotional strings on him, the kind that tied you down, but had caught him up in the other kind instead. Marionette strings. She expected him to do as she commanded. She expected it of everyone. When she called Martin's apartment, she did not say hello. She said, "Matt, please"—two wasted exhalations. If Matt were properly trained, the voice implied, he would have known to answer the phone himself.

And Matt had tired of her friends: they were high-power but low-wattage, their two subjects real estate and clothing designers. Matt's descriptions of them were either affectless or scornful and sickened. He seemed to be afraid of them, though he wanted to be among their number. But surely he was used to such people by now. Hadn't he worked for that couple who owned a club downtown?

"Different," he said.

It seemed to be affecting his health. The sniffling cold would not go away. He would run to the bathroom in the middle of meals. When he came back to the apartment at night, he might be sedate or he might be almost shaking with tension. Stella, hearing the description, at once said *coke*, but Martin couldn't believe it was that. Too trashy for someone like Matt. And too expensive.

He wondered instead if it had to do with sex, which Martin heard about at great length. The lingerie, the locale, what she wanted him to do. No detail was too small or perverse to share, apparently. But what she and Matt actually talked about when they weren't copulating, Martin could never determine. Surely Matt had nothing to say about real estate or clothing designers. And yet he'd drop phrases about one or the other into conversations with Martin, as if for practice. "Do you think this building will go condo?" he asked.

And Martin had to explain once again the difference between condo and co-op.

Matt was lost. In the oblivious woman he could not find his place. He looked to Martin. He kissed him on the stairs in the subway. And what did Martin do to support and confirm this step toward him? He stepped away.

Martin marveled at his own perversity. What caused the mind to play tricks like that? Could the mind train itself against its natural bent?

And so, in the train, after an agony of indecision, Martin put his hand atop Matt's as they sat. But Matt shook it off. "They're watching," he mouthed.

Paying tonight? the waitress had asked Martin in her disinterested, cruel, melodious voice. Paying tonight. Tonight and always. She had never left. Hers was the face he could not face, but neither could he ignore it. He could only leave surreptitious gifts and hope to appease her, hope to delay her next recurrence. But her face was in the blank sun that kept showing up for breakfast, and in the yellow light of traffic signals that warned you to stop, but never did to go. The round frosted bulb in the refrigerator at night, which spared no more energy on you than it must: there she was, too. And in another's cold eye.

You always paid. That night, in bed for the hundredth time, he paid again. "Shall I visit you in Williamstown?" he asked.

The pause was exquisite. "Sure," Matt said.

"Not if you think I'd be in the way."

"Must you reject yourself? You give people ideas." He turned off the light.

And Martin, quite naturally, thought of his father.

IT WAS father-and-son night at the Science Museum. Having passed already through the Grotto of Gemstones, the race-car exhibit, and the weather station, the noisy crowd of boys and their slow, uneasy fathers finally arrived at the miraculous, three-story-high human heart.

"Everyone, everyone," the harried guide cried out. He rapped on his clipboard. "First, fathers, I'm afraid you're too big to fit through the veins, so would you please wait over there by the descending aorta to pick up your boys?" He pointed to a big red tube that emptied into another room. "Now, boys," he went on, "this heart is not a toy. Please walk slowly, single file, and read all the signs so you get something out of it."

The heart was dark and narrow, and the stairs within it steep. A single bulb in a cage lit each chamber, casting long shadows through the mitral valves. Martin was frightened, but curious, too, for the red walls were almost completely obscured by words cut in with pencils and knives. I LOVE STEVEN, one wall said. I LOVE AMY. A thousand conjunctions of the same few initials marked their paths: DM + JE, JM + DR, MM + RE, on and on. No adult, it appeared to Martin, had ever squeezed himself in to see just how profusely the heart had been annotated. If he had, he would long since have overpainted the litany of abuse gouged into the plaster: FUCK and COCK and I HATE THIS MUSEUM! There must be a million words, thought Martin, random greetings, unfinished statements. THIS IS— YOU ARE— THE— said the walls; and peace appeared, too, overstruck with an *X*. Love, which showed up occasionally in the butterfly form of a heart, crudely drawn, looked nothing at all like the heart it was actually in.

At first, as instructed, the boys moved slowly, crawling up through the inferior vena cava, taking the steps one at a time. Then, from somewhere behind, what could only be called a pulse welled up. The single file doubled and then broke apart. Suddenly boys were racing into the atrium, filling it up as if with blood. They stamped up the steps, whooping and shouting, until the whole heart shook. Off they spurted toward the lungs, kicking at the shoddy steps with their sneakers, punching the shoddy walls.

Martin slipped, terrified, into the bottom of the ventricle, and waited for the stream to pass. The shouting grew distant, and then louder again as the boys returned from the lungs. They were flowing past him now, on the other side of the wall: the footsteps muffled and retreating, like thunder. It was probably safe to move again, but he waited until he could hear them pour into the hall outside and disperse.

At last it was peaceful. He studied a word on the floor beneath his nose. He sang a verse of "Lavender Blue." A sign informed him that a man would have to be two hundred and twenty feet tall for this heart to fit him. It was fifteen thousand times larger than life.

"Martin?" a voice finally called. It was his father. The voice was friendly, tempting, concerned, and Martin had no desire whatever to answer or follow it.

He'd only leave of his own accord. But there was plenty of time. He sat himself up in the engraved, empty heart, and scratched his initial into the wall.

IV THE GUEST HOUSE

For a moment after Martin woke up, everything was still beautiful from his dream. In the dream, a ring of naked babies had been dancing around a fire in the woods. Each baby had a circle of berry-shaped bells wrapped around its ankle on a leather strap, as if they'd all just escaped from a chain gang. The fire, comic-book yellow, leaped up in discrete, triangular flames. It roared as if in agony, growing bigger, wanting to die. But when rain came, delicious and cool, it refused to be quenched. The babies shook the bells on their feet and kept dancing.

The blinds were open, and somewhere outside, a single bird was chirping its single pair of notes at right angles. The familiar man across the street was making his sofa bed, as Martin had seen him do a thousand times. The sheet bellied up like a sail before collapsing on the mattress, wrinkled but true. Then he moved from side to side, tucking, pulling, smoothing, adjusting. In a minute he was done. He shoveled the whole thing up into the sofa's maw.

The sky turned from the color of butter to the color of blueprint, and the first mean horn of the day was sounded. The light was getting harder, sharper. Martin's beautiful dream was receding fast into the pores of the air. What was it about? Babies? Fire? He looked at his clock. There were still ten minutes before the alarm would go off, but the day had crept in, incontrovertibly.

In the bathroom he performed his dull ablutions. Soap, deodorant, toothbrush, comb. He plugged his shaver into the surprised-looking socket and buzzed away his incomplete beard. His alarm went off.

It was Bastille Day, July 14, or so his daily planner said.

CARY, the religious roommate, would have been scandalized by the contents of Martin's fantasies, but not by the contents of his bureau. No pornography lurked beneath the underwear there.

175 ■

For three years, no matter how often he tried, Martin could not bring himself to buy the forbidden thing he so much desired. In the ratty, gated magazine shop near campus, he would nod toward a soft blue cover, unable to call it by name. The clerk would seek to determine which one he meant. This one? This one? He would glance at Martin. His chubby hand would brush lightly over the pictures of posing men, one with his top pants button undone, another with no pants at all. But Martin could not do it. The damp little store made him sick. The air was thick with something, and he felt the walls of newsprint and bright covers might lean in together and trap him. Before he fell, he would ask for *Time* instead. He would rush to his room and read it cover to cover, even the statement of ownership.

In New York, however, such transactions were carried out shamelessly, in public. On weekend trips to the city, Martin cased the newsstands at Port Authority or Grand Central Station as if he were planning a heist. The clerks were overworked and spoke a foreign language. Customers felt free to pick magazines from the spreading displays, to test them, reject them, choose different copies. From a few feet away, it might have been a farmers' market, with its cornucopia of bright, fresh produce spilling beyond the stalls. Only when you got closer did you realize just how ripe this produce was. Even so, the faces Martin studied were unembarrassed. They stared at the covers familiarly, with the expression of old Italian women who devise an evening's menu by contemplating a tomato or pepper.

He was sure there were answers in these magazines: charts and lists, mysteries demystified, tested ways of living. Each magazine had its own important message; you had only to choose the right one. If you were hesitant to touch, you would fail. Men in fine suits bought incredible things without flinching. The rule seemed to be: Look like you know what you're doing; do whatever you must.

Finally, in his senior year, Martin made his first purchase; the magazine burned in his briefcase all the way home on the train.

For days he dared not look at it, not until Cary was safely ensconced in a three-hour class. The deprivation had been exquisite, but when Martin finally managed a little privacy and inspected the goods, he was shocked by how much more exquisite was the revelation. The magazine was completely erotic and completely safe. There was no evil to it. The man taking his pleasure in front of the camera was clearly not faking and clearly not forced. Perhaps it was different with pictures of women, but the pictures Martin kept gasping over did not glorify subjugation. They glorified self-reliance. Even the man laboring frantically toward another man's joy was laboring toward his own as well.

Perhaps it was mischievous, perhaps it was an intuition, but when Martin grew tired of the tattooed sailor, the youths by the pool, the terribly unlikely orgy in the stable, he buried his copy of the magazine beneath the sweaters and winter coats at the bottom of Cary's steamer trunk. Then he waited for his chance to buy a new one: a chance he would only take, to this day, in train or bus stations, on his way into or out of New York.

AS THE BUS pulled into its dim, green berth on an upper floor at the Port Authority, Martin could see it through the waiting-room window. On cue, the scraggly line of would-be passengers contracted toward the conductor at the gate. Children and packages were suddenly lifted up, or dragged, resisting, across the linoleum floor. Well-wishers shuffled shyly away while those in line held their tickets out like tongues.

But the natty conductor wasn't ready to board them just yet. He'd neaten the line first, announce all the stops. "Yonkers, White Plains, Danbury, New Milford." The list ran on. Meanwhile the bus fumed, waiting behind glass, shiny and wormlike, with a driver high up in its head.

Finally the conductor accepted Martin's ticket—for Martin was first among those waiting—and admitted him into the boundless garage. Stingy light made the concrete rafters look as if they'd been wrapped with foam. Martin made a mental note: Use this some day, something brutalist, maybe Brecht.

The side of the bus lay open, but Martin had no luggage to stow. He walked straight up the stairs and said good morning to the indifferent driver. Then he bent down to fit in the aisle. He had his choice of seats, and could not choose.

Eventually he selected a window seat, halfway back. He arranged his overnight bag and decrepit briefcase on the seat adjoining. Then he withdrew them. In the past he'd have left them there to discourage people from sitting beside him, but it only discouraged the shy and polite. The rude, the loud, were drawn to the challenge, and so Martin always ended up passing a journey with exactly the people he most hoped to avoid.

Despite this reasonable strategy, the seat remained vacant. Martin decided this was because he now appeared too desirous of company, so he fished a Berkshires visitors' booklet from his overnight bag and pretended to read it. Nevertheless, at eleven o'clock when the door sucked shut, he was still alone. The bus spiraled its way out of the building and emerged into daylight made sickly and brilliant by an emerald-green coating of plastic on the windows. He returned his bags to the empty seat.

Martin had had high hopes for this trip—for the trip itself. He'd seen it as a kind of pilgrimage, valuable as much for the journey as for the end. But when the bus started creeping through the Upper West Side a block at a time, he realized his hopes had been absurd. An empty nausea slid over him. He felt as if he were trying to digest a rock that kept turning over in his stomach. The hardship of pilgrimage was supposed to produce a reward of self-knowledge, but it was clear already that the self-knowledge gained would be yesterday's news: *I do not travel well.*

Stella had warned him. "If you insist on going, which I wish you would not, at least rent a car. Don't be so stingy with yourself. Live it up."

"But I want to see New England," he'd said.

"Rent a convertible."

"But I want to see it more leisurely."

"Rent a horse."

He *had* taken Stella's advice in researching accommodations. He read the listing of Small Inns and Lodges in the Travel section of the Sunday *Times*. There must have been three hundred entries. They filled up several pages with their slight variations on the same information—much like tombstones, Martin observed. Appletree Inn, Edgartown Commons, The Lodge at Bretton Woods. Some offered stained-glass windows, some rhubarb waffles and strawberry jam. Whatever they offered, they sounded alike. The same person might have written them all. Martin imagined some chain-smoking intern in the ad department hooting with laughter as he came up with "individually knotty pine cottages," or "a tiny touch of graciousness."

In Williamstown alone there were seven such places, aside from the hotel Matt recommended. It was clean, he'd said, but Martin claimed he was looking for character. This was a lie; he wanted both. He wanted the perfect combination: old, warped furniture sitting on flat, spotless floors. The weight of the past made visible but sanitary. He knew it never came that way, but it's what he wanted.

So he'd settled on a place that called itself the Victorian Guest and Americana House. The name amused him. "President Coolidge," the ad asserted, "often stayed here. Charming, quiet, 'yesterday' rooms, where antiques surround you. We feature a rose garden: 100 colorful varieties. Historic feeling, where comfort is yours. No food."

No food: Martin had liked that. It was as cold and clean as Coolidge was antiseptic. Complementing these was the profusion of roses, both colorful and enumerated. Even the proprietress was just what he'd hoped for. Her name was listed as Miss Faye Mapes.

Well, not exactly what he'd hoped for. In fact he had hoped to stay with Matt, but that, it appeared, was not to be.

▪ ▪ ▪

MARTIN fell asleep, and when he awoke, someone in the bus was smoking. But so was the driver. There was nothing to do. He forced open the oblong window instead of complaining, and got smacked in the face with the wind. It was warm and acrid, slightly stinging, like pepper. Speckles of dirt flew by.

His booklet on the Berkshires had as its theme: *We're not just quaint anymore!* It showed pictures of couples dancing, of motorboats on choppy lakes, of Robin Williams at Tanglewood. The scene it described bore no relation to what Martin saw going by out the window: Lincoln-log fences, the rails all split and dropped at angles. Red barns whose silos were topped with roofs like Prussian helmets. If that wasn't quaint, what was? Outside of Sheffield, hand-painted signs on the side of the road flew by at intervals, getting ever more desperate. FRESH EGGS, the first announced, then BROWN AND WHITE EGGS, then EGGS! EGGS! ¼ MILE. A rickety shed soon materialized, beside it a turquoise truck filled with crates. All those eggs! And no one stopping. The bus passed by three more signs, but these faced the other way, offering their importunate message to southbound travelers, Martin presumed.

Occasionally, quaintest of all, there were cows. What was the name of this breed, Martin wondered, the ones that seemed to be wearing pointy glasses? He took out his sketch pad to see if he could get this image on paper, but it kept coming out like a bad cartoon. He waited for a different image to strike him. Miles went by. Cows, he determined, look mostly the same. Finally he saw one munching slowly and started to draw as it came into range. At first it was fine, but then, when he'd passed it, he kept adding strands of hay until it looked like a cat with a walrus mustache.

He flipped the page.

A woman got on at Stockbridge carrying only a book. She pointed to Martin's bags and said, "Anyone sitting here?"

"No," he said, removing them.

"Coming from New York?"

He looked at her and nodded, smiling. She had apple cheeks but a tall, narrow face. Her long hair was iron gray and tied back in a ribbon. He couldn't figure out how old she was, or what she might do. She wore a polo shirt and jeans.

"And you?" Martin asked.

The woman laughed. "I'm coming from Stockbridge," she said very slowly.

"Oh, of course," Martin stuttered. "I guess I'm a little—not used to—that is—"

But the woman was now making sniffing motions. "Is someone smoking?" she asked severely.

"Off and on," Martin said. "Someone in back."

She got up. Five rows behind, a thin old man with bad teeth and a birdlike scowl was taking drags on a Lucky Strike. "Put that out," the woman said. "Don't you know there's no smoking on a bus?"

The old man looked at her briefly and made a sour face, but she'd turned back down the aisle without even watching to see what he did. Martin, however, saw that he extinguished the cigarette.

"Thank you," he said.

"It's the squeaky wheel that gets the oil." She opened her book, which proved to be *Walden*.

Martin sketched. Just beyond Pittsfield, a big, round lake passed on the right. He blindly drew its shape on his pad, not caring. The *Walden* woman looked up from her reading, smiled briefly, and looked back down. Martin wondered what she thought he had drawn: an amoeba, a potato, a fried egg without its yolk. He scribbled it out. Then he searched for better samples of his work in case the woman should look up again. Slowly he paged through bedrooms and buildings, coffeepots and Queen Anne chairs. Everything here was functional, for this was the Book of Objects. But sometimes they glimmered with life.

He was getting better. Three weeks into the course at the Y, the instructor had taken Martin's hand roughly, had forced his palm open and realigned his grasp. He placed the pencil so it lay almost slack in the web of Martin's thumb, then threaded it between his middle and ring fingers. He forced Martin to draw that day without closing his palm at all. It was completely unnatural, but his line loosened up immediately. The classroom studies—kept in the Book of Life, as he called it—improved even more than the objects did. And he began to find ways of combining the two. This toaster on a table, for instance, with distorted reflections of Martin's own profile, was particularly good. But the *Walden* woman was deep in her reading.

Martin flipped back past the toaster; behind it there was a face that made him turn the pad away. It was in the wrong book, and done in a completely uncharacteristic style. A little had been colored in. An ear blushed slightly yellow, a marble curl of hair glowed umber. He'd laid in a plane of pink on the cheek, a fish of lavender above one eye. The eyes themselves lacked irises, like Roman statues. They appeared to look up, but you just couldn't tell. That was the only real way to do it. Empty, empty, open to anything.

Now of course the woman finished reading and closed the book on her finger. "What a lovely drawing," she said. "Is it from the Met?"

Martin was startled. He thought she'd said Matt.

"Is it from their antiquities, I mean? When I lived in New York, I always saw artists drawing those statues. There's something timeless about them, don't you think? All the young men? But you know, they're all so noble, so beautiful, and you have no idea if they were Hadrians or Neros. I mean, look at that face." She pointed to it with her book. "Is that a tyrant or a slave, for instance? All it says about itself is beauty."

"Well, it's from life," said Martin.

SOME THINGS were so relentlessly beautiful you just didn't know what to do. The face of a lioness. An iris. A Turner. And other things, not beautiful, could produce the same confusion.

When he talked to someone at a party, or in the street, or a stranger in an office, a pause in the conversation could make Martin feel, whoever the person he was speaking to was, *I must kiss you.* There is nothing for it, when the skein of words has been broken, but to hang on to each other for life.

Moments like this made beauty and love seem wily, protean. What you didn't value was as valuable as what you did. Was beauty so shiftless? Or was something deeper than beauty the issue? And what could be deeper than beauty? Martin wondered. It was only skin deep, perhaps, but that was deep enough for him.

It took great feats of attention to keep things in their places. This person I love, this person I like, this person I don't know from Adam. A pear is beautiful, a banana is not. The minute you loosened your grip on these facts, the world started slipping around. You might paint the banana instead of the pear, or love someone you didn't know.

Martin had once met a man at the opera, and as his name turned out to be Malcolm, their fate was set. They had slept together and gone their separate ways the next morning, then met at the opera again the next night. It was *Figaro*, the second cast singing. Malcolm took Martin's hand during "Dove sono" and whispered a translation into his ear: *Where are the beautiful moments of sweetness and pleasure? Where have the promises of those lying lips flown?* It was all Martin could do to remember Malcolm's name and who he was and what he was like.

Later, on the subway, heading to Malcolm's apartment in SoHo, he did remember, all too completely. Malcolm, holding on to the strap, was letting the motion of the train throw him around like a go-go dancer. He laughed out loud, almost a shout, and then whispered intimately into the heart of Martin's ear. Anyone who looked could see what they were. It made Martin nervous, but he did not protest. He wished he could just swing out and touch this smiling man's chest, as his tie did now, so casually in the aisle.

But affection had to be reserved for darkened rooms. They would crawl into bed and only then be permitted to kiss. They'd hum "Dove sono" while making love. Martin would examine Malcolm's face in passing, the big flat airstrip of a nose, the delicate eyebrows like circumflexes. Down below, something would be going on that he could not watch, but up above, he would be discovering that Malcolm was exactly what he wanted in life, whatever that might be.

Now, Malcolm barged through the accordion passageway into the next car of the train. He looked back at Martin through the webbed glass windows as if paying him a visit in prison. He pressed his face into comical shapes: flattened his nostrils, stretched an eye diagonally across a warped panel of cheek. Then he kissed the glass quite fully. His lips went pale and curled up like shrimp. He repeated the kiss and repeated it again, leaving smudges, slightly superimposed, on the glass. He seemed to ask Martin to return the gesture, but Martin, horrified, couldn't do it. He grinned then grimaced, did both at once, as if to say, "I can't! This window is covered with dirt!"

Malcolm laughed and ran ahead through the car, his trench coat flying open around him like a cape. He turned around and waved. When the train stopped at Spring Street, he pointed for Martin to get out there.

Martin stepped onto the platform, promising himself he would not be squeamish. He would do what he desired, not what he thought was decorous. He would reach his hand into the finger paint, and baste the page of his life with it.

Up ahead of him, the tan trench coat was swaying invitingly. Martin approached slowly, wanting to make the gesture a surprise. He took the glove in his hand from behind. He pressed it firmly so there would be no mistaking his intention and, as if he were a spy in a movie, merely kept walking, looking straight ahead. He spoke as if a conversation had been going on already. "I want you," he said. "And I don't care who knows it."

Twenty feet ahead on the platform, Malcolm was doubled over, laughing. The woman in Martin's grasp merely smiled.

THE PERFECT lover, Stella contended, was perfectly alien. You would not understand a thing about him. His assumptions would be different and his needs unknowable. When you woke up in the morning, his arms reaching through you, you would be shocked to find them there. And again his smell, his inscrutable design, would rivet your attention. Then, when he spoke, his English, even if native, would be marginal. You might understand him, but you'd never be sure.

Martin disagreed. "This is perfectly theoretical, of course, but I imagine someone as much like me as possible, except of course better."

"But how long would whatever pleasure there is remain if you're just so completely the same?" Stella asked. "I mean, you're both male, so why do you want the same personality, too? I can't imagine it—but then no man I sleep with would be like me, ipso facto. Don't you want to hit up against something? What you're describing, I'd be afraid I'd pass through and out the other side. Like passing through a mirror."

"No, I'd just feel safe and familiar."

"If that's what you want, you should sleep by yourself."

"Just so," said Martin.

In practice, however, he found the safety unnerving. Malcolm, who was as much like Martin as possible, but better, bored him to death after a week. His bow ties, his glen plaid suits, his straight hair: they offered no resistance. Like Martin, he folded his clothing obsessively and wanted his pillows to face cool side up. Turning down the bed at night, the two of them could have been mistaken for chambermaids, preparing the room for guests.

So Stella was right about too much similarity, but her own adventures did not recommend the merits of too much difference. It was exciting, no doubt of that; Martin became uncomfortably interested in her descriptions of the various foreign moans her lovers made. But soon enough it would be Stella moaning, and not in pleasure. It was never clear exactly what had happened: she got fed up; he disappeared; a wife materialized just before dinner. Whatever the provocation, Stella's response was definitive and cool. Take your boots and go.

It wasn't that she was heartless; in fact, she wore her heart on her sleeve—but the sleeve of a dress she'd now put in storage. The new sleeve had her power pinned on it instead. She might have been raising or lowering paintings, the way she dismissed the men who had failed her. "Helen of New York," she called herself. "The face that launched a thousand shits."

But a man had danced with her at a wedding in June. He lived in Bucks County, made frames for a living. He often came to the city on business, so they dated awhile and then became lovers. Mornings, Stella was shocked—not by the feeling he was alien, but by the consistent, warm touch of his fingers upon her hair. He spoke English well, but tersely enough to remain mysterious. He smelled like pine.

It was the closest Stella had ever come, but she was not happy. A man she could not pass through, she found, she also could not broach. His life was so even, his demeanor so calm and true and accepting, he kept disappearing within Stella's view. The sounds he made during love were white noise. She had to slap him to hear him.

There was no blame to be apportioned, so Stella could not disengage in her usual fashion. It illuminated and confused her, both. She came back to the city from a weekend in Pennsylvania and met Martin for lunch in a Village café. She looked radiant in a knit vermilion sleeveless top, a rare adventure in color for Stella.

"You've gotten sun!" Martin exclaimed.

"Have I ever."

"Your skin is glowing!"

"Yes?" she said, and lifted the vermilion top up to her breasts, peeled it up like a banana skin to reveal, on her perfectly white stomach, a constellation of pink stars.

Martin shuddered.

"We swam in a lake, if you can imagine. There was some sort of algae."

She lowered her top and said she'd decided to end the affair. "Just in time, too. He was almost done making the frame, if you know what I mean. And, doll, I do not want to be framed. I don't want to live my parents' life. In a frame house, a camouflage house." She switched to a gun-moll voice. "I was framed once, Sister, but got away, and only criminals go back to the scenes of their crimes. I'm no criminal. I don't commit crimes. I just happen to like the getaway part."

"You're an outlaw, yes," Martin said. It was an old routine.

"I sleep with my car keys in my hand."

"Even though you don't have a car."

Stella smiled. "I hate that you know me."

"I have to know someone."

Despite the banter, the breakup was painful, though not nearly as much for Stella as it was for the man. Weeks afterward she was still receiving surprise visits and passionate mail. Next came a string of laments on her machine. She couldn't stand it. Eventually she changed her message to say, "This is Stella. I'll never be home"—a greeting that remained on the tape to this day.

Martin had never met the man, but grieved for his banishment more than Stella did. He had sounded so good. Still, Martin tried to keep this to himself, because he knew you could not judge how, and what-in-the-world, a person found to love.

Stella knew it, too. Martin could see how she restrained herself from criticizing his involvement with Matt. She commented on it, she expressed particular dissatisfactions, but when Martin got upset she immediately stopped. His trip to Williamstown she found absurd, she told him so directly. But she dropped her objections when he made himself clear.

"I know the situation," he said. "I still want to go."

"Then go," said Stella.

And so the bus turned from Route 7, and Martin could see, in the parking lot of the Williams Inn, a dark, impatient figure waving ironically.

"CHANGE of plans," said Matt, approaching, as Martin disembarked from the bus. "We've got to rehearse straight through dinner, so we'll drop you off at the place you're staying. Then we'll see you after the show."

The bus wheezed gigantically and took off for Vermont in a mist of exhaust. Matt started walking with Martin's bag.

"What?"

"Sorry, I'm running a little behind. We have a tech rehearsal in just a few minutes, so Joanna and I will drop you off. Then we'll see you after the show."

"Joanna?"

Matt pointed to a woman waiting in the red convertible toward which they were headed. "I mentioned her in the letter, didn't I?"

"What letter?"

But they were standing at the car already, where Joanna seemed anxious to get on the road.

"Ready?" she asked.

"Ready," said Matt.

Martin was hardly in his seat when the car took off. The strange, undular hillscape blurred. They were going sixty, and within a minute, they passed the bus.

"Sorry about the rush," Matt yelled from the back of the car. "How was your trip?"

Martin mouthed "fine," a little angrily perhaps.

After no more than two minutes' driving, Joanna stopped and said, "Here we are." She did not bother to move the shift from drive.

"Your ticket is at the box office," said Matt.

"See you later," Joanna added.

Martin's bags were handed out to him, and the car went roaring back down the road. "Hello," he said to a passing squirrel. "And whose little boy are you?"

THE FIRST thing was the American flag, beckoning limply from the top of its pole. Then the house itself appeared. Part of it looked like a converted barn, part of it like a prairie fortress. It had hip roofs and mansards, a stone chimney and a brick one. White louvered shutters on every window, and gray clapboards on every wall, held the whole thing together. Otherwise you would have thought it was several unrelated buildings.

As Martin approached, the place seemed more and more abandoned. Short white curtains blew straight out through the windows on the porch. One panel was stuck by its delicate hem to a sprung coil of wicker on a camelback settee. Martin detached it, tried to push it back into the room it had come from, but it flew right out and got stuck again.

He tapped on the screen door and two German shepherds galloped barking down the hall. They were full grown, with black glistening coats like mink. Martin ran ten feet off of the porch before he realized that the door was latched and the dogs couldn't get him. They had their snouts pressed up against the mesh so it bulged out of its frame as if it might rip. They growled continuously, one picking up where the other left off. Martin tried to return to the porch, but they started barking as he reached the first step. They sat up on their hind legs and poked at the door with their paws, which overlapped in a *W*.

"Margaret! Mary!" a high voice came calling. "Back to your room." Immediately the dogs dropped off the door and retreated out of sight down the hall. The figure of a very tall, very thin, antique-looking woman materialized in their place. She unlatched the door. "Welcome," she said, "I'm Miss Mapes. Welcome to the Victorian Guest and Americana House." She waved Martin in, then dropped the hook back into the eye on the jamb. "We keep it latched for Margaret and Mary."

"Ah," said Martin.

"And you're the man in from New York for the night?"

Martin nodded, though it was odd to hear himself referred to as a man.

"Now look around while I fetch a pen."

The floors were shiny and dark where they showed at the edges of the wine-colored runner. You could see delicate pink footsteps in the plush, like a ghost would make. But you could also see clots of hair and dust creeping along the baseboard. It wasn't very tidy. A skeletal sprig of baby's breath had been stuffed in a Lydia Pinkham's bottle. It shed little white buds on the floor, like popcorn.

Martin could not make sense of the space. There were too many doors off the hallway, and the doors were not where they should be. On the other hand, they had crystal knobs shaped like patty-pan squash, and these were worth drawing. They would surely be useful for something someday, the salon scene in a musical, perhaps.

Miss Mapes reemerged from behind the stairway. "Well," she said. "I think it's time we took you to your room. Will you walk this way?" She swept down the hall as if operated from above by strings.

Martin laughed to himself at the setup. *If I could walk that way*—but he had no punch line.

She led Martin up a flight of steps and into a room on the second floor. "Our loveliest suite," she said. "It's all original, all antique." She parted the curtains. "Batiste, don't you know."

"It's perfect, I'm sure." Martin was suddenly very tired from the ride, and wanted a nap before the day ran out.

"Yes, indeed," Miss Mapes went on. "And the Queen Anne desk. Calvin Coolidge wrote his inaugural address here." She opened the shallow drawer as if the address itself were stored inside. "He was my grandfather, don't you know."

"Really," said Martin, with a trace of disbelief.

She pushed her finger along her eyebrow, over and over as if trying to straighten it. "Yes," she said eventually. Then she went fuzzy and silent, like a television station signing off for the night.

Martin nodded and smiled encouragingly. He knew there was no point contradicting. Nanny had gone senile, too. When she claimed she was married to Martin's father, you just ignored it.

But Miss Mapes looked merely frozen, in an attitude of error or loss. She stood at the window and scrutinized the view through the passing screen of her fingers. She was beautiful, Martin decided. Her skin had not dropped or hollowed, her posture not sunk. She stood perfectly erect. Her eyes were watery, like a dog's, but clear.

Martin said, "This will be fine, then," hoping to move her. There were two sleigh beds with embroidered coverlets, a table worked with a pineapple motif, and the Calvin Coolidge memorial desk. All of these would be worth drawing; they could be useful in a hundred plays. But Miss Mapes wasn't moving.

Martin wondered if there wasn't a password he could produce to unlock her. "It's all so *charming*," he tried. "I'm sure I'll *enjoy* it." He was still in the doorway, holding his bags. "Well," he said, "shall I pay you now?"

That must have done it, for she slowly revolved from the window and spoke. "Wait," she said. "You're only just one?"

"Yes, just one," Martin admitted.

"Then I really apologize, you can't have this room." She went straight out the door.

Just one, just one. And sometimes less.

Martin lingered in the room he could not have, but Miss Mapes was impatient to correct her mistake. "Walk this way, please," she commanded. "I'm going to put you in the parlor." She started down the stairs without looking back. "I don't know what I could have been thinking. Old age, you know. It gets you in the head. But really, really. That's too much."

Martin watched her navigate the stairs, touching neither the wall nor the banister. She turned a perfect ninety degrees at the landing and went right on. "The parlor," she said. Then she turned back. "The parlor is on the porch, don't you know!"

Actually on the porch?

He marveled how her stout black heels sank barely at all into the runner. She couldn't have weighed a hundred pounds. Even if she did, the weight was no burden to the floor below her or the air around. She pressed on nothing, and nothing pressed back. She was loosed from all constraints. Her black skirt hung unconcernedly from her waist, crooked, or she crooked within it. It was on backward, Martin eventually determined. But it didn't matter. She was free from designs, free from the correct angles of even her own outdated fashion. Had she always been that way? Martin wondered. Or had she learned it—and, if so, how?

Miss Mapes was added to the long list of people Martin at some point had wanted to be. How admirable her accommodations seemed. To forget what was inconvenient, to fabricate what gave pleasure. Not to care what anyone thought. To have no weight. This was the life.

Maybe gentle curves of the mind could be learned as curves of the hand and tongue once were: by mechanical practice. If he stepped as lightly as she down the stairs? If he turned at the landing without looking anywhere? If he *walked this way*?

He tripped, and his briefcase flew from his hand. He watched as the torn old zipper gave way, and everything inside got jettisoned out. It seemed to be happening in slow motion. Onion-skin sketches hovered and then dropped in descending Cheshire smiles to the floor. Martin lunged to catch a magazine before it hit Miss Mapes.

"No!" he cried.

An hour early for his bus, he'd wandered around the Port Authority, pretending he didn't know where he was headed. At the newsstand he'd perused *Theater World* with uncommon interest. He'd considered the merits of a new ballpoint pen. A dollar they cost now—that was too much.

He'd walked away, as if indignant, to a coffee shop, where he'd distracted himself by watching donuts dive off a platform and fry. But he knew he'd return to the newsstand in time, return to buy the magazine he'd spotted, with the handsome man on the cover, the man with eyes so insolent, so threatening, that no briefcase could ever be zipped carefully enough against him.

Still, Martin had not lived in Providence four years for nothing. Someone was looking over him. Miss Mapes walked straight through the rain of paper without taking notice; she passed just in time through the door of another room. "No, indeed," she muttered, disappearing, as if his cry had actually been hers. In the meantime, Martin raced around the hall, collecting his things, stuffing them back into the gaping briefcase as fast as he could.

"Here we are," Miss Mapes said. "Welcome to the parlor." Martin joined her in a room of remarkable wallpaper. "You see," she continued, "here's the porch, just like I told you." It was the same room he had seen from the other side, with the curtains blowing out of the windows. He put down his bags, carefully.

"The bathroom, I'm afraid, is down the hall." A spray of white hair sprang itself from Miss Mapes's bun; Martin averted his eyes. He did not want to see it. It was like the discovery of a compromising letter among family mementos, or the admission of any infirmity—you instinctively turned away from it. That way the infirmity did not exist. And indeed, when Martin looked up again, Miss Mapes had fixed her hair. "I'm sorry to have to move you," she said. "I don't know what I was thinking. You see, there's such a great attention right now for the room upstairs. But this will do."

Martin only vaguely understood what she meant, but he humored her. "May I ask what all the attention's about?"

"Attention? Did I say attention? That's not the word I want. It's, you know, you know." She stared at the carpet as if the word she sought had been scratched there in the nap of the pile.

"There's such a great what, you know, great what? Attention? Attention? This time of year."

"Need? Fuss?" Martin tried, and then sarcastically, "Personage?"

"No," she said, waving him off. "You know, it's interesting what the mind does. I'm seventy-seven years old this March, and I sometimes can't remember the silliest words. It's so—"

"Oh, don't be embarrassed. I'm twenty-seven and I forget almost everything."

"I didn't mean embarrassing, I just mean silly. And there's some connection. *There's such an attention*—no, I can't get it." She clapped her hands together and smiled. "Anyway, whatever it is, there's such a great, oh, *demand*, that's the word. For the room upstairs. Because it's a double. I'm glad I finally got *that* out. Isn't that silly? Demand: attention. There's always a connection. But this room is nice."

"I really prefer it," said Martin, lying. "I can go in and out without disturbing anyone."

"Oh I hope it's *we* who don't disturb *you*," she corrected. "That's my mother's room, you see." She pointed to a door in the back wall of the parlor, next to the bed. "It's a party wall, so come join the party! We play cards at night, Mother and I. She of course was the president's daughter. And I'm *her* daughter. Some people find that hard to believe—well, that's all right. But anyway," she said, looking stern, "she's a very religious woman, don't you know."

Martin did know. He knew exactly. The phrase was a warning and the warning meant: *Bring no one to this room.*

"You may hear her sing," Miss Mapes added. She went to the window, as reluctant to leave this new room as she had been to leave the last. Was Martin to be moved another time? To the basement, perhaps?

"I could charge you less," she finally said. "Charge you less for the room, don't you know." She lifted her face in a mask of anxiety. "It's not as nice as the one upstairs."

Martin blinked to cover his surprise. "Oh, well, that won't be necessary." It was ridiculously cheap to begin with. The Williams Inn would have been three times as much.

"That's very kind. And now will you sign this?" She produced a blank piece of paper from her pocket and held up a pen, like a carrot, or stick. While Martin signed she said, "We have a rose garden out back, you know. Please help yourself. Why don't you go there now? You must be hungry from your trip. Would you like a cheese sandwich?"

"No, thank you."

"All right then," she said. She looked at the paper. "That's fine then, Mr. Gardner. Have a nice nap." She left the room.

Have a nice nap. How had she known? Or had she meant to say *day*? Was it she, herself, who wanted a nap?

Martin studied the room. It was not set up for regular use. It could accommodate a guest but clearly preferred not to. There was no closet, just a hook on the back of the door. The bathroom, of course, was down the hall. The curtains were inadequate for the windows; Martin could see right through them all the way to the road, and the road could see right in just as clearly. Worst of all, despite the ad, the furniture could not be considered antique—not like the furniture in the room upstairs. These were knockoffs, the kind you got from Montgomery Ward, where tabletops were advertised as Genuine Faux Marbre.

Not the real thing—but what was? It was all real enough, Martin supposed, all real knockoffs, all really purchased, all really there. He could see too easily through the inadequate curtains, but what he could see—the porch and the lawn, the sun and the shade—what he could see was lovely. You could sit in the chairs, put clothes in the bureau, sleep in the bed. Did it need to be gouged out of pine to charm, whorled of antique cherry to please? Did it have to sit on real ball-and-claws, real griffin feet to suffice?

But Martin had wanted to find the real thing. He could have stayed at the Williams Inn to see Matt, if that was all he had come for. Instead he'd chosen the Victorian Guest and Americana House. Now that he thought of it, even the name was off. What did it mean? Victorian Guest? Americana House? Real things don't have that aura of doubtfulness about them. Real things are complex and perhaps even contradictory, but never confused. They sound right, they have authority. Their names are a part of their stature, and stand as adequate symbols for them. Martin thought about the Met, for instance. The three elegant capital letters in its name stood handsomely for the place itself: the columns, the stairs, the grand facade. But Victorian Guest and Americana House sounded like a bad translation, a compromise hammered out in committee.

On the other hand, perhaps Miss Mapes—or was it her mother?—had named the place aptly. Maybe she thought it was quaint, just the thing to snare nostalgic New Yorkers. If so, it had worked; Martin had been snared. But he should have known better. Victorian Guest and Americana House: it had to be fake. Had the place been the real thing, it would have been called, more simply, the Guest House.

But this was where Martin was. A Victorian guest in an Americana house. He tried to look at the bright side; it wasn't all bad. There was a wild baroque mirror, gilt lions stalking the glass. There was a painting of a little girl, with two drooping blades of palm stuck behind the frame, like rabbit ears. All this was charming. And there was the wallpaper, too, so creamy and clever. He could use it in a set someday, a drawing-room show: something lovely, something ironic. He took up his sketch pad. *Candida*, he thought, or maybe *Misalliance*.

He leaned the sketch pad against his knee and roughed in the skeleton of the pattern with a very hard pencil. He drew the vertical trellises of lavender twining like DNA up the wall; between them, posies of peach and lilac flowers. He looked back and forth from the pad. When he looked away, the flowers seemed to drift. When he looked back on them suddenly, they stopped drifting and bloomed. When he looked away again, they followed him like Mona Lisa's wandering eyes.

He named the colors in the margins of his drawing. Cream, ivory, lavender, mauve, peach, lilac, Wedgwood. Each word was connected to its piece of the sketch by a pencil line finer than hair. He began to whistle—that is, to purse his lips and blow through them noiselessly. In charcoal he fleshed out the petals; with a rub of his finger he suggested a shadow. He wrote, in cursive, at the top of the page: *It covers the entire room, like skin.*

He looked back from his pad to the flowers, which froze in place. Rung up like this at random heights among the stripes, they appeared to be the only image on a defective slot machine—no lemons, no cherries, always only flowers—a defect whereby every gambler breaks the bank, and life offers universally the winner's bouquet.

But the moment he closed his pad on the drawing, the moment of contentment closed, too. He laughed to himself, thinking: What on earth am I doing here? Surely there was a more important role to play than Matt's duenna. After all, he had seen Matt through three girlfriends already, and now apparently a fourth in Joanna. What was the point? The experiments came to nothing; Martin came to less. He was the lab assistant, the janitor. When the beaker exploded, he swept it up. Or: he was the beaker.

Of course it was his own fault. He believed too much in the value of love, not only his own but anyone's. But, like beauty, love seemed to be an overadvertised, overcrowded amusement. It came to nothing. None of it did. Stella's illusionless *fleurs du mal* picking, Matt's optimistic maid of the moment, least of all Martin's hound-dog fidelity. This last had all the ridiculous Hollywood hopes of the other two, without the Hollywood seal of approval. He would give it up. Chastity of thought as well as deed—and a good time for it, too.

This decided, he combed his hair. Surrounding his reflection in the mirror, the lions eyed his head hopefully, an instinct for defenselessness sculpted into their muscles. Beneath them an eighteen-inch statue stood on the overwrought bureau: Saint Anthony. In his tiny hands, the porcelain saint held a tiny book, and—could it be?—in the book sat baby Jesus. Is Our Savior a bookmark? Martin wondered. An engraved legend recommended this prayer to all in need:

> *Holy Saint Anthony, your love for God and charity for all his creatures has made you worthy to possess miraculous powers. Encouraged by this thought, I implore you to obtain for me* (fill in request). *The answer to my prayer may require a miracle: even so, Saint Anthony, you are the saint of miracles.*

Martin prayed that the little Savior would crawl out of the book before it shut on him. He prayed that Miss Mapes's mother would not sing too loud, that Miss Mapes herself would remember the difference between *demand* and *attention*. He prayed that nothing would change, that everything would change. These might all require miracles, Martin thought, but how, even if you believed in them, could you *require* a miracle?

His mother had said it was a miracle that Martin survived the accident with Eric Hayes. Holy Saint Anthony—Martin wondered—on top of the bureau, did you require that one? Even if not, do you require me?

Religion was supposed to give comfort, was supposed to direct and confirm you, but didn't. It only made things worse. It was another Hollywood, complete with stars. What was Jesus—a leading man on a Cinemascope stick. Martin rejected him, rejected religion, except its most useless, absurd components. He was impressed by all its excesses and distortions, its cathedrals and threats, but by none of its saving graces. He selected from its precepts only what would hurt him. God's love and the serenity of belief had eluded him, but purgatory, for example, he knew to exist. Retribution he had felt. Dangerous pills, like the one that says people can belong together, as good bone china and sterling silver do, he'd swallowed whole. That this had proved untrue—well, religion cannot be held to account. Religion is just an idiot child.

Compared with life itself, the idiot child is welcome, because life—life!—is a comatose one. You spend a lot of time grieving, then hoping vainly, then waiting for the tiniest sign. Maybe his eyelash will flick momentarily, or a pinkie curl up on itself. Maybe he will wake and remember his name, or yours, or anyone's. Then you accept that he won't. You grieve some more, and settle in for the long haul.

Still, Saint Anthony, there on the bureau—Martin was truly praying now, perhaps for the first time in his life: What I have seen! And barely touched! The seams of beautiful skin through which, if anywhere, one might enter the—*attention!*—of another human soul and require—*demand!*—a miracle. Please, Saint Anthony, Martin prayed, make me worthy to possess miraculous powers. Oh, let me touch one beautiful thing that lives on this earth—one beautiful thing—and have it not shrivel away.

AFTER his nap, Martin visited the rose garden, which had nowhere near the one hundred varieties promised by the ad. Still, it was lovely. Fuchsia, scarlet, lemon, coral, antique, and tea; tight, unforthcoming, or blowzy and shameless; pert little beauties luxuriating above thorns. The air was thick with their provocative bouquet.

Also in the garden was a couple eating lunch at a wrought-iron table painted white but chipping. In two minutes, Martin learned they were friends of actors in the show that night, they were pretending to be on their honeymoon, and thus they were staying in the room from which Martin had just been ejected.

"Have you heard much about the production?" Martin asked.

"No," said the man. "But it's avant-garde."

"Yes, so I gathered."

"We're very excited."

Martin nodded and walked to another part of the garden. He sat on a small wooden bench, which immediately tipped backward, depositing him in a bed of day lilies. He lay there, feet in the air, head among their broken necks.

The couple eating lunch ran over to help, but Martin waved them off. "I'm fine," he said.

"Are you sure?" asked the man.

"I think I would know."

The couple retreated.

If he was a little defensive, he had cause. He had been reading up on the heart and its ailments, and the more he read, the more afraid he became. Sometimes the diagnosis was Marfan's syndrome—the condition that killed the basketball player. Weren't Martin's hands a little bit webbed, as the article suggested was often the case? Other times it was an insufficient valve that plagued him. *Episodes of syncope, especially after unusual physical or emotional stress.* The idea that he was suffering from a genuine ailment at first seemed liberating, but now caused him dread. And because he dreaded it, he suspected it was true.

He tried not to think about it. He disentangled himself from the lilies, brushed the dirt from his hair, and walked into town. The museum there featured as many beautiful flowers as any sensible person could wish.

AVANT-GARDE did not begin to describe it. The play was called *Viruses* and Matt had the role of Virus Number One. The advertised nudity had been replaced by tights, but maybe the nudity would have been better. As it was, Matt's head was completely enclosed in a box.

His co-virus was played by Joanna, of course. They did creepy little viral dances and humped and withered while other actors offstage said words that were meant, presumably, to be their thoughts. Yet another group, painted with dirt, made music on coconuts and melons and rocks. Martin had the vague impression that the three groups represented three aspects of life, but what they were, and why material inadequate for one person had been parceled out among an entire troupe, remained to him a mystery.

Even the simulated sex struck Martin as unerotic. Oh, the loins were interesting enough, he supposed, but the boxes on their heads kept tilting and hitting. It was ridiculous, and yet it was also in some way suggestive. Martin could not help reading his own agon in the clumsy dance of the viruses.

Still, he felt certain, he was reading an unintended message. There must be a more salient heterosexual meaning that floated past him to more receptive antennae in the audience. The couple he had seen in the garden, for instance, sat two rows in front of him, hunched intently toward the stage. They looked at each other from time to time and nodded their heads or grunted approval. At any rate, when one virus said to itself, in a disembodied voice from offstage, "I wonder what my mother would think?" only Martin had laughed. The man in the next chair threw him a dirty look.

Maybe the subject was AIDS, Martin thought—an idea he refused to consider further.

To distract himself, he studied the design, a stratagem that kept him busy for all of seven minutes. The set was even more minimal than the one he was designing for *Six*: a platform or two and an unpainted drop. The costumes looked as if they'd been designed by a microbiologist. Only the lighting—as was often the case in such productions—was proficiently done. Martin counted the lamps and categorized them by the color of their gels.

He had attended bad shows before, God knows; *most* shows were bad. They had ranged from five-million-dollar fiascos to inept Strindberg done by waitresses in kitchens. But all of these productions had something to offer, if not beautiful costumes and breathtaking sets, then at least a charming lack of pretension. Here, it appeared, pretension was esteemed. And yet, he thought sadly, it was better that way. Without pretension these people would have nothing.

Perhaps that was a good moral to draw from the whole experience. Certainly Martin saw his sadness as a pretense clung to: his abandonment, his faintheartedness, his hatred, and his love. Whatever they were, they were over. They had no more actual existence today than the memory of the view of that lake the bus had passed. They could be made to float away like the purple dots on the inside of your eyelids. If you could separate yourself from their supposed importance, you could let them go.

Only disconnect.

The play progressed, like a disease, and after some indeterminate time, was apparently over. During the curtain calls, the audience stood. Matt and Joanna removed their boxes and clutched them at their sides. They looked like astronauts, back on earth, excited but grave, as protocol required. They clasped their free hands. The musicians rose from their mound on the floor, and the disembodied voices appeared from the wings. The applause went on. When the author was called from the audience for a bow, Martin was surprised to find it was a woman. He had imagined only a man capable of writing and promoting such obvious drivel.

The director, too, it turned out, was a woman. From this fact and others, Martin began to develop an uncharitable theory of Matt's employment. He had been hired because experience and talent were here unimportant, were possibly even drawbacks. The director and author would require, he imagined, merely what excited them. They had something like music to suggest the souls, and offstage voices to utter the thoughts. They wanted a body, and a nice one at that. No one could doubt that Matt would provide it.

Though this was indeed uncharitable, it was no more uncharitable than the interpretation he now constructed for his own interest in, and employment of, Matt. The director had the excuse, at least, of an audience seeking pleasure. Martin had wanted Matt only for himself.

Well, that was all over. Martin was letting go of the strings. They could be friends, if that's what was wanted. They could be strangers. The only thing they could not be is what had never been possible anyway. And that thing they could not be seemed so paltry, so beneath consideration, so helplessly mechanical, Martin was glad to find himself bereft of its desire. He clapped louder. "Bravo!" he cried.

THE HEAD of the theater was a little Greek man who honked like a goose. He ran the place as if it were a ship—so Joanna said—with dowagers and menials assigned to different decks. Matt and she were somewhere in between, at the highest rank of sailor: neither indulged compulsively nor made to clean toilets. Toadying was reserved for the stars, who, in their staterooms, kept themselves ignorant of what transpired down below. They saw their experience at Williamstown as a delightful summer cruise in temperate climes; the Greek wore a captain's hat and deck shoes to reinforce the image. As a result, the stars loved the time they spent here. They did good work and kept returning year after year. Of course, they played Medea or Vanya on the Mainstage, not viruses in a gym. For them it was easy to love the place. They had no idea that the young men and women who made the ship run were required to pay for the privilege of serving—and then subjected to constant abuse. It showed, said Joanna, the lengths people went to get near their art. And the lengths others went to keep them from it.

Tonight the Greek had exchanged his naval uniform for a white linen suit and a red bow tie. He looked to Martin like a bowling pin. All around him at the party people hoped for an approving honk. They tried to get near but were kept at bay by the strange witchlike woman who held on to his arm, her dead eyes blinking slowly, her hair a mortician's dream.

Martin sat with the viruses and strained to hear them speak.

He had hoped dinner would mean dinner alone, but it didn't matter. He was trying to abandon each grudge as it came his way. As a result he was considerably more gracious than he had intended to be when he got there. He even complimented their performances, albeit vaguely, and then changed the subject.

"Tell me all about your work up here," he asked Joanna, surprised to find how interested he was. And Joanna, who had seemed impatient in the car, now warmed up. She told about the rehearsal process, how they'd argue for hours about philosophy, and then eat pizza until they got sick. When she said something intended as funny, she pulled her long tendrilly hair back over her ear, tilting her head. Then she'd smile a bit.

"Oh," she said, taking Martin's hand. "How's work going on *Six* so far? Will it be marvelous? Or are you disappointed? I heard they were thinking of going minimalist."

Martin looked at Matt and smiled. "I'm disappointed, but I'm trying to allow for more design. So far, I've convinced the director to paint the floor white. Who knows, with enough persuasion, I may achieve ecru."

Joanna laughed. "Matt never let on you were *funny*." She looked at Matt with mock severity. "Or said anything about your eyes. That marvelous green in the middle of the brown!"

"What *did* he tell you?"

"Oh, you know, the pertinent facts. The résumé—those shows you designed. I'm so impressed. And of course that you're a marvelous cook. He always says, when we're eating pizza, 'I don't think I've had junk food in months.' Though why you let him come over so much is a mystery to me. He's such a glutton. You should open a restaurant and make him pay!"

Martin scratched his head but said nothing.

"How's the place?" Matt interjected.

"The place in New York?"

"The place you're staying."

Martin imitated Miss Mapes and explained how he'd been moved from the room upstairs. "Now I'm right on the porch, don't you know. There's no bars on the windows, but I suppose it's safe."

"Oh yes," said Joanna. "We've slept outside. It's wonderfully safe up here, don't worry."

A champagne cork popped and flew past their table. In another room of the restaurant, a piano struck up a Broadway tune, a bass fiddle entered, and then a soprano. People rose, inappropriately, to dance.

"Isn't that from *Cats*?" asked Joanna. "They must be playing it for you!"

Martin was perplexed and laughed.

"What was *that* like?"

"What was what like?"

"Working on *Cats*? It's such a marvelous set."

Martin stammered. "I didn't actually, you know, design it."

"No, of course, but you worked on it, right?"

"No, not really. I wish I had, though."

Matt put in, "You told me you did."

"I guess I lied, what can I say?"

Joanna, mercifully, laughed and said, "My résumé deserves a fiction award. *Hang gliding?* Really!"

Martin knew such fabrications were par for the course. Both women and men added inches to their height. Ages got trimmed. Brown eyes became green, and gray eyes blue. If an actor's experience was inadequate to fill up the eight-by-ten inches of history permitted, he merely invented the balance. Unlikely, uncheckable productions of Shakespeare got appended to the list of productions he had performed in, and innocent teachers were blamed for his training. Martin himself had toyed with this once. He typed up a résumé that let it be believed he'd designed a production which in fact he had only drafted. But the spurious credit was insufficiently impressive to counterbalance the guilt its inclusion caused him, so he tore the whole thing up.

Joanna was saying, "I'd like to go hang gliding sometime, though. Doesn't that count?"

"I'd like to play Hamlet at Lincoln Center," Matt said sourly, "but I didn't list it."

"And you, Martin? What would you like to have on your résumé?"

"Age twenty-one."

"No, really, what?"

Martin had never considered the question but found himself answering immediately. "I'd like to say I designed a production of *La Traviata* at the Met."

Joanna began to sing "Sempre libera" at full voice, and Martin joined in occasionally with suggestions of the orchestra part. Matt accompanied on glass and silverware.

"What a lovely voice you have, Joanna!" said Martin when the song had unraveled.

"And Matt makes a lovely percussion."

Matt hit himself on the head with his spoon, and Joanna kissed him.

"So," she said.

Perhaps it was natural, given the work they were doing together, that Matt and Joanna had become a couple. But Joanna was not the type of woman Martin expected Matt to get involved with. She was regal in a way that would tend, Martin thought, to make Matt feel defensive, and yet not so unapproachable as to make her an obsession. She wore elegant, simple clothes, like Stella's, but they weren't all black. Tonight she was dressed in shades of dark green. She was educated and well informed but not incapable of sloughing that off. Perhaps she was a bit over-eager that Martin should like her, that things should go well. But this was a fault, however annoying it might be to Matt, that Martin could not help but approve.

Given this, he wondered whether the same fate awaited Joanna as had befallen Chloe, Kim, and the English one. For although each of these women was nominally responsible for the dissolution of her bond with Matt, it was Matt, Martin thought, who had really engineered it. As if, in reverse of the sitcom cliché, he got himself fired before he could quit. And then, too, he seemed to jump directly into a new relationship as soon as the last one had ended—no, sooner.

Stella believed he was just incompetent at managing his entanglements and so left the work entirely to others. Martin could see from his own experience that there was truth in this. But it did not explain the way Matt grieved at each loss—a convoluted grief that as often as not expressed itself without words. The night Kim had fled from the dinner table, Matt ate her roast beef but threw up later; the call from the English one exacerbated the series of unshakable colds.

Never having met her, and disliking her from Matt's description, Martin felt no pangs of remorse to find that woman replaced by Joanna. Of all Matt's girlfriends he had known or inferred, he liked her best, and trusted her most. It was Matt he found he did not trust, to hold on to Joanna.

The Greek sailed by, with his girlfriend in tow, and Matt launched into a derisive imitation.

Joanna hushed him. "Matt has to be more careful where he honks. The walls have ears."

Matt honked louder, defiantly.

"And the ears have walls," said Martin.

THE PARTY switched gears when the Mainstage show—*The Cherry Orchard*—let out at ten-thirty. An older group of actors arrived. The chatter became frenetic, the music unlistenable. An actress generally recognized as the finest interpreter of O'Neill in the country flung herself wildly across the dance floor, two acolytes attending.

Martin leaned forward to make himself heard. "What are your plans after the summer?" he asked.

"Well, we'd thought," Joanna began, looking toward Matt, "to go to France. We'd really like to see Matt's Maman, and some folks in Paris. Simone de Beauvoir."

Martin laughed. "How will you meet *her*?"

"Oh, don't you know? She's a friend of Matt's." She turned to face him. "Didn't you meet through Jean-Pierre Barrault?"

Matt looked miserable but nodded quickly.

"Oh yes," Martin said. "Now I remember."

He went on chatting, trying not to glance at Matt. *Without their pretenses, people have nothing.* He included himself and, in doing so, felt a new emotion. Sympathy.

It was one thing to exaggerate Martin's achievements, or to disguise the fact that they lived together. These made sense in the circumstances, and were innocuous. What Martin couldn't understand was how Matt expected to avoid tripping up in his own pretensions. Surely, if they went to France, Joanna would soon discover the lie. Or maybe he had no intention of going.

On the other hand, it could all be true. It was presumptuous of Martin to assume he knew everything. Perhaps Matt kept certain things secret because Martin showed no interest in them. Perhaps, like the putative thousand-dollar suits, Simone de Beauvoir was waiting in a closet. Certainly Martin had kept things from Matt, and not for such reasonable reasons.

It didn't matter: it was Matt's prerogative. And Martin, filled from somewhere with a spirit of generosity, wished him only well.

"Why don't you two dance," he said. "I think it's time for me to make my way back."

"Why don't *you* two dance," said Matt.

"Yes, let's do that," Joanna said. "Then we'll drive you back to the place."

Martin made his usual protests but eventually gave in. Joanna was so insistent, and Matt seemed to want it even more.

"Take your jacket off," he said. "Live it up."

Was it better or worse that the dance was slow? Martin did not have time to decide. Joanna led him to the middle of the floor. She put an arm around his waist and a hand on his elbow—she could not comfortably reach his shoulder. The bluesy song modulated from verse to chorus.

"I really don't know how," Martin said.

"Don't worry. Just follow me. Watch your head for the mirror ball." And Joanna started moving slightly.

Her face came up to Martin's heart, but she didn't seem capable of looking within it. Nor could he look down at her head and determine what was going on there. It was just as well. What could a person do with the information he gathered? It barely made sense and was never complete. But you could feel a hand at the small of your back, or your own improved body twisting and stretching within a crisp white shirt.

"I just want to thank you for coming," said Joanna. "It means a lot to Matt. I know he has a funny way of showing it, but he's very grateful. For everything."

"Really?"

"Maybe too grateful. You know Matt."

Martin considered this and decided he did not.

Soon the dance was over and the unlikely pair returned to the table. Matt was finishing another beer. "Let's get to the dorm before everyone comes back," he said. He nuzzled Joanna's neck and put his hand in her lap.

"Stop it, Matt," she said, turning red.

The waiter delivered an exorbitant bill, which Matt and Martin fought over. Explaining he wanted to charge their dinner and use the receipt for his income taxes, Martin took his wallet from the jacket he had left on his chair while he danced.

"Let me pay for something for once," Matt said heatedly.

Martin conceded; he withdrew his wallet. Matt left bills— nearly all that he had.

THE TOP was down, the wind was cold, and the radio played music Martin would never have suspected Matt could endure. Yet he had chosen it. Heavy metal. Joanna shrugged happily. "To each his own," she screamed.

They pulled up in front of the guest house and sat in the car with the radio on. "There's my room," Martin said. A light was shining inside the window, and the same batiste curtain was blowing through it. "I think it may be chilly tonight."

"Will we see you tomorrow?" Joanna asked.

"I have to make the early bus. But I've so much enjoyed getting to meet you."

Matt, cramped up in the narrow backseat, made a face that combined boredom with scorn.

"Oh, me too," Joanna said. "Marvelous. And I know we'll see you a lot in the city. Maybe you'll cook one of your famous dinners."

"Marvelous," Matt echoed.

Martin looked down. "I'd enjoy it. Absolutely."

"Absolutely."

Joanna said, "Is something wrong?"

Matt was silent.

"What's wrong with you? Don't be such a baby." She was neither shrill nor condescending.

"You haven't said anything about the show," Matt said, addressing himself to the side of the road.

"But he did," said Joanna. "He said he liked it. Right at the start."

"But he was lying," said Matt.

Martin took a deep breath. "I didn't care for the script, it's true, but I thought you both did admirable jobs under the circumstances. And then, the more I thought about it, the more I found things that interested me, that spoke to me."

"Well, that's all we wanted," Joanna said.

"Maybe all you wanted," said Matt.

"Look, I'm sorry I caused a problem here. You two really did excellent work." Martin heard his praise escalating, but didn't know what to do about it. "The play is provocative intellectually and at the same time sensual." He looked to Matt to see if this was enough but got no response.

"Well, Joanna, really, I mean it, a pleasure to meet you." He leaned over the stick shift and kissed her on the cheek. "And Matt, what can I say but good night."

"Matt, please!" complained Joanna as Martin unfolded himself from the car.

"Good night," Matt said feebly, then offered his hand—his left hand, Martin realized with a pang.

Martin shook it as best he could. "Sleep well," he said, and started walking.

The car sped off, its music trailing, but Martin was not ready to go inside. For one thing, he was afraid Miss Mapes would identify him with the unholy noise. A moment's pause might remedy that. For another thing, the night was beautiful, and he wished to see it. So starry it was—a Starry Madderlake.

In the scarred black sky, the waxing crescent moon hung lost, an index tab flung loose from a dictionary. What letter would it be, Martin asked himself, what letter but *M*? The letter of his life and the letter, perhaps, of the love of his life. The veins in his right foot spelled it plain as could be. They have been intent upon it, have pulsed with it; on their evidence alone he has waited for years. Waiting for a letter from far away.

But what's to say, Martin now thought, it isn't a *W*? Or something entirely different, a *3*? What would a *3* mean: *You are meant for a robot?* Or if he turned his foot around, a sigma appeared. Was he meant for Socrates? Was he Socrates himself?

And had he looked, might he not have found his body depicting the whole world's alphabet? Everything on earth making its claims, staking him out as its own? The *Y* of the crotch, the *O* of the mouth, surprised, the *U* of the curled tongue within it. You, of course, Martin thought. My body spells you. And yet you do not respond.

If he could thumb the moon, and open the night's dictionary there, what would it tell him? It would tell him *moon*, that *M* stands for *moon*. That's all it would say. In the night sky, the moon needs no definition, and offers none. At best, the stars like asterisks may lead the reader to related ideas. *See also,* they say. See also *Man.* For *M* stands for the man in the moon as well, his face half-obliterated, like a waitress behind her pad. See also *Waitress, Woman, Maria, Mirror.*

The night splits open, and out of it pours a shower of words. They jangle down like pellets of sleet, drumming on everyone's bedroom windows, hitting their roofs. Oh, how free the night is with data, how stingy with direction! It closes over itself, like Pandora's box, before offering up its long-imputed treasure. We fall asleep, our minds still buzzing: What was the word I was trying to remember? We look for clues, messages in our dreams, but there are no messages, no word has been left. We wake up exactly where we left off last night.

If only the sky, Martin thought, could be opened up further— that *M* in the sky—so that cool, soothing milk might rush down and drench us. As it is, we must drench ourselves with whatever will suffice.

IN THE WINDOW above his window on the porch, two figures passed in shadow. Pretending to be on a honeymoon, they'd said. And Martin was on his. He hugged himself, whether from the chill or the first shy stirrings of a feeble self-love, he could not say.

The guest house seemed less peculiar by night. It was just a house, Martin considered, and a simple one at that. It had rooms you slept in and then left forever. They did not of themselves project a morality or a plan for living. These were reflected onto it by its owners, but could not then further reflect onto you. He had nothing to fear from its puritanical mien, and nothing to gain from it either.

He tapped on the door and the dogs came running.

"Mary, Margaret, hush," said Miss Mapes, arriving out of the dark in the hall. She unlatched the hook and let Martin in. The dogs immediately started sniffing at his crotch.

"Would you like to join us? We're playing bridge."

Martin followed her into a room whose walls were covered with religious drawings. Amidst them, a truly ancient woman sat in a wheelchair with cards laid out on a table in front of her. Miss Mapes made introductions and begged Martin to sit. "Do you enjoy this music? I can change it if you like."

The old radio, as he almost suspected it must, played old tunes. "Oh no, that's fine."

He watched a few minutes as the game progressed. The women's voices knitted together like yarn. *Pass. One heart. One no trump. Two hearts.* Then only the music remained, floating around on its sea of static, while the two played out the hands they'd been dealt. For the life of him, Martin could not figure out how a game meant for four could be played by two.

At a pause in the action he asked Miss Mapes's mother, "Do I understand you're President Coolidge's daughter?"

The woman stared at him as if bewildered, then started singing "America the Beautiful" in a loud, unbroken voice. Martin listened with interest, especially to the bizarre second verse. *O beautiful for pilgrim feet, whose strong impassioned stress a thoroughfare for freedom beat across the wilderness!* Martin had never heard these words, and they filled him with unexpected patriotic feeling. Was he not himself a kind of pilgrim? Was he not an American, in his own perverse way?

The feeling was short-lived, however. Soon enough, God reappeared in the lyric, supplanting freedom; self-control was invoked as a greater virtue. Martin cleared his throat, bringing the song to a sudden halt.

"She's not all there," Miss Mapes explained.

But she was enough there, Martin noticed, to keep winning tricks in the mysterious game. It seemed more likely that Miss Mapes herself was not all there. But then, who was?

After a while Martin made excuses. "Such a long day, and a long day tomorrow. Have a good night."

Miss Mapes's mother looked up from her cards. "And may the Lord Jesus be with you always," she said, in tones more appropriate to a curse than a blessing. Martin almost jumped into the hall.

It was half past eleven; too early to sleep. In his room, he took out a mystery novel he had brought in his bag and sat down to read it. An hour passed, and then another. He finished the book, though he did not understand the solution when it came.

He undressed slowly, folding his shirt, bundling his socks, laying them next to his wallet and keys on the ornate bureau. He took his nightshirt from his overnight bag, then put it aside. I will sleep in the nude, he decided with pleasure, let Coolidge and Queen Victoria think what they like.

He got into bed. The pilgrimage had worked perversely, but well. He felt washed of his sins—the sins of belief.

CARY had been cured of his lisping several times, and once on TV, but never for long. Eventually his father had realized there was no hope of his preaching the gospel effectively and, in a display of pragmatic tenderness, allowed his son to attend art school in Rhode Island. The idea was to develop skills that could eventually be turned to the service of the Lord, and for a while that was all Cary wanted. But he must have come to want more, Martin figured, for Cary had killed himself upon returning to North Dakota after graduation. This Martin discovered when a package arrived at his mother's house the following summer. A note explained that the items enclosed had been found in Cary's steamer trunk—*after*. Terrified, Martin undid the twine, tore the brown paper. But inside he only found five pairs of underpants, carefully labeled *Martin Gardner*, and his high-school crew clothes, maroon and gray.

TAPPING. Tapping? What? No. Wait. Martin looked at his travel clock. It was three o'clock.

Then silence again. He lay still as the dead, except for his eyes, which searched the room wildly. Nothing. The door was shut, Saint Anthony still on the bureau, reading. The windows, which he had lowered for bed, were lowered still. He could see the shadows of their mullions on the batiste curtains. But he had not bothered to latch the latches.

Had it been Miss Mapes? Or Miss Mapes's mother? No light slipped under the party-wall door. And the radio, too, had been extinguished. A woodpecker? But Martin didn't even know what a woodpecker sounded like.

Tapping again; and now a new shadow arose on the curtains. An absolutely definite head, looming, distorting, and now arms reaching. The window slid open.

The familiar breezes blew through Martin's ears; the bed was spinning. A leg stepped through the window frame, and quickly thereafter a familiar body.

"Martin?"

For several moments he could not speak. Strange noises of relief and terror escaped him.

Matt stood at the bureau, facing the mirror and the statue of Saint Anthony. He seemed to be praying, or doing something with his hands. It was too dark to tell.

"What are you doing? Why are you here?"

"Must we talk about it?"

"Are you crazy? You almost gave me a heart attack. And what if they'd seen you?"

"Well, what if they had?" Matt turned around.

Martin signaled Matt to lower his voice.

"Well, what if they had."

Matt sat down at the end of the bed and grasped Martin's foot through the chenille spread. "I need to stay."

"You need to stay?"

"Yes. Where's the bathroom?"

"You can't go there, it's down the hall."

But Matt left the room before Martin could prevent him.

And so Matt was in another bathroom, watching the water slide through red and brown whiskers to the sink and thinking, or not thinking: Another mirror, not my own. Martin could picture him there, by sheer force of imagination he could conjure the scene, could see behind himself, behind the purple quilted headboard his back was stiff against, past the sleeping woman in the shrine next door, through three walls and down the hall, through the bathroom door with the crystal knob and through the limp, white towel on the back of that door. If it were all the rooms and halls in hell, he could see it still: the fresh well water blue from the faucet, the porcelain sink, the tiny red-and-brown forest of hair, and the mirror, the mirror, not his own.

He could see as easily into the future. Matt would return in a minute or two, would get into bed uncomfortably. Martin would wrap the sheet around to protect his naked flesh from view. They would not touch and would not speak, would feel their familiar resignations to sleep or wakefulness, would wonder or not wonder why they were there, in this room, in this bed, together and apart. Their two bodies would prove to contain entirely different lives that did not intersect, no matter how similar they were as bodies. Their dreams would dig through the bed in entirely different directions, one toward China, one toward the moon. They would be inches from each other in fact, but they would not know. They would not know.

Deep in the walls, the water squealed.

''YOUR SHIRT is torn,'' Martin said, sitting up and clutching himself. With the window open, it was cold in the room.

"Quiet," said Matt.

"You smell bad. Have you been running?"

Matt continued to undress.

"I see we've got our little problem again."

"Quiet."

"I gather you intend to stay here. I warn you, it's a narrow bed. And I'm not wearing anything."

Matt pulled off his underwear.

"All right, then, get in." He turned to the wall. "You can sleep on the right."

Matt climbed in and pulled the covers over his head. His smell was overpowering.

"Jesus," said Martin.

Matt reached over and covered Martin's mouth. "Quiet," he said. He let his hand droop.

"You *know* you won't be able to sleep with your arm like that."

"Quiet," he said. He put his fingers in Martin's mouth and turned him over by the teeth. They were face-to-face. Martin recognized the smell of his own toothpaste on Matt's breath, lightly covering the smell of beer.

"Stop looking," Matt said. He took Martin's hand and guided it down to the base of his stomach. He closed his eyes and a smile came over his face. They lay there absolutely still.

"I don't know what you want me to do," Martin whimpered.

Matt turned over and nestled backward into the curve of Martin's lap, like a spoon. He replaced Martin's hand where he wanted it to go. He seemed to be asleep, except that he wasn't. He was in a coma, like Eric Hayes, and how long would it last?

Martin felt himself contract to the ends of his fingers. Each finger had its own eye, and with them he explored the ineffable skin of the dreadful man he could not be touching. His words, his thoughts, were utterly gone, sinking, rising, wobbling beyond containment. His newfound independence was gone, his anger was gone, Joanna was gone. Only the view from the fingers remained, as they crept over hot plains and through scratchy thickets. Here was a sudden rise in the ocean, a volcano protected by a scarlet reef. Here was its twin. Here above was a mountain range, shifting with every swallow. Above, the incomparable topography of the face: granite promontory, forested ridge, Luray cavern, Old Faithful steaming.

And then, again, the trail led south, but the terrain was alien, a moonscape of strange forms and plates. The penis, the testes, these were their names, but what were they like? Martin found them baffling to touch. So forbidden, they had no meaning except in their prohibition. Turkey neck, turkey gristle, robins' eggs in elephant leather, but almost scalding to the skin, and salty to the mouth.

What they most were like, Martin realized, were his own. To touch them was to touch himself, with all the pleasure and disgust that entailed. To taste them was to do the impossible upon oneself. To give pleasure was to exaggerate the already absolute separation between lives. You intruded your hand between the legs of another person only to feel more heatedly than ever the demarcation of your skins. Different lives worked feverishly beneath contiguous sheaths of abdomen; the workings could be sensed through the flesh, but they worked for different masters. No intrusion of genital or hand, of tongue or eyebeam could alter that.

Everyone is alone, thought Martin, and everyone is the same.

And yet he was not alone. Life stirred within his hand, and his breathing attained the consistency of sobs. The light from a passing car on the street garbled the room and set the wallpaper spinning. Where would it land? It would land where it must, on flowers, flowers, always flowers, another winning combination.

Matt was silent, a sleeping beauty. The wrong prince was kissing him so he could not awake. But his body worked as the terrible accident of evolution had allowed it to, and out came the burning milk on Martin's hand. He held it up to the feeble moonglow. Here is life—and death as well. Virus bearer, child producer, degraded ichor with a thousand embarrassing names. The cheap wine unceasingly flowing. Renewable blood, donable to all, paler, paler, but just as staining. Is it toward you all life is headed? And from you, too?

Martin raised his arm triumphantly and let the stuff dry and crack upon his hand.

V MILK

Martin burned his finger in the not-quite-boiling water. It had looked inviting, warm as a bath when he went to test it; not possibly hot enough to burn. Now he regarded it accusingly. He stuck his finger in his mouth and sucked, he bit gently into the wrinkling flesh. He guessed this was the price you paid, the notorious hardship of parenting.

But it didn't make sense. Why should you test the water? The baby never touched the water, never went near the pot, not even as a joke. What was it mothers were always testing, then? Martin was completely ignorant concerning babies. He didn't know how to warm the milk. Always before, Maria had prepared it herself, and Martin hadn't bothered to watch. Now he was stuck. David was off at work, and Maria was changing the baby in the nursery. Martin was supposed to have the bottle ready when she returned. "No problem," he had said. Now several minutes had passed. He began to panic. How warm should it be? And how did you know when it got there? The bottle bobbed and hit the sides of the pot. It rose and sank like a buoy in a storm. And inside the bottle, Martin now noticed, the milk was starting to bubble. It looked yellow and thick. This had to be *too* warm.

He considered asking Delia to help him. She was drawing something huge on oaktag on the kitchen table. She sang one of her loud, endless songs. Martin imagined asking her how warm the milk should be, and worse, imagined her knowing. Delia would take over calmly, almost disdainfully; she'd stand on her Peanuts footstool and tend without interest to the pot and the bottle. If she knew how to do it at all, she would do it masterfully; if she didn't know, she'd just yell for help. Either possibility was humiliating, so Martin decided not to ask.

He turned down the flame of the gas, watched it soften to the color of lilacs. Above it, in the pot, the rolling water calmed. The milk in the bottle looked once again like milk, but appearances were deceptive. Martin's whole family had once gotten sick

221

from mayonnaise that seemed perfectly normal. It had even tasted good, better than usual. And milk, wasn't milk notoriously susceptible to change? Couldn't it turn into cheese, or yogurt, or something botulistic? What if he were responsible for poisoning his own godson?

Martin wished Maria could breast-feed the boy as she once had breast-fed Delia, but Stefan had a digestive problem. Natural milk made him sick. Instead he was fed synthetic formula from a bottle. It came as a chalky powder in foil envelopes; you mixed it with water and heated it and served. You would do it a thousand times in the course of one infancy; you would reach and tear and pour it, over and over. Maria's kitchen was littered with the silver scraps of used-up packets. She bought them in bulk, in square, sky-blue boxes, each with a painting of a happy baby sleeping. Maria kept a month's supply lined up on shelves across the top of the kitchen. The happy babies faced out en masse, as in a nursery.

These packets were scientific, where breast-feeding was mystical. They were even called formula, as if feeding were a learnable equation. Anyone could do it. Even a man, even Martin. It was a formula without any unknowns; the unknowns had been removed. The mysteries of the breast were bypassed. You only needed the desire to nurture—that, and instruction.

Still it was not the same. Martin often watched Maria feed Stefan from the bottle, much as if she were taking his temperature. But when she had nursed Delia, at her breast, Maria had been transformed. Never at first, never while opening her shirt; that was just business. She would carry on casually and the baby would fidget. "It's a wonderful dish," she was saying one time. "I had it in a German restaurant. Made with rabbit, I think it was." She started to list the ingredients: onions, noodles, maybe some butter. Then she went silent. She half closed her eyes; a smile rippled beneath her face. The baby had stopped squirming and was feeding dreamily, collapsed on her breast. It looked as if a delicious poison had overtaken them both, an ancient thing known only to women.

Martin thought of Cleopatra and the asp, that sucked its nurse asleep. He thought of mandragora; what was it? They were things a man could never know, but any woman could. Maria glowed with the light of centuries of privilege. Oh yes, women were certainly oppressed; Martin was not unaware, not unsympathetic. But maybe this privilege was the reason. It made every mother a Cleopatra, and whisked her away to a private, impenetrable Egypt. Martin understood how a man might feel, living with it day and night. Though he might be the father, he could find himself superfluous: an arrangement of skin and bones and hair in pale blue pajamas.

It wasn't just Maria. Martin remembered his Latin teacher from high school, who wasn't married and brought her child to class. The baby was about the size of a cat and was kept at all times in a red corduroy sling. Miss Oates would go over the lessons as usual, but occasionally, while Martin and his classmates read from their translations of the *Aeneid*, she would take out a breast and angle it toward her baby's mouth. Sometimes the child wouldn't nurse, and the breast just lay there, making everyone nervous. Martin would run through the conjugation of *amare*, the famous and less famous parts, the indicative and subjunctive, in all its tenses. When that ran out, he might organize papers in neat grids on his desk. Around the room, pencils were sharpened, lunch money counted. But it wouldn't have mattered if they had all just stared; Miss Oates was oblivious. She was back in Egypt, like Maria—or maybe for her it was Troy. Minutes might pass. She might put a finger in the baby's mouth, or speak to it coaxingly. But the baby frequently remained unimpressed. It liked to loll its head over the back of the sling and stare, vacantly, out the classroom window, at cars maneuvering in the parking lot.

Eventually, if she couldn't convince her baby to nurse, Miss

Oates would remember the expectant class. "Oh," she said, looking up slowly, "where were we?"

Martin picked up his spiral notebook and read: "Aeneas returned from the ship, downcast."

"Yes," said Miss Oates, in her soft, disembodied voice. "And Neil, now, your translation please?"

Neil read haltingly his version of the line. "Aeneas returned to the cave and got lost."

"That's very poetic, Neil, yes. A ship can be like a cave, if you're lost—and how sad that would be! Lost in a cave! And Gilbert now? Your translation please?"

Suddenly the baby lunged, and the room filled up with great sucking noises.

"Aeneas returned with—a hole in his shoe?" Gilbert offered meekly.

"Oh, lovely," whispered Miss Oates, starting to rock. "Such a lovely rhythm."

But Miss Oates was in a haze with or without the baby. Her expression was dreamy, her posture ecstatic: broken-necked like the sculptures of sorrowful Madonnas. She walked to school through the mistiest fields available, drenching the hem of her peasant dress. Of course breast-feeding would be a transcendent experience for her; cleaning the blackboard was, too. But in Maria the transcendence came as a shock. On all other occasions, she was cool and practical. She looked over shopkeepers and paintings and produce with the same skeptical, thin-eyed squint. "That's not art," she would say at a gallery, "that's someone skipping therapy."

And yet with Delia at her breast she sat all loose and disconnected like a dreamer under the shade of a giant tree. Martin swept the kitchen and put away the dishes while he waited for her to return. Eventually she lit up without warning and said, "*Hasenpfeffer*, that's the word! A wonderful dish!" She folded her breast back into her shirt, as a businessman replaces his billfold, then took the sleeping baby into the nursery. But Martin, feeling abandoned, would try to jump back into the lost conversation. "Rabbit?" he asked. "I don't think I could eat a rabbit."

Transcendent or not, the breast-feeding had come to an end. Delia moved on to a bottle and then to a safety cup, and soon enough was drinking for herself. She not only refused assistance but denied she had ever received it. That she had once been breast-fed was a ludicrous suggestion. Maybe other children had—but certainly not Delia. She was born, it seemed, sipping through a straw. When the subject came up, she would laugh disdainfully. "Don't you think I'd remember?" she said.

"Not only did you do it, Delia, but you loved it," Maria explained. "And someday maybe you'll have a baby of your own to nurse."

Delia would run from the room, shrieking with laughter.

It was a shame, Martin thought. Something that seemed so pleasurable, so complete, you could never remember, you were forbidden apparently to remember. When you tried to imagine it, when Martin did, all that came up in the mind's eye was comic metaphor: endless hills looming, inviting, frightening. But if the metaphor was there, wasn't the memory itself hidden somewhere behind it? Wasn't it true you never forgot a thing? Martin believed all of life was dumped into storage bins, and with enough searching, all could be found. A memory was immutable, it had to be: Where would it go? You couldn't *give* it away, that he knew; you couldn't destroy it either. But this particular memory eluded all attempts at recapture, and yet despite being unrememberable, forever lured you to try. It seemed like a test, like the Sphinx's riddle.

Martin had been trying for a year to remember, ever since his mother told him. "I've always loved you," she said. "I've always given to you. I even breast-fed you, Martin, did you know? Not like your sisters."

She had never mentioned it before, and it seemed so important. "You're kidding," he said.

"No, it's true," she continued. "And it wasn't the thing then. It wasn't popular in the fifties, you know."

To which Martin had no comeback.

MARIA brought Stefan in new diapers into the kitchen. He had stopped crying. "It seems he wasn't hungry after all. Forget the milk."

Martin put on asbestos kitchen gloves and lifted the bottle from the pot of water as if it contained spent nuclear fuel. All that work wasted. And what should he do with it now? Throw it out? Put it in the refrigerator? He stood with it in the middle of the kitchen, letting it drip.

"It's so hard to know," Maria was saying. "Always trying to tell us something—who can guess what it is?"

Martin looked over, formulating a reply, but found that Maria had addressed this to the baby. She was always asking Stefan such questions, perhaps because it was impossible for him to answer.

"What, are we falling asleep now, Stefan? Is that it, sweetie, is that what I see?" She smoothed the baby's wisp of eyebrow, traced the cleft in its chin with her thumb. "Isn't that true?" she asked, searching his flat red face for a sign. "Isn't that so?" She walked around and rocked him, then lowered herself carefully into the sofa.

"This woman where I stayed," said Martin, "added 'don't you know' to the end of every sentence."

"Well, don't you?" asked Maria.

"Well—"

"Don't you, Stefan, don't you?"

Delia danced over to her mother, chanting loudly. "My doll is green, my dolly is mine!"

"Delia, pipe down," said Maria.

"Give him one of your noonies, Mommy! Then Martin could watch!" She giggled hysterically and ran behind the sofa.

Stefan had been born at the end of August and was now three

weeks old. In that time, Martin had watched Delia grow more childish as if to meet him halfway. The green doll, long since abandoned as silly, had been dug up from the depths of her trunk. And her performances in *Jet Set* became erratic.

"If you be quiet, honey, he may fall asleep."

"But you never give him your noonies, Mommy, like Mercedes's mom gives Zeke."

"I've explained this a hundred times, Delia. Now sit down."

Delia ran back around the sofa and launched herself onto it. She landed headfirst in the crack at the back of the cushion, her dress and slips and petticoats flowering open. On the other side of the sofa, Maria and Stefan popped up suddenly as on the crest of a wave. Stefan started to wail.

"Sorry, Mommy," said Delia, rearranging herself.

Maria got up wearily. "I guess I'll need that bottle after all," she said. Martin wondered how she knew, but figured that mothers were fluent in the language of babies. Stefan was crying across her shoulder into her hair, fanning through it with his tight, mad fists. This meant he wanted milk, apparently.

"Would you accompany Miss Delia to her room?" Maria asked, taking the bottle from Martin bare-handed. She spoke under her breath. "I need a break."

"I *heard* that!" Delia shouted from the sofa.

"Sorry, honey, but I have to give Stefan his bottle."

"Let Martin do it. You never play with me."

"No, honey. Martin has better things to do than feed the baby. He wants to play with *you*." She made a wry face, minimally apologetic, then turned back to Delia. "Honey, okay?" she called. Martin watched her squirt a drop of the milk from the bottle into her hand.

So that was it, of course! The *milk* you tested, not the water. Martin actually smote his forehead. Maria rubbed the milk on her finger, swirled it around absently like skin cream, until it disappeared.

But Delia was still sitting on the sofa with her arms folded tight. "Come on now, honey," her mother said. "Do me a favor, all right then, sweetie?"

"Can we play Truth at least?" asked Delia.

Maria made a pleading face.

"Sure," Martin answered. "Let's go play Truth."

THEY LAY on Maria's and David's bed, eyes shut and arms folded, as Delia's new rules apparently required.

"Why are you so old?" she asked for openers.

"I'm only twenty-seven," Martin answered.

She hit him. "Why are you so old?"

"Your mother is thirty-six."

She hit him again. "You're not answering the question, and you're risking a double penalty."

This was a new twist. "I'm as old as I am," said Martin, thinking hard, "because I was born when I was."

Delia seemed to accept this. "Have you ever had a baby?"

"No."

"Why not?"

"Only a woman can have a baby."

"Very funny," she said. "Have you ever had a baby with a woman?"

"No."

"Why not?"

"I'm not married."

"So?"

"Usually you get married to have a baby."

"Then why aren't you married?" She hit him. "Don't you want a baby?"

"It's not as simple as that. You don't get married just to have a baby."

"Why not?"

"Well, Delia, because, well—" He considered the question.

She hit him. "Not fast enough. Have you ever kissed a girl? Other than your mother or aunt, on the lips?"

"Yes."

She hit him.

"But it's true!" he protested.

"Maybe it's true," she said, "but it's gross."

Delia, in her sickening way, had somehow come to understand Martin's sadness and its root. For weeks she had been asking what happened to Matt, and Martin had lied—or perhaps not lied—saying, *Nothing.* Now she brought up marriage constantly, as if to suggest he should try something else. Or was this only what Martin was thinking?

"Do you think I should really get married?" he asked her.

"No," she said.

"No?"

"I just think you should have a baby."

"And how do you think I should do that?"

"You figure it out," she said.

Martin laughed. "Do you know what you're saying?"

"Of course I do."

"What then?"

"Didn't you see 'And Baby Makes Two'?"

"No, what's that?"

"Oh, this TV show about people with only one parent. Someone helps you have the baby, then goes away, or they do it in test tubes. It's called an arrangement."

Martin started to laugh. "They show you this on TV?"

"Yeah," she said, "on afternoon specials."

"And that's what you mean? An arrangement?"

"Yes. An arrangement. You should get yourself arranged."

EVEN DELIA did not know that Martin started weeping the minute he was left alone. The first tears had come during a movie one night at the end of August, and failed to stop when the lights came up. He told a stranger, who kindly inquired, that the film had moved him—an unlikely prospect since the feature in question was *Kiss Me, Kate* with 3-D glasses. But the man accepted his explanation without comment. When Martin walked home, he felt the tears making a moving film on his face.

Matt had disappeared the night of Bastille Day. He must have escaped just as he'd come: through the white batiste curtains in the window on the porch. Martin was alone when he awoke the next morning, alone except for the smell all over him. He did not shower, but dressed himself in a cloud of sex. When he went to say good-bye to Miss Mapes, he thought he saw her curl her nose.

"That's thirty dollars, then," she said. "Don't you know."

Martin opened his wallet and noticed that the blue-and-white bank card he always kept with its insignia pointing up was now pointing down. He stared at this for a moment before handing the ten-dollar bills to Miss Mapes. How had this disorder occurred? For a second the answer flashed in his mind; then he forgot both answer and question until his bank statement came, several weeks later.

One thousand dollars had been withdrawn during the night of Bastille Day: five hundred dollars five minutes before midnight, five hundred more just two minutes after. Five hundred, he learned when he called up the bank, was the one-day limit, so the person who took it knew what he was doing. The money was drawn from a cooperating institution, a savings and loan in Williamstown, Massachusetts.

"Does anyone else know your personal identification number?" the phone teller asked.

"Yes," said Martin.

"You should never let anyone else know your number."

"Thank you. I won't."

Immediately he called Matt at the theater, with no idea what he would say. It might have been easier had there not been two weeks of silence between them. The last words Martin had said to Matt were: *I don't know what you want me to do.* And the last thing he had done was kiss him to sleep—on the back of his neck, but a kiss nonetheless.

For a while, back in New York, he had kept the fragile bubble aloft. He had waited for a word from Matt: eagerly at first, then anxiously, then with mounting nausea. The arm he remembered raising in triumph collapsed in stages in his memory, until it was an image of perversity and barrenness instead of consummation. Perhaps that's all it could ever have been. And what could he say to Matt after that?

But the person who answered the phone at Williamstown cleared her throat repeatedly before finally admitting that Matt had left. Joanna was put on the line instead, and Martin asked her where Matt had gone.

"After we dropped you off," she explained, "he and I had a fight in the car." She sounded tired.

"What about?" Martin asked.

"Oh, who knows what anything with him is ever about. But you know he had his drug problem."

Martin was silent.

"You did know, didn't you?"

"You mean the Xtasy."

"I mean the coke."

"Oh. Right."

"Nothing against coke, but some people simply cannot control it. He had stopped for a while—"

"Yes?" said Martin.

"But something started him up again."

Martin immediately suspected himself.

"Anyway, he wanted me to drive him to the bank and then to this guy he knew in North Adams. When I refused, he jumped out of the car. It was moving at the time, but he didn't fall. He just leaped out like a cat and started running. I stopped for a minute and then sped away."

"What time was that?"

"Oh, I don't know, eleven-thirty? Quarter to twelve?"

Matt did not return that night, Joanna continued, and next morning his few things were gone from the dorm. She had not seen him or heard from him since; his understudy took over the part of Virus Number One. A day later he'd apparently returned, contrite and disheveled, but the honking Greek dispatched a minion to boot him back out. "So self-destructive," Joanna said. "He'll never work *here* again. Unless of course he becomes famous someday, in which case it wouldn't matter if he'd murdered an usher."

She went on in this vein, half-bitter, half-dismissive, while Martin tried to piece together how the job was done. First Matt had told him to dance with Joanna, and even suggested he take off his jacket. Then, while they danced, he must have taken the card from Martin's wallet. Afraid the theft would be discovered before it had even proved useful, he'd insisted on paying for dinner himself. Later that night, after climbing through the window, he'd stood at the bureau. He must have been putting the card back in place, but upside down. He'd never understood the depth of Martin's precision. Or perhaps he'd ignored it, on purpose, as a sign.

Matt certainly had his own precision, though. Five minutes before midnight; two minutes after. He had sunk the card in the scanner twice, had twice told the machine his personal code was *M*. Did he think that Martin wouldn't figure it out? When the statement came? But of course he was desperate. Desperate people do insupportable things.

And where was he now? Joanna suggested France. "I bet he's gone to see Maman. She was sick, you know. She offered to pay his way over."

Martin said nothing.

"On the Concorde—but of course. She was rich, you know. She had this big ring."

This all sounded preposterous now. How could Joanna have swallowed it? How had Martin? The only way possible: they'd swallowed it whole.

Maman's illness was fictional—Matt had already admitted that—but now Martin wondered, did she even exist? Rich *or* poor? He slowly dug through Matt's belongings and found the envelope with the fancy stamps. He hesitated to read it—and yet he could no more resist finding out what its message would be than he could resist the message of his dirty magazines. He slid the tissue of stationery from its envelope.

It was in French, at least: a hopeful sign. He read it to Stella over the phone, letter by letter where necessary.

" 'Dear Matt,' " she translated. " 'Yes, I remember you.' "

"So he wasn't lying," Martin said, and then, more eagerly, pronounced the French words.

" 'I am pleased to hear that you are doing so well. Acting is a very difficult profession, so I congratulate you on your success. Do you still play guitar?' " Stella paused. "Did he play guitar?"

"I don't know," Martin said. "I thought French horn."

"Well, it says guitar."

Martin read the next phrase; Stella resumed her translation reluctantly. " 'I am sorry to hear of the death of your father.' "

Martin said: "What?"

"Was his father dead? I thought just poor."

She asked Martin to recheck the spelling—love and death sounded so much alike in French. But no matter how he interpreted the writing, the meaning would not consent to change. "That's what it says," Stella concluded. " 'Death of your father.' Is it possible he was dead?"

"He never said so."

"But *your* father is dead—he knew, I assume."

"Of course. I told him."

"Ah," said Stella, "so he's stolen that, too. Read the rest."

Martin complied, his appetite for the exercise spent. What remained of the letter was just as distant and courteous as the portion already read. Condolence and benediction followed in graceful turn, then gave way to a signature that betokened no intimacy. In any case, it was not Maman.

A long silence ensued, interrupted only by scraps of someone else's conversation crossing the line.

"Shall I come over?" Stella asked.

"Where do you think he is?"

"You don't really care, I hope."

"Shouldn't I? He might be in trouble. There were drugs, you know." And as he told Stella what Joanna told him he remembered the nearly perpetual summer cold, the bloody tissues, the sniffling in bed he had thought was crying.

"It doesn't surprise me," Stella said. "It explains a lot."

"It explains nothing. It's only another thing that needs explaining."

"It explains the money."

"Does it? It explains what he used it for, I guess, but not why he took it. What's a thousand dollars to me? I'd have given it to him, handed it over, no strings attached."

"Even for drugs? I can just see it. 'Martin, I need a bag of coke, could you lend me a grand?'"

"He wouldn't have had to tell me what for. I'd have given him money blindly. I'd have given him anything."

"Then maybe that's why he had to steal it."

Martin took this in and then laughed derisively as if to expel it. "Because you have to destroy what loves you? Isn't that a little old hat? I mean it may explain you and your boyfriends, Stella, but it doesn't explain me and Matt. It wasn't Matt who stole from me, who lied to me, who—" He stopped himself from referring to their last night together; when he resumed, his voice was suddenly strung out with anger. "Who did all that stuff. He wouldn't have done it if he weren't in trouble. People do not change that much. And this is not what he was. I'm the one who lived with him! He was here in this room—don't you think I'd know? We shared—what we shared. Whatever he did was the drugs, not him." And now Martin knew he was contradicting himself. He had switched to arguing Stella's position because it was less painful to think Matt had suddenly changed than to think he had not changed at all.

"I'm coming over," Stella said quietly.

"No! No!"

But she did come over, with cardboard boxes from the supermarket. She packed up what remained of Matt's clothes, while Martin watched, reproachful, unprotesting. Into the boxes went Matt's amber soap, his coffee mug, his threadbare copy of *Catcher in the Rye*. Volumes one through four of the *American Family Learning Book*. A handful of coins. A ticket stub.

Stella surveyed the bedroom for anything she had missed. Her eye lit upon a photograph in a pewter frame, sitting on the table by the right side of the bed. "I assume this is his?"

"It's supposed to be Maman."

"Oh, Martin," said Stella sadly, picking it up. "It's Barbara Stanwyck."

"It is?"

She nodded. "Such a special French lady." She undid the clasp and pulled the photograph out with her nail. "A nice frame, though. You could use it for something." She threw Barbara Stanwyck into the trash. "Is there anything else?"

"No," Martin lied. Nearly a hundred eight-by-ten glossies remained in a drawer in the living room: photographs he would tape to his bedroom wall the minute he was alone again.

Stella folded the boxes shut and dragged them to the door. "Some of the clothes I can give to people on the street. The rest we'll take to Goodwill tomorrow."

"But what if he comes back to get it someday?"

"He will never come back," Stella said sternly, as if somehow she would make it so.

IT TOOK all of ten minutes to rid the apartment of Matt's existence, but nothing could erase from Martin's memory the image he had of that night in the guest house. No matter how he tried to push it away—over the next few days, he threw himself tirelessly into his work on *Six*—it crept into his imagination and took over his body. He would become aroused and have trouble breathing. Even at the theater, in the middle of rehearsals, there was nothing to do but go into the bathroom.

But the physical release, the pop and blossom, was his only solace, and brief at that. He would open his eyes and find his face as wet as his hand. Then when he stood, he could not get his balance. The way he emerged from the bathroom, the cast and crew must have thought he was drunk.

But the cast and crew were too concerned with their own problems to complain of Martin's carriage. They were panicky and fractious. Response during previews had been less than ecstatic. Friends in the audience reported a general feeling of confusion. Who were these people? they wanted to know. Where was it set? Why was everything so abstract and glaring?

Peter White called a meeting on the empty stage, one week before they were scheduled to open. "Gather 'round in a circle," he yelled.

The actors, like children at camp, obeyed; the staff and crew followed more slowly. When everyone was quiet, White spoke.

"All right, look, this is a great show," he said. "We're gonna make it. I want you to know I have no doubts. No reservations. But I think you need to be reminded what we're about. See, no one said this show would be easy. We're challenging our audience, we want to make them think. And the thing about stream of conscience is, it needs careful thought—from them and from you."

Stream of conscience? Martin thought.

"See, the thing about stream of conscience is, you have to understand it."

The leading man, a barroom tenor whose still-good looks seemed ready to depart at any minute, loped forward dramatically into the circle. "Wait right there, Peter, that's where you lose us. What *is* this stream of conscience, anyway? You've been throwing that phrase around for weeks now, and I won't speak for anyone else in the cast, but this is one genius who just doesn't know what the heck you're talking about."

Some other actors nodded agreement in an exaggerated manner rarely witnessed except in crowd scenes from Shake-speare.

"Now, Donald, let's calm down. Stream of conscience. Put simply, it's a method writers can use to tell the story of the interior thoughts and perceptions of a character, as if it were a continuous, shifting, illogical, random stream. Okay?"

Donald stood in the center of the ring, considering. After a series of faces to show he took the thing seriously, he said, "*Now* I understand," and withdrew.

White looked relieved. "But let's not get stuck on stream of conscience. The point I'm making has to do with how you think about your lines. How can you speed them up."

Stream of *conscience?*

White went on to announce some changes in the script, in-cluding the introduction of a narrator, but Martin was thinking: Consciousness is not a stream. It's more like a canal. You're not carried along randomly by currents, you sit in a thought until it drops down steeply into a different thought, discrete from the first. The path is arranged and the water is still. It's not a stream, it's a system of locks.

A cast member nudged him. White had asked everyone to hold hands in a circle and feel the energy of a squeeze pass through. Dutifully, when the pulse came along, Martin trans-ferred it. Mostly he was grateful for the actor's warm hand.

STELLA had to be argued into accompanying Martin on open-ing night. Her excuses were laughable: no dress, no time. Martin knew the real reason was her dread of hating something he had been part of. But finally Martin had said to her, "Stella, you don't have to like it, you just have to come." And so she did.

For the occasion she put on diamond earrings and replaced

her knapsack with a beaded purse. She looked beautiful, by anyone's standards. Martin in his tux looked as good as he got. People turned toward them under the marquee in a way that suggested admiration. Martin saw in the lobby glass that they actually made an arresting couple. When colleagues came over to be introduced, they smiled as if impressed with Martin's taste. Some obviously assumed he and Stella were a couple, and Martin did nothing to disabuse them. People so easily believed anything.

Partially as a result of White's pep talk, the show had improved in the last few days. At any rate, it was shorter. Martin found himself half-excited and hopeful. As the lights went down he took Stella's hand, but she withdrew it quickly as if frightened.

The curtain went up on the bare ecru stage. The narrator descended on a wire from the flies. "And then," he said, "they were singing about the day." Music rumbled up from the pit. The chorus appeared on scaffolding and launched into the opening number. In the middle of it, a very large towerlike object, also ecru, wandered as if confused onto the stage.

"What's going on?" Stella whispered.

"It's supposed to," said Martin.

She stared at him as if to say, "You've got to be kidding," then broke out laughing. By the time the song ended on the repeated word *six* her face was frozen in a rictus of hilarity.

"I'm sorry," she said, clapping reflexively. "But this is the worst disaster I have ever seen." She looked apologetic but could not stop laughing. "And I've seen film of the *Hindenburg*," she added.

But at the cast party later, spirits were amazingly high. The audience—mostly composed of friends, it was true—had responded well and stood cheering at the end. Peter White seemed nervous but reasonably optimistic. He entered the ballroom, raised his arms in a victory salute, but crossed his fingers; then he withdrew with the producers to a plush anteroom. There they stared at phones and televisions that would at any moment convey to them their fate.

The party went into a holding pattern. People drifted from clique to claque, greeted each other, asking questions that called for no answers, then looked expectantly toward the inner sanctum before moving on. Finally, at eleven-thirty, the producers and director reappeared briefly. The show had received gleeful, horrendous reviews on five different channels. The papers were worse, with their punning headlines and formula epithets. One had referred to the score as six notes in search of a composer.

The producers escorted Peter White through the hushed crowd as if he were a criminal. He could still be heard muttering the words *conservative* and *stream of conscience.* One of the producers said, "Oh, shut up, Peter." When they left the room, the party died almost instantly.

In the cab, Martin said, "I know, I know. I knew from the start. But I couldn't say no, could I?"

Stella slowly took off her earrings. "Knew what?" she asked.

"How bad it was. This goddamn stupid avant-garde bullshit, I really—" He was stamping his foot on the floor so hard the driver turned around.

"Sorry," he said, and tears leaped out of his eyes.

Stella sat back. "It's not goddamn stupid avant-garde bullshit. It's just goddamn stupid *old-fashioned* bullshit. What ideas there are, are only half-understood. And no, there's no shame in having done it. Doing it again, however—that's a different story."

He couldn't stop crying.

"Martin? Martin? Are you okay?"

Now he willed himself to laugh. "The tower!" he said.

"The ecru tower. That's where elite gay people live."

The cab pulled up at Stella's building. In the rearview window, Martin could see people walking their dogs at the edge of the park.

"Maybe you should come up."

"No," said Martin.

"Well, don't despair." She kissed Martin on the cheek and said, "Call me, doll."

"I will. I promise."

The next night, a notice went up. Sunday's matinee, it announced, would be the last performance of *Six*. Disappointment was expressed that a show so meaningful had not been able to find an audience advanced enough to accept it. But, wrote Peter White, "I have no regrets." Someone, however, had crossed out the R.

THE LAST performance was of course the best; the sense of powerlessness and futility that had so eluded the actors throughout rehearsals now fell easily into the range of their emotions. Long after the red velvet curtain came down, the acting continued, the tears, the orations. Martin said good-bye to his friends and walked to the subway.

He got out at Christopher Street; it was seven o'clock. What he would say to Matt, he had not determined. For weeks he had restrained himself from attempting this encounter, but now with the show closed, he had nothing left to stay him. He half imagined punching Matt in the stomach, and half imagined just curling up with him in bed. How could both of these powerful feelings be directed toward one miserable person? Because neither would be expressed. There would be no violence, there would be no comfort. There would only be words: terrible, necessary words.

To Martin's surprise, the building that matched the address Matt had given was a four-story brownstone on a well-kept block. He climbed the stoop and read the buzzers. None listed Matt's name, but that would not be unusual. The vagaries of Manhattan subletting ensured that names on doors were hopelessly inaccurate. By the buzzer for apartment E—the one Matt shared with graduate students—an embossed label read BERNSTEIN, R.

Martin checked the torn piece of paper again, returned it to his wallet, then rang.

A man's voice answered.

"Is Matt there?" said Martin.

"No," the voice said, but not definitively.

"Is this apartment E?"

"Yes."

"Does someone named Matt Melodondri live there?"

"No."

Martin always felt self-conscious standing on stoops, talking to intercoms. He was painfully aware that someone passing might think he was crazy or at least unwelcome. Nevertheless he persevered. "Has he moved recently?"

"I don't know who you're talking about."

"Twenty-five, good-looking? This is his address, I think."

"We've lived here five years and there's no one by that name. Do you have the right building?"

"I think so," said Martin. "Could he live in one of the other apartments?"

"I'd know if he did."

Martin could not think of a way to prolong his conversation with the building. Or any reason. "Well, thank you," he said.

He studied once more the address in his wallet, but none of the numbers or letters could be misread. There was no mistake. Matt had written the address himself, and written a false one.

Martin walked to the pier as the sun, gigantic, was falling alarmingly fast above Hoboken. In another corner of the sky, a pale full moon was showing its transparent face. Both at once— but that was impossible. The sun and the moon out together: an unnatural liaison.

And on the twisted deck men talked in pairs, or smoked silently, or just held hands. One couple, a plain man and a beautiful, kissed playfully, combatively, like chickens at their feed. How had *this* unnatural liaison occurred? How did any?

By deception, Martin concluded. And by belief.

Matt had deceived him: he did not live where he said he did. Did he live anywhere? And then there was Maman with her enormous sapphire ring—played in this performance by the lovely Barbara Stanwyck. Martin wondered what else might be fictional. French horn? Guitar? The saintly parents—was one of them dead? The English girlfriend's celebrity set? The couple who ran the downtown club? *Simone de Beauvoir!* How could anyone believe such things?

But Martin, without a moment's hesitation, had chosen to believe, or at least not to question. More than that, he had encouraged the fictions, had let himself get caught in the Chinese finger torture. Leaving well enough alone was not good enough. He had demanded a story, and suffered the fate of having his demand met. He had caused Matt to explain himself so that Martin could bear to want him. It was no more than popes had done, imputing God because the stars were otherwise too beautiful to endure. When the stars turned out to be dead cold rocks, the nonexistent gods were despised.

But the fault, Martin thought, is not in our stars: it is in our fans. Our adoring fans. He himself was to blame for Matt's disappearance—for all the disappearances and disappointments in his life. The truth was, he wanted no one, not even himself. It was not only Matt who had perfected an illusion. He, Martin, had built a magical contraption and made it work exactly as planned. The beautiful assistant, placed inside, vanished, leaving the box intact but empty. And every memory eventually vanished, too: every spangle, every hard bead. There was nothing left but the impermeable wood and the grieving magician.

Martin stepped forward to the edge of the pier. The sun fractured across the rippling water, making fiery stepstones upon it. The yellow brick road. Oh, Dorothy, Martin thought. And there were the munchkins, back behind him, the wee people, employable only rarely.

The kissing couple was smoking now, the smoking couple,

walking. They looked truly happy, but Martin knew their happiness would disappear as absolutely as if it were false. Perhaps more absolutely.

A wind picked up. A short man in battered jeans sauntered toward Martin at the end of the pier. His T-shirt said, in giant black letters, LEAVE ME ALONE. But he smiled as if to deny its message.

It was Martin who should have been wearing the T-shirt. He frowned, but still the man approached. Martin shivered. A wind rose up around him and echoed in his ears. *What do you want from me?* it sang.

He turned around to catch his breath and found himself stepping into the river. The yellow brick road dispersed beneath him.

FOR world cultures class, during a unit on Japan, Martin had made a mobile of origami animals. A boy threw it out the window, and Martin felt himself sail out the window with it, about to be blown into a meaningless tangle by the wind. The contraption of his personality—the intricate folds, the careful design, the precarious balance—could not withstand the drift of it. He knew what would happen to his beautiful project: its coathanger wires would splay in the air, its frogs would unravel, its paper birds would fail to lift their stiff, sharp wings, incapable of flight. But this didn't happen. The mobile landed in a tree, and floated there, the origami figurines spinning and kissing.

MARTIN awoke in a narrow cubicle, surrounded on three sides by sinister machines. One of them beeped while the others cast silent green gazes at each other. On the fourth side of the cubicle a curtain had been withdrawn, and Martin could see across the corridor into a cubicle identical to his. There a woman was asleep, her mouth open, tubes lashing her to various clear, distended pouches. Martin investigated his own nose and mouth, looked beneath his sheet and gown, found himself unscarred, untubed.

But three pads were taped in a horizontal line across his chest, and the pain beneath the pad dead center was excruciating.

In a plastic bag on the bed table he discovered his wallet, still damp. The piece of paper upon which Matt's address had been written was now completely blank. The bills would need drying, but the credit cards were as shiny as ever, though they'd unsigned themselves on their backs. Some quarters lingered in the bottom of the bag.

He tried to review what had happened, but there were more gaps than memories in his memory. Still, he knew he had been in the river. How had he gotten there? And how here? He could see the T-shirt that said LEAVE ME ALONE, but then there was a cut and a dissolve to his own shirt, much later, being ripped from his body. Water was dripping off a table; there was a siren. All he could remember thinking was that the shirt was a new one from Charivari; the buttons went leaping. It would be beyond repair.

Now he was wearing an embarrassing shroud. His body was stiff and his chest hurt as if a stake had been driven through it, but he was pleased to note he remembered his name. After performing a few sums in his head correctly, he concluded he was basically unimpaired by the swim.

A doctor came in, an Indian woman, her hair knotted like a bellpull. Her name was embossed on a label at her breast, but Martin found he could not make it out.

"Good morning," she said. "Do you know where you are?"

"St. Vincent's, I think." And then to confirm this he looked at the doctor's scrubs, at the beeping machinery, at the plastic bracelet around his own wrist, all of which were emblazoned with the hospital's insignia.

"The intensive care unit. Can you tell me your name?"

This he did gladly.

"And do you know what day it is? What month? What year?"

"Is it Sunday?" he said. "The month is September. The year is 1984."

The doctor nodded. "It's Monday morning. And the name of the president?"

This stumped Martin briefly. When he remembered, he made a sour, regretful face, which the doctor seemed to accept as an answer.

"Good," she said. "Do you know what happened to you?"

"I fell in the river?"

She narrowed her eyes. "Did you fall?"

"I think I fainted."

"Do you have a history of fainting?"

"Well, sort of."

"How long?" She started taking notes.

"Mostly as a child."

"I see. Any drugs?"

"Certainly not."

"Prescription or recreational?"

Martin hesitated. "Xtasy," he murmured. "I took it once, in June. But I never took anything else. Ever."

The doctor made a disapproving face and wrote this down.

"It isn't dangerous," Martin said.

"Who told you that?" She did not wait for an answer. "I have to ask you, were you trying to jump off?"

Martin blushed. "I don't really know."

"Then it's not impossible."

"No," he admitted.

She put down her clipboard. "I'd like to listen to your heart now, please." She placed the tips of her stethoscope in her ears and leaned over Martin intently. Her name, he discovered, was Chatterjee.

"It hurts a lot."

"Does it? Where?"

Before Martin could answer, she'd slipped her hand under his gown and caused him to scream.

"Anywhere else?"

She padded around with two or three fingers, exerting a gentle pressure on his flesh. It hurt nowhere else.

"Now let me listen. Breathe deeply, please."

"It hurts."

"Yes, I'm sure it does."

But he breathed and she listened.

"Can you turn over on your side now, please?"

She moved the pad around Martin's back so that it felt as if a slow, cold animal were creeping toward his neck.

"That's fine, then. Turn back over," she said. She scribbled more notes.

"Am I all right?" Martin eventually asked.

"From the water itself you are fine. Would you squeeze my hand, please?"

This he did, but with mounting panic.

"Dizzy?" she asked.

"A little."

"And you're how tall? Six-foot-five?"

Martin nodded.

"Just like Lincoln." She asked him to perform various tasks while she continued to listen.

"Are you a cardiologist, then?" he ventured.

Dr. Chatterjee looked at him as if he had asked a ludicrous question. "Certainly," she said.

Martin could not hold out any longer. "What's wrong with me?" he asked. "It's my heart, isn't it? I have Marfan's syndrome. I have a defective valve."

Martin's research had told him what he could expect: open-heart surgery, a replacement valve made of pig, a lifetime of anticoagulant medicine. He would be frail—deservedly so. He could have fey coughs, he could stay abed; when he ventured forth for a summer weekend, he could withdraw from the punishing sun of the garden to recline on chintz on the shady veranda. These would be articles of his frail constitution.

"You have a broken rib," Dr. Chatterjee said.

"I don't have Marfan's syndrome?"

"The pain in your chest is a broken rib. Probably from the CPR. They weren't professionals, they were a little too exuberant. But they saved your life." She put her stethoscope back in her pocket.

"And I don't have anything wrong with my heart?"

"I'm sorry to disappoint you."

"Not even a murmur?"

She pursed her lips and shook her head no. "You were slightly arrhythmic when you came in, which is only to be expected. That was taken care of with lidocaine. Now we're just monitoring you to make sure you're back on course."

"And my fainting?"

Dr. Chatterjee shrugged. "Sometimes people faint," she said.

But then of course he hadn't fainted all that often. He'd only let people believe that he had.

"Do you know how," Martin asked, but could only stammer, "well, did you, did anyone, happen to say—"

"How you got fished from the water? I don't know. But someone standing around must have done it, because you were back on the pier when the ambulance arrived. I should think more than one. Your clothes alone must have weighed twenty pounds."

"Was I conscious?"

"In a way. You kept crying out what sounded like 'murder.' Or so the police sheet says. They finally figured out what you were saying was 'mother.'" Dr. Chatterjee appeared to withhold a smile. "Do you think you can eat?"

Martin was hungry, which seemed ridiculous so soon after nearly drowning, but it was true. He nodded.

"And is there someone you can call? Your *murder* perhaps? You might want some things from home. A toothbrush, a book."

Martin nodded.

"I'm ordering an X ray to make sure the rib didn't puncture your lung. After that, you can go to a regular room—you'll need to be monitored another forty-eight hours. We'll give you some codeine for the pain. And, on the other subject, may I suggest you consider a psychiatrist? Though in a way it's lucky you did end up in the water. You might not have known about your heart otherwise—that it's fine, I mean."

Martin smiled weakly.

Dr. Chatterjee started toward the door, but paused as if confused by a detail. "Did you never tell your regular doctor about your concerns?"

"I haven't had a checkup in years. I have a thing about doctors."

"We're a terribly frightening lot," she said. "Aren't we?" She hurried away.

A BLACK technician wheeled in an X-ray machine, put down his baloney sandwich, and took a few shots of Martin's chest. "How you feeling, buddy?" he said. "Just hold your breath." When this was done, a tray of food was brought, which Martin devoured with unexpected pleasure. A nurse washed his face. A volunteer offered to make any phone calls Martin might like. Everyone touched him lightly, calmly, on the hand, on the head; his body was open to all who came by. A few hours later, some very large nurses helped move him onto a gurney and into a semi-private room on another floor. His gown, never properly tied, fell off in transit. It didn't matter. He entered the new room naked.

Stella was there already, arranging flowers in a makeshift vase; she turned away while the nurses dressed and arranged Martin on the bed. Even when they had left, however, she could not bring herself to say the word *hello*. She started to cry, and walked away for a moment, standing in front of the strange round windows Martin had only seen from the outside before. Now they admitted a thin, bluish light.

"Which way is north?" Stella asked. Then she tried to sit in a chair next to Martin's bed but could not find a comfortable position.

"I've brought you some Jell-O," she said, jumping up. She

withdrew from a shopping bag an enormous container. "And magazines." She stacked these on the night table. "I've already hung your clothes in the locker. And your toothbrush ..." She trailed off, pointing to the sink.

"I'm fine," said Martin. "I'm perfectly fine."

"You sound disappointed."

"I am, I guess."

She walked back to the bed and this time took his braceleted hand.

"Is my apartment okay?"

"Yes, except—well, Martin, in your bedroom—"

"Oh, my God."

"I took the liberty of taking them down. It was like a shrine in there."

Martin covered his mouth to prevent himself from laughing.

"And here's your Walkman. I brought you some Mozart. Did you want that letter mailed, by the way? By the kitchen phone? Anyway I mailed it. A very strange name."

"Nana Obeng," Martin said. The letter had been sitting there three months at least. "Well, I guess so."

"I ask no questions."

"Did you call my mother?"

Stella made an equivocal noise, but before Martin got a chance to question her further, Dr. Chatterjee had entered the room with a swarm of interns. Stella moved away and let them collect around Martin's bed.

"Mr. Gardner found himself in the Hudson River yesterday evening," Dr. Chatterjee announced. She clipped his X ray onto the light box. "Isn't that right?"

Martin nodded.

"With resultant arrhythmia, acidosis, hypothermia." She went on to detail the case in a monologue Martin could barely understand. He did manage to discern that his fifth rib had been broken cleanly just where it joins the sternum, and that it would heal by itself in about six weeks.

"Patient will be discharged after seventy-two hours of normal EKG," Dr. Chatterjee concluded. "A social worker will be around to make arrangements for a home health aid, though an otherwise fit young man like this should be back in business in two weeks or so. Physically, that is."

She then left the room, the troupe of interns shuffling out behind her like ducklings.

"A regular Benazir Casey," said Stella.

"At least you know where she stands," said Martin. "What about my mother?"

"She said she didn't know if she could get into the city just now."

Martin exhaled a narrow filament of breath. "It's funny," he said. "I want her here. There are decisions to be made. I'm not old enough to make them. A mother should do it."

"She's made hers already."

Mrs. Gardner, like her son, had been overwhelmed, but her son had been saved. His supposedly insufficient heart had proved to be strong and renewable. But what could save her?

"She said she'd pray for you with her prayer group. That seemed to mean she wouldn't be calling, but then she asked for your number, so—"

"What on earth should I do if she *does* call?"

He answered himself in unison with Stella. "Only disconnect," they said.

THE CURTAINS surrounding the man in the next bed were opened that afternoon by his wife, a woman who resembled him almost exactly. They both had hair that was yellowish white, his cropped one inch shorter than hers. Perhaps from the hospital, his skin was paler, but otherwise their faces matched, line for line. They each had blue eyes, the color of Wedgwood.

They were sixty or seventy; Martin couldn't tell. They seemed youthful, or ageless, an impression fostered in part by their silence. They played Scrabble together, barely talking except in praise of each other's moves.

Questioning them, Martin found out that Mr. Buchanan was recovering from gallbladder surgery. They had no children. Mrs. Buchanan had been an editor, Mr. Buchanan a writer, but now they were both part-time consultants, whatever that meant. Mr. Buchanan had never been one for a regular job. In their youth, he had made her support him while he read all of Proust in the original for a year.

"Did you like it?" asked Martin.

"Like it? Is that what you're supposed to do?"

She herself was reading it now for the very first time.

They did not question him, but continued their game, which was at first incomprehensible. Mr. Buchanan lay down the word TOPAZ, though he might easily have scored better with a longer word. Mrs. Buchanan crossed TOPAZ with BEZEL.

"Oh, very nice," her husband said, actually studying the four new tiles. "I'm afraid I haven't got anything so good."

He quickly added ARD to the B in BEZEL. His wife shook her head as if disappointed.

"I notice you don't keep score," Martin said.

"We play our own rules. Instead of points, we try to make the most beautiful words. That's why BARD was such a failure."

Martin laughed.

"You forget, George," Mrs. Buchanan said, "how eccentric we must appear."

"No, no," Martin said, "it's delightful, really."

"And then we try to make a story with all the words at the end," said Mr. Buchanan. "Catharine is better with the words, but I tell the better story."

As if to prove this, Mrs. Buchanan started laying tiles on the board. "I've redeemed you," she said, changing BARD to BOMBARDIER.

"Ah, lovely," Mr. Buchanan replied, eventually surrounding

her final R with the letters of JORDAN. "Proper names are permissible in our game."

"As long as they're beautiful."

The two played on in perfect friendliness. He had bad teeth, she a long scar at the base of her neck. But they looked at each other even less than they spoke.

After considering various possibilities, Mrs. Buchanan connected BEZEL to JORDAN with the word ELYSIAN, and Martin gasped. She raised her eyebrows in acquiescence.

They play their own rules, but who had taught them? What box top had given them the authority to devise their own patterns? Certainly none that Martin had ever seen. No movie, no book, no homily had ever suggested the joys or even the validity of such a union: a union neither sanctified by its fruit nor glamorized by its beauty.

But the dirty river had washed Martin clean of that illusion, or so it seemed to him. It had erased not only Matt's false address, but the false image of their beautiful love. What was left—now that Stella had removed the hundred pictures—was merely a gap. No bitterness; a few scraps of song; an occasional, inexplicable echo of plain affection. This was unexpected, but not unpleasant. Perhaps it was how it should be, thought Martin. For they had kept company and broken bread and done all those simple things that supposedly last. They had slept not inches apart for months. In Martin's closet hung an attractive new suit he would not otherwise have bought for himself. Matt had left him a different person. As a result of their time together, Martin liked his body more, if the world less. In any case, he had no egrets.

But he dared not think further. The memory was best left unannotated; when words crept into the margins, it foundered. In effect, he was resigned not to know what he had never known, and this made perfect sense.

And so, though clean, he felt empty. There was no beautiful, unlikely word for him to lay on the board. He fell asleep in a coin of sunlight from the porthole window, with words of a story swirling around him: bombardiers, elysian, Moses at the Jordan, bezels of topaz ...

DELIA, who due to her age was not permitted to visit the hospital, sent Martin an elaborate card made from fabrics and papers known only to her. She enclosed an enormous letter that detailed the activities of Stefan in the morning, school in the day, and *Jet Set* at night. The letter ended with this amazing sentence: *I wish I could visit you, but I know I can't, so get well quick, and come home soon, or else.*

Martin obeyed. Three days after falling or jumping or fainting into the Hudson, he returned to his apartment. The home health aid, a Barbadan named Lois, carried his bag and led him by the elbow. At his request, no banners or balloons or guests lay in wait. Stella had vacuumed and dusted, however, and left the magazines in a pile so neat it could only be a sarcastic comment. She'd stocked the freezer with chicken soup, the refrigerator with chicken.

Lois was skinny but strong, with eggplant skin and braids so tight they looked almost painful. She brooked no nonsense but was jolly enough. "PJs," she said, and Martin pointed to the drawer where he kept his collection of nightshirts. "What color do you like today? You seem to have one of everything here."

Martin chose blue. "But can I take a shower or something? I feel dirty," he said.

Lois started undressing him. "Too slippery, and I'm not going in there with you. Later we'll work something out."

Martin didn't know what she meant by this, but did not have time to consider. Lois already had her arm around his back and was putting him into bed, expertly avoiding any pressure on his chest. She gave him his codeine. "That'll help you get some rest now," she said. "I'm going to the store. I'll be back in ten minutes. Don't you try to get up now, you read me?"

Martin nodded, but the minute he heard his front door shut,

he slid out from between the sheets and walked haltingly to the living room. He knelt on the carpet and started to cry. His tears were neither of pain nor relief, nor anything he could name or cared to. They were merely tears, and necessary, and unabating. Soon he was coughing them up, and panting. But this was fine. He let himself do it.

"There," he said, when he'd finally worn himself out. "That feels better." He rose carefully and surveyed the room.

The Foo dogs, the drapes: he had made a place fit for a grandmother. The Chippendale chairs, oiled and curvaceous, like their namesake strippers. How had he ever? What was he thinking? The statue of Venus made him laugh out loud.

Out it would go! All of it! He would do it over. A lamp, a chair, bare floors, a rock; he wished he were Japanese. He remembered the lunch Stella had brought him in a neat little box. We should eat that way. We should live that way. But if we could live that way . . .

Still, he would try. He shuffled back to bed and smoothed the white sheets neatly around him. His body, so ornately engraved in the past, was plainer now by far. The *M* on his foot was as nothing compared to the giant **I** he'd make if seen from above. Bold, sans serif, it could not be ignored. He was alone, it said— but, at least, not less than alone.

Lois woke him up an hour later. "Bath time," she said, with the air of someone delivering a much-desired present. She took off his nightshirt, then stood him up in a red plastic laundry basin she had bought at the five-and-dime. She filled a matching bucket with warm water and doused him. Next came shots from a bottle of dishwashing liquid. She wiped him down with great arcs of a giant car sponge, then doused him again. With a nail-brush, she scrubbed the soles of his feet. Delicately she lathered and rinsed his chest. He stood there dripping, his window shades open; what would the man on the fourteenth floor think? Would he think, as Martin did, How lovely? How kind?

"Have we done your ding-dong yet?" asked Lois.

Martin did not know whether to be embarrassed or insulted. They had indeed done his ding-dong, or as much doing as it required. He nodded and giggled.

"Good, then we're done." She wrapped him in towels and combed back his hair.

"Do you think I'd look good in braids?" he asked.

"I think you'd look good in bed," she said, and put him there.

"That's the nicest thing I've heard in years."

Lois said, "Shush. I'll make you lunch."

A DAY or two before Martin felt up to it, Stella gave a small party in his apartment. Lois was skeptical, but Lois came only three hours a day, and Stella asserted her prerogatives. She convinced Lois it would do Martin good. Together they dressed him in a new Charivari shirt—blue silk with black polka dots—and propped him up in bed to greet visitors.

Delia showed up first, running into the bedroom with a heart she had made from felt stuffed with cotton, a Band-Aid pasted over its middle. She looked as if she would jump onto the bed, but Lois stopped her with a hand on her face.

"I wasn't going to," Delia complained. Then, after asking permission, she sat, oddly quiet, at the foot of the bed. She stared at Martin, as if trying to see if something was different. After a moment she remembered her gift, and handed it over, wordlessly.

Stella ushered Maria in next. She leaned over and kissed Martin, her hair falling in front of him like a screen. "Where's Stefan?" he asked.

"Oh God, it's the first time we've been parted, and I just don't like it." She stopped for a moment to adjust the blanket where her hand had disturbed it. "He's with David," she added.

The doorbell rang and then kept ringing. Colleagues and actors from various shows arrived. Each came up to Martin and presented a gift—a book, a bag of Pepperidge Farm cookies. The bedroom wasn't large enough for everyone, so Stella admitted them one or two at a time while the other guests mingled in the living room. Martin could hear their chatter over the music on his stereo, could hear his name occasionally, too. What were they saying about him? he wondered. And then gave up caring. Delia, her initial reserve now overcome, ran from room to room making announcements.

"There's a tall guy here with, like, no hair."

This turned out to be Chris, the painter. He brought Martin a sketch pad and a box of Crayolas. "I thought you might like to draw," he said, opening the lid to reveal the crayons all in formation, like a U.N. army.

"How did your show go?" Martin asked.

"Sold out," said Stella, bearing champagne flutes. She handed one to Lois, who was sitting by the window reading the Bible amiably.

"It's your doorman!" yelled Delia, running into the room. "And some girl!"

"I feel like 'This Is Your Life,'" said Martin.

"Just wait," said Stella.

For a moment he had the awful thought that she'd dug up Matt and caused him to come, but it was soon apparent she meant someone else. A young woman stuck her head in at the door. She was slight of build and not very tall, and had vibrant red hair caught up in a green headband.

"Kelly?" said Martin.

"Jane, actually."

They looked at each other and everyone watched them. Not even Martin knew for sure what their looks contained. There was an element of surprise, naturally, on both parts; curiosity, too. Eventually, Jane walked to the bed, but whatever energy had propelled her there at once gave way. She looked as if she would lean in and kiss him but touched his hand for a moment instead.

"Hello, Martin," she said tentatively, as if forced to give an answer to a question she wasn't prepared for.

Stella, Chris, and Lois turned away from the scene, but Delia stared openly.

"Will it heal completely?"

"So I'm told."

"You'll be better than ever?"

"New and improved."

"And you're not in too much pain?"

"No, not *too* much."

Jane lapsed into silence, then said, "Look at this!" She examined carefully the heart Delia had made.

"Do you like it?" said Delia. "I designed it."

"And what a clever little girl you are!"

Delia made a weary face for Martin's benefit. "Are you Martin's sister?"

"One of them, yes."

"Where's the other?"

"She's back at school. I was just about to tell you, Martin, that Kelly sends her best wishes. She's got—"

Martin was content to listen without hearing. He tried to compare the woman speaking with the chipper, brittle girl he remembered from Rye, but the exercise seemed pointless. It was enough to see her as the chipper, brittle woman she actually was now, a woman who was no more his sister, he thought, than—what? Than Jesus was his savior, is what came to mind. And he felt completely free to think about this. His saviors had been a bunch of gay men, who up until the necessary moment had been smoking and kissing on a condemned, rotten pier.

For Martin had been the recipient of a random act of love, as others are of violence. If there was a God, he thought, it was only the electricity, the chemical connection in someone's brain, that made him jump after someone else in the water, or made her dare to listen carefully to a man's absolutely unimpaired heart.

▪ ▪ ▪

LATER that week, on a day Stella could not come to visit, Chris showed up as a substitute. "What a pleasant surprise," said Martin, as usual with the wrong intonation.

"Didn't Stella tell you I was coming?" Chris looked perturbed. "Apparently not." Then he laughed. "Well, anyway, I've brought the *Enquirer*." He held up and brandished the ink-soaked tabloid. They looked at it together.

"I used to love this in high school," Chris lamented, his bottom lip thrust out. "I used to cut it apart and decoupage my notebooks. I was such a queen."

"Really?"

"Does it amaze you?"

"It's just I spent so much time desperately trying not to be. I wouldn't even try out for chorus."

"Well, you could get away with it. I couldn't, so I went the other extreme. In college I called myself Crystal." He laughed.

"But why?"

"I actually believed it was a political statement. I called everyone by women's names, except women. The idea was that names are the primary site of attachment people have to their rigid ideas of the world. I called my parents Mummer and Dud. I was a little Mao without a revolution because my friends could pass and were happy with that. And I was a little embarrassing, I suppose. My watch cry was 'Be fitful and mortify.' Then I grew out of it."

"How?" asked Martin.

"Well, look," he said, putting down the *Enquirer*. "I made my revolution in other terms. But I don't disdain what I did, not a bit. Do you want the spiel?"

Martin nodded.

"We wouldn't have a women's movement if it weren't for loudmouth, pushy women. Bella Abzug begat Gloria Steinem begat Geraldine Ferraro. Yesterday's terrorist is today's elder statesman. I just found that I could do as much without the affectation. As the movement found out, too. Still, I think it would only be fair to let the drag queens lead the parade instead of the politicians. But that's part of growing up, too. You have to let people do it however they can."

"Now you do it in your paintings."

Chris had a handsome face—the kind Martin always wanted to have—but it was pitted with scars from what must have been acne. It was difficult to watch closely, at first, but soon Martin adjusted.

"I don't think of it that way," said Chris. "I'm not attempting to shock, though I know it happens. I'd prefer not to, in fact, but I can't control it. The avant-garde is grotesque to me—so often it's only avant-garde in the abstract. In real life, they're as intolerant and selfish as anyone else. I only mean to say I hate all schools. And all pretensions taught in those schools."

Martin nodded. "I was visiting Matt this summer," he said, presuming Chris had heard all about it from Stella. "And I stayed at this peculiar place called the Victorian Guest and Americana House." He went on to describe Miss Mapes, her mother, Calvin Coolidge, and to his surprise, the night spent with Matt. "The whole time, I had the feeling of being trapped in a foreign architecture."

"Victoria wasn't even American, for heaven's sakes," said Chris. "We *left* there. The pilgrims came to New England—*New* England—only to install a new intolerance. What I want to know is, where are the new pilgrims? Who's going to lead us from today's tyrannies?" He smiled at himself. "I'm getting oratorical."

"And what tyrannies are those?"

"Well, Victorianism, like your guest house. Romantic expectation. Beauty."

"Maybe it's you."

Chris laughed, tilting his head at just the right angle so the sun hit his crew cut and made it light up. Crew cuts, to Martin, were inevitably associated with rowing crew—the desire for normalcy—and being well turned out. How odd that the style had been appropriated by gay men, especially by activists who were now appearing on the news almost nightly. Were they mocking the Boy Scouts in their uniforms? Or perhaps they were saying: We are good boys, too.

In any case, Martin found himself wanting to rub his hand across Chris's scalp—but who knew what might rub off if he did? You must not touch, lest you be touched, he thought. And Chris was so involved with the world—a world Martin had spurned from early youth. With what excuse? None that held water. My constitution, he told himself now, is unimpeachable. There is nothing I lack to make a full life from. I am merely spoiled. I have not traveled well.

But Chris had moved from one version of himself to the necessary next with fortitude and good humor. He was scarred, it was true, but this was just the sign of life upon him, a difficult message he had no choice but to read.

"Maybe it's you," Martin repeated.

"Maybe it's *us*," Chris said, and for a moment Martin thought he meant the two of them. "We've already started. Think of all the teenage boys you see who wear earrings now, and shirts cut off to bare their little midriffs. Five years ago you wouldn't see anyone straight caught dead like that. Now they don't even know what it meant."

"That's fashion, not morals or politics."

"But that's just what morals and politics are: trends like clothing and coiffures. I mean, we must be here for a reason, don't you think? One out of ten?"

"I think we're here for the same reason or lack of reason as the other nine. I see no difference except we don't have babies."

"There are other ways to procreate," said Chris, but Martin looked baffled. "Maybe when your rib is healed, we can do a little experiment," he said.

IN TWO WEEKS the pain departed; soon thereafter, Lois did, too. On the last day of September, Martin ventured out on his first wee errand.

"I want to change my code," he told the clerk.

"May I see your card please?"

The clerk dipped it into a machine and pressed various buttons. He then turned the keyboard toward Martin. "Six characters or less," he said. "And make it something you'll be sure to remember."

Martin had considered the names of friends, the year of his birth—even the word *penis*, since he would never be tempted to reveal that code to others. But in the end, uncertain, and hurried along by the fidgeting clerk, he pressed the buttons that spelled out MARTIN. Six characters in search of an author, he thought.

MATT leaned almost out of the TV screen to promote the juiciest night on Broadway. The commercial came on while Martin and Stella were watching the local news one night. Martin screamed comically. Stella changed the channel.

"I wonder where he is," said Martin.

"Do you really?"

"Only in a curious way."

"Then I'll tell you," said Stella. "He's with his parents."

"How do you know?"

"How many Melodondris do you think there are in Buffalo? I called them up. The late Mr. M answered the phone."

"Did you speak to Matt?"

"Just long enough to tell him he should never attempt to contact you again. If he cared to pay you back, I said, he could send a check through me. But he wouldn't admit to stealing the money. He went all nutty. He referred to himself in the third person. 'He was exploding,' he said. 'He was a little boy who wanted candy.'"

For a moment Martin felt nauseated, but overcame it. He was not after all so angry at Matt. How could he be angry at a perfect stranger? And if the perfect stranger had to keep lying to keep going, was that so unusual? A new mother here, a ring, an address? Martin knew all too well how a life could be woven, and limited, too, from such paltry, thoughtless materials. He himself had practiced deception, practiced for years and then mastered it. He had made himself delicate because his mother said he was, but Dr. Chatterjee pronounced him a "fit young man." He had obeyed the advice of the *M* on his foot, but it wasn't an *M*. It was the random overlap of four little veins that contained no message.

Who knew what else might be pure fabrication? His tastes? His affections? It was as if he had never chosen a thing for himself, never taken time to decide what was right. He had lived his life in a stream of conscience, repeating certain hand-me-down words until they took on power from the repetition itself. *Family*. *Love*. And most of all *beauty*. He had said the word, in all its forms, over and over, millions of times, not sure what it was, believing it absolutely.

And wasn't Matt as much the victim as the purveyor of such lies? Loved instantaneously for no achievement, treasured for beauty? Forced to comply with the story built up around him? The Chinese finger torture works both ways: The more you struggle, the more it conforms. Matt was written by Martin's desire. They were a perfect fit. For all Matt actually contributed to his personality, he might as well have been a projection, and naturally enough he had thus disappeared.

"You should have told me," Martin said mildly.

"Should I?" said Stella. "I'm telling you now."

Martin, upon reflection, agreed. "My faint heart, you know."

"Don't be silly. You're coming back."

"As what? As what?"

Stella tickled him until he was gasping for air and they both got frightened. "Oh, my God, are you all right?"

"Yes, I'm fine," said Martin, panting. His eyes were wet. "It's just I get this image sometimes that my rib will break again and pierce my heart."

"You know what they say: The bone is stronger where the break has healed."

"I think that's a wives' tale."

"Really?" said Stella. "Then I must be your wife." They lay on his bed, each with one pillow, staring up at the ceiling and holding hands. The television proceeded in pantomime. Nana Obeng, framed in pewter, observed uncritically.

"COME this way," the receptionist said, wiggling toward the psychiatrist's inner office.

If I could come that way, Martin thought, I wouldn't need the shrink.

But he had not made the appointment in hopes of finding a doctor who knew how to turn him straight. The problem was not so much being different as it was being too much the same. He wanted to be fitful and mortify—to produce in himself that feeling of embarrassment that at least was a feeling. To break his rectilinear geometries—explode the Oak Ridge grid in his head that said: Life is here, work is there, a beautiful mountain is outside the fence. No more boxes! No more being ruled by rulers! He wanted, not to produce, not to deploy, not to exact, but to *draw* a curve.

"Martin?" said the doctor, for he had been staring out the window. "Martin? Martin?"

"Sorry. I'm here. I'm here," he said.

DELIA sat at the breakfast table pouring herself a glass of milk while Martin stood in the corner. He knocked a picture out of alignment and then kept trying to straighten it. He was only half-awake. Maria had called him at seven to take Delia to school; David had an emergency law thing, and Maria herself had an appointment with the obstetrician. "Sure," he had said, talking woozily into the earpiece, "I'll be right over." Then he had dropped the phone among his sheets and forgotten about it until it hissed its dial tone.

On doctors' advice he was taking it easy, and anyway there were very few jobs to be had. He filled his days with walks and the shrink, with museums and baby-sitting. The city looked different, the people only vaguely familiar. Walking around, he felt as if he were attending a reunion of a school he had attended erratically long ago. On the way to Maria's that very morning, it had taken him nearly a minute to recognize the familiar man from across the street when he stepped onto the same crosstown bus. They tried to place each other's name, but couldn't, of course. So they made introductions.

When he did arrive, Delia said, "What's wrong with your hair?" Stefan was wailing in the nursery and robots were blamming each other on the television.

"I don't know, what's wrong with it?" He went to a mirror and saw that the left side had all been pushed forward in a wedge and the top had sprayed open like a peacock's tail. "Slept on it wrong, I guess," he said. He tried to pat it down and mold it into place, but it kept springing back.

"Go fix it," said Delia. "You can use my brush."

"Right." He wandered around the room, looking at nothing. He sat next to Delia at the table and watched her watch television.

"These are Gobots," she explained.

"Right," he said. He folded his arms on the table and dropped his head upon them. When he awoke, Maria was in the room with Stefan, and everyone was talking or crying at once.

"I want to be on the milk carton, Mommy," Delia demanded.

"No, you don't, honey," Maria said sharply.

"Yes, I do so!"

"Don't start with me, Delia, I told you those children are missing. They're gone, they've been abducted, do you understand? They've disappeared. That's what it means. That's why they're on the carton at all. Do you understand me?"

"Missing?" said Delia.

"Yes, all right? Now please let me take care of your brother." Maria disappeared into the kitchen to check on a bottle.

"Missing?" Delia repeated. She continued to stare at the chil-

dren on the milk carton. There were two of them, a white boy
with buck teeth and a girl identified in the copy as Hispanic.
She had two stubby braids rising up from the back of her head
like antennae, and she smiled as if she received happy messages
through them. The photographs were printed poorly in blue,
with the dots so far apart they barely cohered as images. You
had to work not to think of them already as ghosts. You studied
their data to make them more real: what they were wearing,
where they last were seen. But they were *not* real, not real any
longer, not real in the form of those pictures, at least. They were
long gone—two years, one of them—gone into new, perhaps
terrible lives, or gone into death. They would not come back,
and even if they did, who could dare ever know them again?

Delia started to cry. She dropped her spoon in the bowl of
cereal and her face turned red. This was new. She slid off the
chair and heaped herself under the table.

Martin got Maria from the kitchen. "Delia," she said, "get out
from under the table. You're not missing. I told you not to look
at those pictures."

But Delia would not get up. "Look," Maria said, "I have to
feed the baby. I can't help you now. Do you understand?"

"Let Martin do it."

"Martin has better things to do than feed the baby."

"No, he doesn't!" shouted Delia with shocking authority. "No,
he does not!"

"All right, then, all right," said Maria, "I'm coming." She
handed the baby, stunned silent, to Martin. "The bottle should
be ready now," she told him, "but test it. Take him in the nursery. Try to get him to sleep when he's done."

Martin repeated her instructions to himself, as he repeated
phone numbers he was too lazy to write down. "Test it, nursery,
sleep," he mouthed. "Test it, nursery, sleep."

Maria was climbing under the table. "All right now, Delia,
okay, sweetie," Martin could hear her say. "Aren't we feeling
better now?"

He had baby-sat for Stefan before, but the child had already been asleep on those occasions. Now he was charged with the responsibility of getting him there. This was frightening. Babies were notorious for not following orders, and their elders were notorious for reacting strangely.

Martin hardly trusted himself. He remembered Nanny, an apparently sensible, upstanding woman, who suddenly went crazy when Martin was twelve. But even before she went crazy, she was odd. To begin with she was Irish, while most of the nannies in Rye were black. But Martin's mother had wanted someone Catholic. She had heard about Nanny—Martin never knew her real name—from a friend in Boston who had used her for years. "I had to act quickly to get her," Martin's mother told him later. "The right nanny was hard to find. We sent her five hundred dollars and told her to move as soon as she could."

Nanny had showed up with four suitcases in a cab. Martin was six. He was introduced and made to shake her hand, which was damp from carrying her luggage to the door. Martin's mother took her into the nursery immediately. The girls had just been born and she didn't know what to do with them. "Thank God you've come," she said, almost racing down the hall. Martin played with her luggage in the foyer until she returned and told him to help her move them.

She was more for the girls than for Martin, but the girls were up only a few hours a day. After they were in their cribs for the evening, Nanny would sit in the kitchen and watch Martin do his homework. She'd have a cup of tea she liked, yellow and astringent. They didn't talk much. Sometimes she gave Martin a piece of sour candy from the pocket of her uniform.

It was through Nanny that Martin discovered there was something wrong with his parents. She'd stand around the bend of the pantry, speaking quietly into the black wall phone to her people back home, as she called them. She'd slip half out of her squat, white shoes. "Danny?" she'd say. "Gone for the worse? And Caroline?" Then she'd slide further into the pantry. "Well!"

she'd say. "You wouldn't believe. The fighting! That woman, well! Two times now! Two!"

She was talking about his parents, Martin knew, and not respectfully. He found this exciting. But she was completely deferential when they were around and, to Martin's regret, unbearably servile. She called his father "sir" and his mother "missus." When one of them came into a room, she nodded silently and walked away. If Martin was with her, she'd take him away, too. "It's their sofa," she'd say, "not ours," encouraging Martin's view that he wasn't part of the family. Then they'd go to the kitchen or nursery.

These rooms she considered her own, and here she was more domineering. In the nursery, especially, no one could touch her. She wasn't the least bit deferential there. She arranged the girls' things just as she liked, moved their cribs around, demanded different diapers. Other adults were considered unwelcome. She watched Martin's mother like an intruder who might do damage.

Martin felt thrillingly disloyal to his parents when he sided with Nanny against them. He did things with Nanny he was sure they wouldn't approve. Once he helped her rehang all the pictures in the nursery. She plucked the prints of flowers and horses and birds off the wall, then handed their nails down to Martin to hold. "Now don't drop a one," she said. He counted them over and over in his palm, while she hammered in new ones, two feet higher.

He couldn't wait for his mother to see. He waited in the room all afternoon, in case she would wander by, but she didn't. Finally after dinner, she got up from the table and said, "I'm just going to go kiss the girls good night." Martin ran down the hall ahead of her and into the nursery.

Nanny was cleaning the baseboard heaters, which collected more dust than they were worth, she always said. Martin pulled at her white, stretchy skirt, but she ignored him.

His mother looked at the uneven row of prints high up on

the wall. A pained look passed over her face. Her mouth opened, but nothing came out. Martin was ecstatic. Finally she managed to say, "The horses, Nanny."

"Too low, they were, way too low. One of these days they'll hurt their tiny heads." She walked into the bathroom to wring out her sponge.

Martin's mother twiddled her rings with her thumb. "But Nanny, dear, we can't see them up there." She looked so tortured, Martin began to regret having done it. "Nanny?" she said.

Nanny did not return from the bathroom. She cranked open the hot water tap. Martin's mother smiled and shrugged. "Well," she said, looking at Martin and whispering. "Nanny knows best, isn't that what they say?"

Nanny did know best. When the girls were crying, she could always get them to stop. "Give me them," she'd say. "I know how to do them." She'd take both at once, drop them down on her big doughy shoulders. She'd walk around with them, not holding on. Then they'd fall asleep. "I have secrets," she'd whisper to Martin, and wink.

Martin saw one of Nanny's secrets once. He was playing ghosts in the nursery, between the two layers of curtains at the window. She lumbered in, frowning, with his baby cousin Paul, who was screaming and twisting in her hands. Martin knew she had taken him forcibly away from Aunt Carol; he could see her out on the patio shaking her head. His mother was pouring a glass of iced tea. The girls were curled like slugs on the grass.

The house was silent except for Paul's intermittent screaming. In between his awful peals, Martin could hear the air conditioner churn and cough. Paul seemed to listen to it, too, for a moment. Then he resumed. Nanny shook her head and put him down on the changing table. She took off his diaper. "Clean you up," she said through pins. "Then you'll stop your racket."

She cleaned him with a washcloth but he didn't stop crying. He beat the backs of his hands on the mat, and squeezed his eyes shut like fists. Nanny said, "Cripes, stop your racket, child!" She watched him for a moment and sighed. Then she bent her head suddenly over his belly and put his penis into her mouth. The screaming almost immediately subsided. It turned into something else: gurgles, burbles. After a minute Paul was asleep.

"Now *that'll* do you," Nanny said. She shoveled him into Kelly's crib.

STEFAN was wriggling on Martin's shoulder as if trying to crawl up into the vast, empty air. Martin knew he had about thirty seconds before the wailing would start again, and then wondered how he knew this. He lifted the bottle from the water with a glove, squeezed a drop of it on his finger and swirled it around as Maria had done. Here's hoping, he thought as he hurried himself into the nursery and closed the door.

It was not a nursery like the one Nanny had ruled, but merely a den converted to the purpose. Nevertheless it had more of the feeling of comfort and optimism one associated with babies, or wanted to. Drawings of every kind—Delia's, Matisse's— festooned the walls, catholic and generous of color. Every species of animal toy was welcomed into the cubicular ark. Books unreadable for years piled up on the sill, recommending any life at all over none. This baby, the room ambitiously hoped, would be truly free, never tyrannized, never consigned to a beautiful lie. The plastic shade of the night-light threw stars across the ceiling and walls, even in daylight. You may have both! Sun and moon! Night and day! There is plenty!

But this was a child, if not of great wealth, of privilege at least. It would be wrong, Martin knew, to generalize from his luck or character. Childhood should not be romanticized. A child's love as much as its cruelty was completely unknowing, and then, too, they did grow up to become adults. It was hard to say which group was asked more of, and which failed most. Nana Obeng, despite the promises made on her behalf, had not written back.

Had not been *able*, Martin decided. If it had taken him three attempts and a dunk in the river to reach her, what must it take for her to reach him?

Pen pal or not, Nana existed—on this point Martin arranged with himself to suspend cynicism. They all existed: Nana, Stefan, Delia, too; unknown children, unknown adults, even Matt, who seemed to be both at once. It was almost painful to wish him well, but this is what Martin tried to do.

"You suffer from memory," the shrink had told him, memorably, and it was true. He suffered from things he could not remove. But Martin had seen his own heart now, a shadow on the X ray of his broken rib, and knew he suffered just as much from what was lost and could not be re-created. He suffered amnesia. Pleasure he could not remember. Whatever love his parents had managed, he could not distill from his mental image of their strangely terrified faces. His own achievements, such as they were, produced in him only the faintest satisfaction. And what it was like to be kissed, to be touched? He couldn't remember. He'd never remember. All that could be done was start over and pay more attention.

Pay more attention! *Demand* more attention! *Require* a miracle! Martin would do it; he'd do it, but how?

Stefan started whimpering cyclically as if revving up to yell. Martin formed his left arm into a stiff, shallow cradle and plucked the boy off his shoulder like a bug. He offered him the bottle, and without prompting or cajoling, Stefan reached his little mouth toward it and took it in at once. He began to suck rhythmically as Martin watched, rapt. You could look at a baby as long as you wanted, Martin realized; a baby wouldn't mind your stares. Stefan seemed even to enjoy the weight of these different eyes upon him, the touch of a different finger on his soft, mackerel cheek. He made a noise that sounded like *more*.

What I say here, what I do, thought Martin, is part of what this child will be. He acquires his identity from others. What will he be like? What is he trying to learn to say?

Oh, it's passing! Concentrate!

So Martin thought instead about what *he* was feeling: the surprise of the warmth of Stefan's bare back. He made himself look at the white ghosts of fingerprints he was leaving upon it. The blood so close to the surface, the surface so pure. He studied the baby's beautiful skin: splotched and patterned like pale spring apples. It covers his entire body, he thought, like wallpaper. Does it never end? This is a life, twenty inches of life. It has unique properties and shared ones, too. It squirms in some kind of unconscious pleasure, it warms and cools.

"Mary had a little lamb," Martin crooned, leaning into Stefan's face. He buzzed to emphasize the *M*s, but the song had no charm. What would I have wanted to hear? Martin wondered. What do I want to hear now? He realized at once.

> *Dove sono i bei momenti*
> *di dolcezza e di piacer?*
> *Dove andaro i giuramenti*
> *di quel labbro menzogner?*

He began to rock Stefan gently and walk around the room. He swung him in rhythm but got confused and stopped. This was about feeding, Martin reminded himself, not music appreciation. He stood still in the center of the oval rag rug, instinctively bending the bottle higher as the milk got swallowed. My God, he thought, my arm knows what to do—but then he became self-conscious. He felt creaky and stupid. Still, the baby didn't mind; he drank in the milk till he fell back in the crook of Martin's arm. Even then he did not completely stop; he pulled the bottle with him. He closed his little sequin eyes, but his mouth stayed open.

"Still drinking, is it, and already dreaming," said Martin as he started again around the oval. "That's a baby, don't you know?" Dust hung about them in the light like a curtain. "Already forgetting, are we?"

J e s s e   G r e e n was born in Philadelphia, graduated from Yale University in
1980, and worked for several years as a
music coordinator on Broadway shows.
He is a journalist and National Magazine
Award finalist whose articles have
appeared in such publications as *The New
York Times Magazine, Premiere, Mira-
bella, GQ,* and the late, lamented *7 Days.*
For that New York City weekly he also
created, with novelist Meg Wolitzer, the
popular Nutcracker puzzle column; a collection of their most diabolical efforts was
published in 1991 by Grove Weidenfeld.
Green's short fiction has appeared in
Mademoiselle, Mississippi Review, and
The American Voice. He lives in New
York City.